Also by Celia Gittelson

SAVING GRACE

This Is a Borzoi Book
Published in New York by
Alfred A. Knopf

Biography

BIOGRAPHY

A NOVEL BY

Celia Gittelson

ALFRED A. KNOPF   NEW YORK   1991

THIS IS A BORZOI BOOK
PUBLISHED BY ALFRED A. KNOPF, INC.

Library of Congress Cataloging-in-Publication Data
Gittelson, Celia.
Biography / Celia Gittelson. — 1st ed.
p.   cm.
ISBN 0-394-58712-X
I. Title
PS3557.I83B5   1991
813'.54—dc20   90-27681   CIP

Manufactured in the United States of America
First Edition

147257

For my mother,

NATALIE GITTELSON,

and my father,

MARK R. GITTELSON,

with boundless love,

and gratitude

The dead can only live with the exact intensity and quality of the life imparted to them by the living.

JOSEPH CONRAD

When God is squeezing the breath out of you is the time to sing. E. L. DOCTOROW,

The Songs of Billy Bathgate

Biography

ONE

On Alter's desk the telephone rang, an unwelcome alarm. He jumped; then, as was his habit, let it ring a second time.

"Raphael?" A female voice, warm as drawn butter. Slightly scorched.

A month earlier Raphael Alter, biographer, chronicler of literary lives, had placed a query in the *New York Times Book Review*, a simple request, a few short lines:

"For a biography of the poet Maxwell Leibert, I would appreciate hearing from anyone who knew him or worked with him, and has information or documents. Raphael Alter, 7 West 84th Street, New York, NY 10024."

Within a week, responses arrived.

A letter from Noel Perl, former member of the Romance Languages faculty at the University of Wisconsin, rambled on for five closely typed pages. Perl composed on an old manual, the keys loosened by time and lack of maintenance. The tops of *h*'s were chopped off to resemble *n*'s; the *p*'s had also lost their heads; *y*'s, their tails amputated, masqueraded as *v*'s. The letter, a catalogue of defeat, was even more poignant for having been hammered out to a stranger on this crippled instrument with its broken characters, some decapitated, others torn out at their roots—the epistolary equivalent of an all-night bender.

Alter picked his way through Perl's account of a misspent life: his recently failed third marriage to a woman half his age, his crumbling finances, the dismal state of his current employment at a junior college in Boca Raton where, besides teaching intermediate French, he had the responsibility of coaching the women's swim team. He confided to Alter a paralyzing fear of the water. Perl got to his point at last, concluding with the tale of a drunken snowball fight in Madison during which the late poet had tried to smother the much smaller Perl in a snowbank. "To force, in fact," he wrote, "a fistful of hardpacked, freshfallen snow down my throat."

Curiously (or perhaps not so, as he invited Alter down to Florida, practically begged him to come, offering to arrange a speaking engagement to defray the costs of travel), Perl failed to mention an incident with which Alter was already familiar. Maybe it was Perl's intention to speak to the biographer face-to-face about the death of a young woman. It had happened in the winter of 1956 when Noel Perl, Maxwell Leibert, and a female student, Elise Sprung, were involved in an automobile accident near the campus. At midnight, the car in which they were traveling passed over the center lane of a highway, plunged down an embankment, turned over, and came to rest upside down in a gully. Trapped inside the wreck, the three of them lay there until morning, when they were discovered by a passing motorist. Elise Sprung was dead. Leibert and Perl walked away with hypothermia, cuts and bruises. Leibert admitted to driving, but an investigation turned up insufficient evidence on which to base a prosecution.

Although Perl had included his telephone number, Alter replied in writing, thanking him for his reminiscence and promising to be in touch as his research took shape. He did not refer to the accident.

But when he had completed the note and sealed the envelope, he withdrew from a file folder a photograph of Maxwell Leibert taken sometime in the late 1960s at Grand Central Terminal. Leibert posed in the vaulted main concourse in a dark overcoat and battered fedora slouched over one eye, his right elbow hitched on the marble ticket counter. Drooping from the corner of his mouth was a cigarette, its long ash smoldering precariously. The play of light and shadow deepened a crescent scar on his left cheek, evidence of the crack-up.

Alter studied the print; it was fuzzy, as were others he had collected, suggesting that at the moment the shutter snapped Leibert had moved imperceptibly, perhaps anxious under the camera's cold gaze or fearful of being captured too clearly. He had several times proclaimed his distaste for being photographed, writing that "in the wrong hands—which is to say in insensible or incapable or ill-intentioned hands—the camera tends to magnify every blemish until the smallest anomaly becomes disfigurement."

He was no doubt sensitive about the scar, which ran from cheekbone to jaw, but Alter thought it added interesting character to the poet's pale moonface with its widely spaced almost Oriental eyes, bee-stung womanly lips, and high broad forehead. The angry slash, Alter imagined, was God's afterthought, a reconsideration of Leibert's physiognomy, the last-minute punctuation that made the sentence of his face *work*.

Other, more romantic imaginations might have ascribed the wound to a duel; indeed, Leibert *had* been a connoisseur of bladed exotica: sabers, rapiers, scimitars, basilards, hunting knives from around the world. In his lifetime he amassed a large and valuable assortment, a portion of which was auctioned off after his death, bringing nearly sixty thousand dollars to the estate.

Another letter came—this one from Fred Friedman, owner of a Buy-Rite liquor store in Greenwich Village laid siege to by Leibert during the last year of his life when he occupied a small apartment, a third-floor walk-up on Jane Street. Friedman, retired now and living with his daughter and son-in-law in Port Washington, inquired whether Alter was in a position to make good on a debt of some six hundred dollars still owed him by the poet all these years later. "I extended him and a few other steadies credit," Friedman scrawled, his fountain pen leaving blotches like tiny blue bloodstains across a sheet of seamed and grease-stained loose-leaf paper. It was probably excavated from some kitchen drawer, the biographer thought, buried under old dishcloths, a screwdriver, rolls of electrical tape, a bit of twine, extension cords permanently snarled. Alter stopped reading as he envisioned the old man searching for a scrap on which to compose his missive, burrowing in a home without paper or pens; too old to drive himself to the store for a writing tablet but too proud to ask his daughter to take him; his shame at his dependency so heavy that he wore it like jackboots, hardly able to lift his legs, confined in a suburban prison, and forced to end his days in his grown grandson's bedroom. It was no wonder then that Friedman's letter went on, "I would forgo the interest on the money if I could just have the six hundred. It would come in handy right now."

Sorry to refuse the man, Alter answered that he was neither Leibert's accountant nor the executor of his estate but that, being acquainted with the executor, he would see what he could do. Had he the money to spare, Alter might have sent it himself.

A poem arrived; rather, a photocopy of a poem. Reproduced on the slick greyish paper disgorged by the equipment in public libraries, it reeked—an eye-watering chemical stench. Poorly typed, with misspellings throughout, the words themselves were bloated, as if, like a victim of drowning (somehow more criminal, Alter thought, than accidental), the verse had lain long on the bottom of the harbor, rising suddenly now, borne to the surface on its own necrotic fumes.

The sender claimed to have the handwritten original, as well as fourteen more poems, all of which had had their genesis on the backs of paper placemats taken from table seven at the Washington Irving Diner in Poughkeepsie, New York. Maxwell Leibert, during two semesters he spent as poet-in-residence at Vassar College, had formed a profound taste for—not to say a neurotic attachment to—the meat loaf, mashed potatoes, and limp green beans served at the diner. Table seven, a large booth at the back, hard on the men's room and pay telephones, became his court where nightly he ate his own dinner and the remains of his companions' meals, washing everything down in rivers of Schlitz.

Eating and drinking, he regaled an audience of students and faculty with slanderous tales of the famous. Leibert

seemed equally to enjoy cutting both enemies and friends—
even his heroes—down to size. "My memory is of watching
a crazy boxer," one of Leibert's former students wrote, "bi-
cycling around the ring.

It didn't matter to him where he landed his blows, or
necessarily how hard he hit—just how *often*. And he appeared to have the goods on everyone. When he ran out
of steam on the subject of other writers, he lit into pol-
iticians, movie stars, mobsters, even the royal family. No
one was exempt. And if one suspected that some of his
tales were spun from whole cloth it didn't matter. It was
a glorious weave, shot through with the silver thread of
brilliance, fantastically imagined. He compelled you to
believe in them so fervently that they became truth.

The poem's sender, Florence Siminovski, still a waitress
at the Washington Irving Diner, had been presented with
the poetry by Leibert upon his departure from Poughkeepsie. Never a munificent tipper (often the poet's annual income only flirted with the low five figures), he regularly
offered his work to unlikely parties in exchange for services
rendered or sometimes as security on loans that were never
repaid. The recipients, suspecting that the manuscripts
would someday be worth a good deal more than the labor
performed, were usually content. And so, in the years since
his death poems had turned up in many hands and in various parts of the country: from a bartender in Tulsa, a
restauranteur in San Francisco (the poems composed after
long evenings of food and drink were among his less worthy
efforts), to a dry cleaner in Pittsburgh. And the mortician
in Cincinnati who had presided over Leibert's mother's funeral had accepted five sonnets in place of his more custom-

ary fee. With a fair degree of accuracy Alter was able to trace Leibert's peregrinations by tracking this tossed-off verse, as in fairy tales children find their way home (or to the witch's hut) by following a trail of breadcrumbs. The poet's integrity may have been open to question in other areas, but he was scrupulous in dating even the least of his oeuvre.

Often the poetry only confirmed what Alter already knew, that Leibert had been in a certain place at a certain time. But sometimes he was surprised. A cache of doggerel that came to light in a hatbox in Paris caused Alter to fly across the ocean. He met and interviewed a middle-aged Parisian prostitute with whom Leibert had spent a night; not in her small rooms (conscience-stricken, he had been unable to complete the act), but wandering under the stars at the cemetery at Montparnasse. They had visited the tombs of Baudelaire and Saint-Saëns. At the tomb of Maupassant he had collapsed to his knees, weeping. Later, over supper at the Brasserie Lipp, Maxwell Leibert gave the streetwalker the poems as payment for her time and for the use of her silk handkerchief, ruined with his tears. Generously, she entrusted them to Raphael Alter, who flew back to the United States with the pink hatbox on his lap.

From a fat man who sidled up to him following a panel discussion, "Whither Biography?," in which Alter had participated, he received a name and telephone number scribbled on the back of a program. Alter called the number and it put him in touch with the fat man's brother, a college roommate of Leibert's who, long ago, had presciently rescued from the trash two palinodes in which the fledgling poet retracted sentiments in two earlier poems. He then apparently had a further change of heart, retracting the retractions by throwing the work into the garbage.

Alter did not have the poems to which the palinodes

referred but, reading backwards so to speak, he determined that they concerned an older, married woman living in Baltimore with whom the twenty-year-old Leibert had had a brief liaison. Until then, Alter knew neither of the affair nor that Leibert had ever been in Baltimore. That trail led him eventually to the woman's daughter, from whom he learned that Leibert had suffered a broken ankle after falling from his lover's fire escape while trying to escape her husband. Maryland court papers revealed that, a month after the accident, Leibert was cited as corespondent in the divorce.

Florence Siminovski asked a thousand dollars for the original of the poem that lay, stinking, on Alter's desk, and thirty-three hundred more for the entire fifteen. How she had arrived at precisely these figures she left a mystery. What yardstick of literary merit had she employed? Or was there an item she coveted—a used car?—that the forty-three hundred would cover? Alter wondered and worried. There was little doubt that the poem was the genuine article and all the more precious for never having been published or indeed seen by another soul save himself and the waitress. He wanted the work, all of it. Yet he was in no position to meet the woman's price and doubtless his publisher would not agree to foot the bill. A day passed and then the night. On the morning of the second day he decided to enter into a protracted negotiation with an eye to getting Siminovski to lower her financial sights. He wrote, saying, "While I do not for a moment question your sincerity or the authenticity of the material you possess, I need more time to study the poem. In the meantime," he continued, "I will consider your terms for parting with the rest of the cycle." In this way Alter hoped to buy time with her, and to begin a correspondence that would take them through the bitter Poughkeepsie winter and into the early blush of spring when—having won first her trust and then, if all went well, her affection—he would propose a drive upstate to dine and talk.

(He imagined Florence Siminovski alone, boarder in a single room with a single bed, a hot plate, a small black-and-white TV her only link with the world beyond Pough-keepsie, one weak station for the news, which didn't make much sense but only irritated her, as there was too much of it, all bad and nothing connecting to anything else, stories told for a few nights and then abandoned—half-told tales, falsely hinting that the fighting had abruptly ended in Central America or Beirut, or the budget had been balanced, or the children in Africa whom she had seen only the night before with flies crawling in their noses and ears, feasting on snot, suddenly had enough to eat. But the news didn't really reach Poughkeepsie, not the effects of it anyhow, except in the accelerating supermarket prices, the occasional drug bust over at the college, and the odd weather conditions, which frightened Florence a little and for some reason revived her flagging faith in the Almighty, or at least in the power of His wrath.)

Alter would recommend to the waitress a country inn he knew of near Poughkeepsie, an inn with a broad veranda overlooking a rolling lawn and, in spring, banks of flowering dogwood. At twilight, on the veranda, they would sip cocktails before repairing to the dining room. He pictured her preprandial beverage as sweet and rich, a brandy Alexander or something with crème de cacao or crème de menthe. His would be a vodka martini. As the sun sank she would grow tipsy with the liquor and the unaccustomed attention, the sugary concoction crusting on her upper lip. She would order another, then perhaps a third (by this time it would be growing dark and colder but she wouldn't notice, warmed by the alcohol and his presence beside her), and at last they would speak of their mutual acquaintance, so to say, the dead poet Leibert. She would feel in control of their dialogue, more in control the drunker she became, and would remind Alter again and again that *"I* knew him personally and *you* didn't." This was incontrovertible fact, he would concede, and the reason he had come to her. With that simple observation she would relax, the muscles in her knotted jaw slackening. In other words: *she had not come to him.* And the biographer's way of listening, the gravity with which he invested the occasion, the miles he had traveled to this moment, would give weight to her memories, to her *self,* which until now she had kept hidden and had spoken of to no one, afraid of being crushed or, worse, that these memories which constituted herself were lighter than air, hollow as a tube, nothing.

For a time she would be silent, he thought. Alter would look at her sideways, then in deference to a privacy he had willfully invaded and churned up, he would avert his eyes to the rolling lawn—the area closest to them still in light from the windows at their backs, the rest cloaked in blackness. That part could only be known by extrapolation, by the sounds of the crickets living in the grass and the rustle of a breeze stirring the dogwood. He could imagine as well what Florence would be feeling in her silence, remembering Max: it would be like coming back to a familiar house after a long and transforming illness, an illness that had begun in that house and from which there had been no guarantee of re- covery. And through her struggle with the illness or within it, her relation to the world and to her home place would be transfigured, so that everything remained exactly as she had left it and looked the same, yet different.

At the end of the evening, back in her room, as Florence dug in a bureau drawer for the missing poems (now freely given, no strings attached), she would confide that she was—had always been, naturally—in love with their author and had imagined that the poems were written with her in mind; that the possession of them had elevated her beyond her meager status, had graced her life. There is something angry in me, she would say, handing them over, and that's the only reason I wanted to sell. Mr. L was greatly fond of me and then went away, leaving me these poems but never calling, never writing me a proper letter. I know I had no right, no right at all to expect it, but a person can't help the way she feels . . .

Then she would sink onto the bed, hoping the biographer would join her there to complete what had been left undone by his subject, but knowing he would not, could not. As Alter left, at the door, *sneaking away*, he would commend her for her inestimable and selfless contribution to the history of American letters. *Mmmm*, she would murmur, rolling over, but I was never loved, not for an instant. Alter would leave her there, lonely to the marrow of her bones, staring at the blank wall, staring at her loneliness in the blank wall.

He made copies of the Siminovski letter and his reply, started a new file, and put it away. The biography was still a long way from completion—he had not yet even begun to write. But he was certain of his eventual success with Florence Siminovski; she would open herself to him, if only to forget for a few hours her solitude, filled with thoughts of

death, or merely to talk with another human being. More-
over, when all was said and done, she would thank him for
giving her the opportunity to hear her own true voice.

A parcel of brown paper contained a pair of Maxwell Leibert's eyeglasses. They had been left behind at the Arlington, Virginia, home of a friend sometime between 1940 and
1942 when Leibert paid visits there during trips he made to
Washington. The poet whispered that the journeys were of
a clandestine nature but in the same breath boasted openly
to his Virginia friend, and anyone else who would listen, of
top-secret government assignments. He hinted darkly of
relations with the OSS, mentioned a previously undisclosed
gift for code-busting, and sometimes when intoxicated
talked of cryptanalysis, redundancies, Probable Words, re-
enciphered messages. Alter had confirmed that Leibert told
these stories but could not turn up any evidence that they
were true. More likely, he discovered from a reading of
army documents, Leibert (excused from active duty because
of acute myopia) had only participated in writing army
training manuals; one, on the use of light antiaircraft guns,
another on close-formation drill, and a third on the avoid-
ance of venereal diseases, updating and revising already published material.

The friend in Arlington had died in 1975. His son, now
in his forties, having seen Alter's newspaper solicitation,
conveyed the eyeglasses with a note: "Been in the family for
years. Thought you might enjoy having. Good luck with
the project."

Alter gently folded out the earpieces. The one on the left
was still secured to the frame with a bent paper clip and old
Scotch tape that crumbled away at his touch. He perched

the heavy tortoiseshell horn-rims on the bridge of his nose and reveled in the heft of them. As he looked about the room he noted with a palpable thrill that he and Leibert shared similar deficient vision. He stood up, tried the view from the window. It was only mildly distorted. Alter was able to make out passersby, if not quite their sexes. He wore the glasses for several hours until by evening, while making himself a peanut butter and strawberry jam sandwich, he became nauseated and had to remove them; they had worn a deep ridge in his nose.

A trove of adolescent love letters sent Alter scurrying down to the Lower East Side, to the Lillian Wald Houses on Avenue D, where he spent a July afternoon sifting through the contents of Belle Krinsky's closet. One of Leibert's childhood sweethearts, she had hoarded the poet's outpourings since their days together at P.S. 33 in the Bronx. The closet was filled from floor to ceiling with mildewed cartons. As Alter dragged one after another into Belle's sweltering living room in search of the prize, it occurred to him that his work involved *digging in more ways than one* and that all these various artifacts of the biographical quest—and the people who came attached to them—were as compelling as the biography itself.

Alter's telephone was unlisted (the biographer's precaution against embittered late-night monologists) and so he received few calls.

On a morning in the middle of December, an unexpected blizzard dressed the world outside in white. Alter, looking from his bedroom window, saw a car appear, ghostly, moving at a creep, then a single pedestrian walking headbent against the wind; after a few seconds they dematerialized back into the shroud of snow. The entire city seemed sound-proofed, weirdly hushed, as if during the night, as he slept, it had vanished altogether and only he and a handful of others remained, forgotten or deliberately passed over. He imagined, standing at the window, that at the right time the survivors would be called together, led by a psychic command to a subterranean location, there to learn what they had in common and what they were supposed to do next. Until then, they were not to speak or acknowledge to one another their circumstances. The prospect of being al-most completely alone in the void quiet of this snowbound world did not disconcert him; instead it filled him with wonder: would those who were left discover something mi-raculous about themselves?—for instance, that they could communicate without speaking, pass right through each other like phantoms, reconstituting all their connections and imbuing this new life with transcendent signifi-cance? . . . He was a writer, passed many hours alone, and was prone to daydreams.

In bedroom slippers Alter made his daily pilgrimage to the lobby to collect the mail. He owned the small, five-story building in which he lived, an inheritance from his father, who had purchased it twenty-five years ago with money won in a week-long poker game.

"It's falling down around your ears," Alter's mother wailed in her phone calls to him. "You are running your birthright into the ground. I remember the old days when your father kept it like a palace, he was so proud, a Persian rug in the lobby and a doorman, he paid a doorman around the clock to guard the door!"

"Birthright, Mama?" he wanted to snort, but never chal-lenged her.

Grace Alter's memories were largely fiction. And those

recollections that were not wholly invented were based on gross misreadings of the truth. It *was* true that in the early years his father, a gambler and womanizer, had plowed back a portion of his winnings into the upkeep of the premises; and yes, for a time he *had* been proud. There were lavish parties, and Abraham Alter had even let some of the apartments to his gaudy friends. But the rug was "hot," payment on some debt, and the "doorman" was a lookout, employed first to warn against cops with a nose for illegal card games and, later, as protection against certain "associates" who came around regularly to pay brutal collection calls on Alter's father. Finally, as Abe Alter's luck and fortunes faded, he took whatever profits the building generated and left them at the gaming tables or with loan sharks. His flashy friends abandoned their deteriorating apartments. Grace had also not known about (or, her son suspected, had turned a blind eye to) the presence of Mrs. Estroff, the pretty blond widow who occupied a second-floor apartment, his father's main mistress. There were others too, he knew, in other apartments around town, and in other cities.

The facts were these: Alter's father—his father's life—at once fascinated and terrified him and turned him inward by degrees. He thought of his parent as a big and a little man at the same time: grand in appetites and dreams, but dwarfed in achievement. Abraham Alter's existence was a series of petty wagers with himself and others: driving a car with the gas tank on Empty past a gas station, betting he could make it to the next town without filling up; drinking strangers in bars under the table; starting ill-conceived skirmishes with business colleagues that he could not hope to win but seemed to relish waging. He thrived, in his son's mind, in pointless adventure, against heavy odds. Alter grew up not knowing from one day to the next when the odds would turn, when their fragile little world would finally collapse.

As a teenager he seemed to himself always to have an ear pressed against a door, listening to his mother on the other side negotiating—tearfully or shrilly, depending on the severity of the threat—with legitimate and shady creditors. The closed door was meant to shield the boy, but fear and curiosity drove him to the espionage (and, he surmised years later, also to the pursuit of biography, drawn as he was to closed doors and to exposing the dramas enacted behind them). While *home* was a place fraught with uncertainty in one respect, in another it offered shelter from the wide, crazy world inhabited by his father. Alter as a youth spent most of his free time in his room, on his bed, reading and rereading boys' adventure stories. He sometimes wondered if he *was* his father's son, or if some mistake had been made. As the years of his parents' marriage wore on, he and his mother took most of their meals in each other's company. He wished to free himself of these memories, to consign them to dust, but knew that no man can separate himself from his history.

One unseasonably warm May afternoon, Abe Alter's heart stopped at Aqueduct during the running of the third race. The following week, Raphael Alter moved from the fifth-floor apartment where he had lived as a young man back into the owner's ground-floor flat where he had come of age. By August, he had established his mother in Hollywood, Florida.

Alter knew the building's contours as well as he knew the structures of his own body. The ten apartments, two to a floor, were tenanted by people mostly much older than himself, paying rents well below market value.

". . . I tell you what you must do, Raffi," his mother

counseled long distance, "kick them out, those deadbeats, and raise the rents! Fix it up, put a man back on the door, otherwise you will be left with nothing, *nothing*. Is this asking too much, that you show a little initiative?"

Every week the same thing, a mantra. He listened politely, saying "Ummm, ummm," his mantra. His mother did not seem to notice that he never said more than *ummm* to her anymore.

He could not, as she demanded, raise the rents—bound by laws that prohibited it, bound hand and foot as it were. Yet there *were* legal remedies. He could go to court, appeal, apply by means of endless documents for special dispensations, pleading ruinous conditions and hardship and surely he would prevail: the bottom drawer of his desk was stuffed with citations from building inspectors, elevator inspectors, health inspectors, HUD, the fire department. But he did nothing, sought no relief, and the building operated at a loss, a terrible bone-crushing loss. In at least one observation Grace Alter was correct—it was falling down around his ears. Around all their ears.

On his way down the hall to the lobby Alter examined a new crack in the wall. It extended from the ceiling just to the level of his head. He ran his hand over the ragged seam. Perhaps on the weekend I will spackle, he mused. That would not solve the problem though, only conceal it. The problem was bigger, much bigger, gigantic. And getting worse. For years he had been able, with minor cosmetic and Band-Aid fixes, to keep the structure tolerably operational. But this would no longer do: he had recently discovered that the foundation was rotting underneath them and the entire edifice was shifting and sinking as if into a bog; the problem was that the sinking and shifting had caused other problems in the heating and electrical systems, in the gas mains and water pipes, in the very brick and mortar that held the place together. The roof leaked. Only last week Mr. Bloom on the top floor had complained. Mr. Leipzig on four and Miss Eres on two said their windows no longer fit tightly. The boiler needed cleaning, the furnace needed replacing; the elevator needed new cables and many of the floor indicators were out; the radiators leaked too, spewing driblets of water and scalding steam. The building had taken on a flatulent, derelict life of its own.

I'm running a death trap here.

To Alter's occasional mortification this outing from his apartment to his mailbox, an excursion he could have taken blindfolded, signaled the high point of his day. Otherwise, weeks could pass during which he might barely stir. Often he saw himself as a bear, his apartment a cave, and his biographies as a form of hibernation. He lay in deep sleep, all bodily functions becalmed, awaiting a thaw that never came.

Whatever treasure he hoped to find in the postbox also did not come. Money? God, he wished for it!—even found himself, to his chagrin, praying for funds. He had inherited the building but nothing with which to run it, and after twenty years it was clear he was no businessman. As the building sank so he sank, deeper and deeper into a vortex of debt. A love letter? There weren't any, though these perhaps were what he craved most. Hardly knowing it, never daring to acknowledge it, Alter was afflicted with a formless, inchoate longing for a dart sent with God's grace to lacerate his heart.

Yet never altogether daunted, always fanning the embers of anticipation, the biographer delayed his odyssey to the lobby until after lunch, often until dusk, so as to feed the flickering flame, to heighten the delicious expectation. Merely to receive them, he subscribed to periodicals he only leafed through, then left to accumulate mountainously in his bedroom. He sent for circulars offering free merchandise to discover what he would get back. He filled out irrelevant questionnaires. He had once consented to be a Nielsen family during television "sweeps" week and, in a little booklet, charted his viewing habits in meticulous detail. He entered magazine sweepstakes too; by nature superstitious, not above pinching pennies off the street, he believed that the one time he did not enter a contest could be the occasion Fate had decreed for him to win. (How this would work was not entirely clear, though, for if Fate had decided his triumph, then would not Fate also prevent him from tossing away his entry form?) Finding the small steel cubbyhole of a mailbox filled beyond its capacity to hold one more thin envelope, well, there was some pathetic pleasure in it.

This morning, restless with the day's work, Alter broke with custom and ventured out before noon.

He met one of his second-floor tenants, Clara Eres, just alighting from the elevator. She was a reed-thin woman with hennaed hair who, summer and winter, night and day, wore dark glasses. Today, in spite of the frigid weather or, he guessed, in defiance of it (and of him, the landlord, who did not supply sufficient heat), she wore a sleeveless blouse, pedal pushers, and high-heeled open-toed sandals. The nails of her hands and her feet were painted the same metallic purple. Under one arm she carried a tiny apricot poodle in a red sweater who wheezed asthmatically, its lungs juicy with fluid. Miss Eres drew up short when she saw him. It was too late to retreat. Even through the opaque lenses of her glasses Alter could read the reproach in her eyes; it rose off her like a mist.

"My windows, Mr. Alter."

"I know, Miss Eres, I know."

"When?" she asked.

"Soon."

"With you it is always soon. Soon we'll all be dead."

She sighed and went off down the hall to knock on the door of her friend Mrs. Pompanazzi, leaving Alter bobbing in the wake of her voice.

In the lobby Angel Muñoz, the part-time superintendent, a former Golden Gloves bantamweight contender, swabbed the floor with a strong disinfectant that stung the air and started tears under Alter's eyelids. The use of so powerful a cleanser was unnecessary, but Muñoz had worked for years as a porter in a municipal hospital where stringent sanitary precautions were routine. Alter could no longer afford to pay him a full-time salary and had reduced his regular employment to two days a week, but Muñoz showed up on his off days just the same, his sense of duty so deeply bred in the bone he could not stay away. No natural circumstance, neither rain nor snow nor sleet nor a firestorm if it came to that, would prevent Muñoz from waging his losing battle with the decaying building. He seemed to derive moral energy from the campaign even as he was driven back, forced to retreat to the rear in the face of an implacable foe. During the blackout of 1977, the superintendent had stayed through the night, helping tenants up and down the stairs with his flashlight, bringing candles and food to their doors. A transit strike that lasted months did not deter him from appearing every day though it meant walking six miles to and from the Bronx. And in August of a long hot summer when his neighborhood had been torn by riots, he showed up for work one morning with a gash in his scalp. He had come directly from the Montefiore emergency room where thirty stitches were taken to close the wound. Blood still oozed under the white bandage that rose like a tumor from the side of his head.

Yet superintendent and employer were not precisely friends. Muñoz had never been inside Alter's apartment except to make a minor repair or to collect his paycheck. They had never shared a meal or a cup of coffee, did not exchange small talk or intimacies. A devotion transcending language pertained, each man a constant presence, immutable and unchanging, in the other's life. And as Alter cherished that which was immutable and unchanging, so, he thought, he must cherish Muñoz. Was it love? He knew that something fluttered in his chest when he saw him, some twinge seized his gut.

Alter hiphopped between the muscular strokes of Muñoz's mop. Muñoz looked up.

"Laundry room's flooded," Muñoz said. They exchanged mournful glances. "Water all over the place. Too much soap, machine back up. Need a new part now, it's a mess."

"These are old people," Alter said, shaking his head, uncomprehending. "Old people live here and yet they treat things like vandals, like hoodlums. Even the washing machines they molest."

"Three times this month," Muñoz said without inflection.

A long silence followed, then Alter reached into his back pocket for his wallet and withdrew a twenty-dollar bill. "Can you take care of it before you go?"

Muñoz nodded, crumpling the bill in his fist, the same

fist, with its permanently scarred knuckles, that brought Billy the Kid Ortiz to the mat in 1960. He resumed his mopping as Alter crossed to the bank of mailboxes set in an anteroom off the lobby. Nick the Mailman, halfway through the day's sorting, stood in a puddle of brackish water, melted snow. He worked swiftly, sending each piece of mail to its slot with a practiced, mechanical flick of his wrist.

Alter hung back, unwilling to disrupt the man's labors. When he looked down at Nick's heavy black galoshes he felt small, naked, and impotent in his bedroom slippers. He made a sound, an involuntary rasp of affection for the other immutable figure in his life, the mail carrier, who always showed up and never failed to bring dispatches. Nick turned and smiled, sympathetic to the plight of the thin, pale man before him. He was uncertain of the exact character of Alter's work, but aware that he did it at home, in solitude, and since he could count on a handsome Christmas gratuity he did not make him wait. The postman reached into his canvas sack and scooped out a fistful of envelopes and magazines, bound with rubber bands. Alter accepted the bundle with the downcast nod of the supplicant and hurried away.

On his way across the lobby, the biographer ran into Miss Eres, stepping back into the elevator. She held the door. It pumped jerkily back and forth against her shoulder, trying to close.

"And by the way, Mr. Alter," she said, "*this*, the elevator, it doesn't know up or down anymore. It goes where it goddamn pleases."

"I'm working on it, Miss Eres," Alter lied. "But perhaps if you pressed the Down call button when you wished to go down and the Up call button when you wished to go up, instead of pressing the Up button when you are *already* up and the Down button when you are already down—"

"I don't know what you are talking about."

"I'm talking about logic, Miss Eres."

"Logic?"

"Irrefutable logic." Alter shifted the pile of mail to his other arm. "If you are upstairs and you press Up, the elevator will naturally believe that you want to *go up* and so—"

"Nonsense."

"I have seen you do it," Alter accused. *I have seen you all do it, every last one of you, summoning the elevator, thinking 'I am UP. Come get me UP HERE.' You are so imperious in your demands, you make allowances for nothing—*

"You have seen me do what?" she asked, angered and unnerved at once. "*What* have you seen me do?"

I have seen you masturbate, Clara Eres. I have seen you peel off your pedal pushers and do yourself.

"Just remember that you must tell the elevator where you want to go," he said, feigning patience. "Suggest to it gently—not by pounding on the button a hundred times, hammering on it as I have also seen you do—what are your intentions, in which direction, up or down, you want to travel. It will generally go where you ask, if you ask correctly—"

"You are truly crazy, Mr. Alter, and I'm not alone in this opinion. To stand there and tell me that this machinery *thinks*, it reasons, it has feelings . . ."

"Feelings I don't know about, but it operates on simple principles. Violate those principles and it won't work for you and finally you'll destroy it."

"If I have to walk, if I die on the stairs, if my heart gives out on the stairs, I will hold you personally liable and responsible to the full extent of the law! My heirs will hold you responsible. They'll see that you pay."

He stared at her dubiously, peering into the depths of her sunglasses. "You have heirs, Miss Eres?"

"A niece." Her voice quavered. "You think I am all alone? I have a niece in New Hampshire with two beautiful children and an attorney husband and they will all hold you responsible. You live on the bottom, Alter, on the ground floor, and only come up to take our rents. You come up like a fish, like a whale, to feed on us, and you don't ride the elevator. You are scared of it yourself. I know. I hear you on the stairs. So what do you care—"

"I care, I care." He took a shuddering breath. "There are problems. Problems with money."

"Words," she remonstrated, at last getting on the elevator. "Show that you care. Let us see. A little demonstration would be refreshing."

He reentered his apartment with the relief of the hermit returning to his lair. Sitting at his desk he examined the mail piece by piece before opening any of it, an established ritual.

A Con Edison bill, one from the cable television company, another from MasterCard. A foldout notice from the Museum of Natural History announced the start of a six-week seminar series, Health and Illness in Cross-Cultural Perspective. Alter, a hypochondriac, briefly considered enrolling. He studied the titles of the lectures and the impressive curricula vitae of the participants. He asked himself: might you meet a girl? He also asked himself: do you want to meet a girl? *What would you do if you did?*

A creamy card addressed to Friends of the Library invited him to a preview of a new exhibit at the main branch on

Forty-second Street and Fifth Avenue. But the thirty-five dollars per annum he donated did not entitle him to become a Bosom Buddy. The elegant black-tie affairs that piqued his interest were restricted to the library's well-heeled patrons, most of whom, Alter was certain, rarely cracked a book and never set foot on the premises save for these glittering events. And although he viewed the occasions with a jaundiced eye he nevertheless longed to be a Literary Lion, or at least to be asked. To be one of the writers who once a year were doled out to host tables of real estate developers and junk bond tycoons and their attenuated wives, these guests having contributed several thousand dollars for the privilege of watching a Lion eat, drink, make idle talk, and maybe spill soup on his evening clothes. All the Lions got to wear medals on silk ribbons around their necks. He wondered what was inscribed on the medals and what they celebrated? Courage? Heroism in action? Bravery in word or deed? Yes and no, he decided. They were for the loneliness of the long-distance writer, for seeing it through the clubhouse turn and not fading in the final stretch. As a Lion, this is what the medal would mean to him, even if those bestowing it had no such idea, thought it simply a "nice touch," an impressive souvenir, or just an amusing way to distinguish the Lions from the others in the room.

A letter from the Albert Einstein Fund asked for an additional donation. According to the request, the Doomsday Clock had crept to within three minutes of midnight since the Fund's last communication. The appeal was urgent; the Fund needed money to hold back the hands of Time. He made a mental note to send ten dollars more. A mailing from an African wildlife federation pictured a dead bull elephant collapsed to its knees; where the trunk and tusks should have been, a gaping slash spewed muscle and fat and sinewy white tissue. Alter debated whether he could spare another ten or so to help prevent the extermination of these magnificent animals. The envelope he next turned over screamed BANGLADESH DISASTER: COUNTDOWN TO SURVIVAL. He searched his mind: which disaster was this? famine? poison gas? quake? war? flood? Ah yes, the rains, villages buried under mud; diarrhea, fevers, starvation. Twenty? Ambulances for Nicaragua. The American Civil Liberties Union. American Foundation for AIDS Research. Retinitis Pigmentosa. Lupus. Klanwatch. PEN Freedom to Write Committee.

He set the rest aside unopened and began to browse through an article in the winter issue of a literary review to which he subscribed. The story concerned a Polish writer, dead since 1965, who had spent a large portion of his life in self-exile in Buenos Aires. "Little did he know that those few steps down the ship's ladder would lead him into an abyss of obscurity. He was to stay in Argentina not for several weeks but for the next twenty-four years . . . forgotten by some, ignored by others, and unknown by most. . . ." Alter loosened his hold on the little magazine and it sprang shut. *How about we form the PEN Forget-Me-Not Committee? I volunteer to chair.* A reminder from his dentist informed him he was due for a cleaning. He stuck it in the latest issue of *The Nation.*

An intriguing envelope, squarish in size, stopped him. It was hand addressed, pale pink in color. He sniffed, thought he detected a hint of lavender or violets. A return address in a neighborhood not far from his own appeared on the back flap but no name was appended, just an apartment number. The postmark indicated it had been mailed two days earlier.

I am probably invited to a dinner, Alter thought. Of course I will go. Even if I do not want to go, even if the invitation has been extended insincerely, which is to say by a couple who wish me to understand that I have been asked, I have been *thought of*, but who prefer that I do not actually attend. As the poet Larkin writes, "My wife and I have asked a crowd of craps / To come and waste their time and ours: perhaps / You'd care to join us?"

In point of fact, these people do not want to see me at all. They only want me to *think* they want me. So they have made the motions of inviting me, and I will pretend to accept with pleasure, owing to a weakness of character that does not allow me to decline the few invitations I receive, however insincere. And when finally I arrive at the appointed place at the appointed time (having dreaded the engagement for weeks), we will all pretend to be delighted to see one another, smiling, shaking hands heartily, claps on the back all around, and exchanging kisses, while hiding our deep dismay at the whole affair: mine, that I could not stay away and now must endure this evening; and theirs, that I have taken them up on the false summons, obliging them to play gracious hosts. Nonetheless, by the end of the night I will have served my purpose, as will the other guests, the interior purpose for which we have all been invited, *to paint over the cracks in their life together*, as I spackle the cracks in the walls of my building, concealing but not healing.

Unable to be alone, alone with each other—indeed more lonely together than they are apart—my hosts hold court amiably over tables of not quite welcome guests, hold them hostage, actually, to their decaying marriage. And they can expect (the other hidden purpose of the party) that these dinners of theirs will net them x number of invitations in return, which will get them out of the house and out of each other's company, where they will in turn serve *their* purpose at another couple's table, spackling over the cracks in *their* disintegrating union.

But my hosts will receive no invitation from me. I am only one, truly alone, part of no union, decaying or otherwise, and do not give dinner parties. I am a writer, a *published writer* (published if not widely read), one of the pegs in the evening's entertainment, a divertissement. My hosts will put me on display just as they have put their artwork on display, their furniture (Biedermeier? Louis XIV?), the obtrusive floral centerpiece on their table, the exotic and unappetizing food, the heavy wines. So I ought to refuse this party where I am to be exhibited like a newly acquired painting or Fabergé egg. But I haven't the will to resist, to turn from blandishments even if fake or fleeting. Craven, base in my needs, I embarrass myself . . .

However, when Alter opened the scented pink envelope that had evoked the fantasy dinner party, he found not an invitation at all but two heavy sheets of pale pink letter paper. His heart dropped, just a little.

The handwriting gave nothing away. It evinced a strange control, the script perfectly uniform as if the writer wished to disguise or dissemble. Or was it the hand of one who had learned to form letters again after a grave insult to the brain? He read:

Dear Raphael (if I may), I write in response to your notice in the *New York Times* of several Sundays ago. At first I was not going to write at all, but at last realized that my motives for keeping silent any longer were at best foolish, and at worst criminal.

I have information regarding Maxwell Leibert that I believe may be of interest to you. There is no doubt in my mind that his life story cannot be called complete, or accurate, without it.

I am aware of your reputation as a scrupulous biographer (your 1973 work on Randall Jarrell occupies a place in my modest library). Nevertheless I feel I must assure myself as to your character, and that I will feel comfortable with you, and that you will treat whatever I may tell you in an even-handed and judicious manner. To that end, kindly write to me (if you are interested), enclosing your telephone number. I have discovered it's unlisted. I will call you at my earliest convenience so that we can arrange a time and a place to meet.

The letter was unsigned.

Alter read it a second time, struck by the stilted turns of phrase, wondering if they were more subterfuge. He replaced the letter in its envelope, took out a sheet of stationery from a box at his elbow, and positioned it in the roller of his typewriter.

"Dear Apartment 7-N . . ."

The wind howled, rattling Alter's windows as if someone were trying to break in. Through one of them he caught sight of Mr. Muñoz in the arctic cold and snow, wrestling a large metal garbage can to the curb. He set it down so hard that the lid popped off and a cloud of ash billowed into the air.

TWO

"Raphael?" came the female voice again. Buttery. Scorched.

The biographer luxuriated briefly in a sensual memory of rice pudding fresh from his mother's oven with a crusty cinnamon top. His spoon, as it were, pierced the lightly burnt shell and sank slowly, slowly into the warm gooey heart of the dessert.

"This is he." Silence. "Hello?"

"This is Chloe." Then, after a beat, "Apartment seven-N?"

Alter cleared his throat. Since noontime he had not spoken; and then, only a few words to a small girl who had been allowed into the building by Muñoz and had appeared at his door selling Girl Scout cookies. He had put three boxes on reserve. Now a clot of phlegm lodged in his larynx; from the feel of it, had taken up permanent residence there. He wanted to spit, but swallowed hard.

"Is this a bad time?" The hot-pudding voice.

"Not at all," he replied. *You are my first human contact all day, not counting Muñoz and Nick, one irate tenant, and an eight-year-old selling cookies.* "So glad to hear from you. I wasn't certain . . ."

"Neither was I. Believe me, I've been looking for a way out."

Why did Alter get the feeling that the faceless Chloe was balancing, psychically speaking, on one leg?

"You received my letter, then," Alter said.

"Of course. Where do you suppose I got your number?"

Another strained silence, during which Alter tried to situate the name within his research: *Chloe.* He riffled through some notes on his desk. No, these were from an interview he'd conducted the week before with a Park Avenue internist who had treated Leibert for colitis, persistent headaches, a rash on the backs of his arms and legs. Leibert's children. Benjamin. Jonathan. Ulysses, known to family and friends as Lee, and Hannah, Leibert's only daughter, the baby, living now in Toronto and trying to eke out a living as a painter. Wives. There had been two: Edythe, the mother of his children, whom he had divorced; and Tamsin, his second wife, who had left him suddenly under circumstances that were still unclear to Alter. Chloe. He could not place the name.

"Would you like to get together?" she said.

"Huh?" Alter blurted. "Yes, yes, very much."

He heard the sound of a match, a sulphurous burst. He listened as she inhaled and in his mind's eye saw the stream of smoke as she exhaled, hitting the receiver and splaying out to engulf her face. What sort of face? Young? Middle-aged? Gaunt? Round? Her voice revealed little but indecision.

"I work, you know." Her tone turned sharper, as if he were somehow responsible for her enforced employment.

Alter was often held vaguely accountable for the burdens, and sins, of his subjects. Had Max Leibert owed her money, in his customary fashion? Or, as so many other women, did she feel cheated, or betrayed by his lies? Or indeed by his assurances (*Leave everything to me / We can go on like this forever / I love you*) in which had been suspended, like drops of oil in water, the lies? What had the poet done to her?— for surely he had marked her, acted upon her, hadn't simply slithered across her life leaving no trace. As the boot track left in sod by the escaped convict eventually leads to his capture, so Leibert left his imprint too.

"Where can we meet?" asked Alter. The line popped with static. "Hello?" he said, certain he had lost her.

"I'm here."

"Perhaps we might meet some evening, after work."

"Sure." She sounded melancholy now, her voice striated with sadness. If it was as Alter suspected, she had some old dry bones to pick with Leibert, who was dead but not gone. He could very nearly hear them crack. She mentioned a bar a few blocks from his building. "Say about six, Thursday?"

"Perfect."

"Or a little earlier. Maybe you could get there a little earlier and find a table. I don't like sitting at bars."

Interesting—Max had loved to sit at bars. He flitted from one to another, pollinating and cross-pollinating; there were men in bars who knew other men in bars only because they all knew Leibert. Barroom friendships had been made, broken, and mended through his intercession. Bars were his sport and his pastime, his passion; they had become his vocation. Of the poems he had written to the grape the best known was "Monks," in which "arrayed down the length of the altar / sticky, smelling faint of spilt wine and blood / we sit in silent contemplation of the whiskey god."

"I'll be there," Alter said. "How will I know you?"

"I'll know you. Your photograph is on the book jacket."

"The Jarrell? That was years ago."

"You can't have changed so much."

"The beard's greyer." *Whiter*, he amended.

Alter worked a plumber's snake down the toilet.

"Hurry hurry hurry, I have to go again."

"I'm working as fast as I can, Mr. Bloom."

The eighty-year-old Bloom, emaciated but for a hugely distended belly, hung at the threshold of the bathroom in a stained undershirt and pajama bottoms. He had come knocking on Alter's door, ten-thirty at night, seeking assistance. In the basement Alter found Muñoz's snake, a plunger, a can of Drano, a jug of Liquid-Plumr. He arrived at Bloom's door prepared to blast a hole to the center of the earth.

The air in the apartment smelled of rancid feces, an unwell aroma, sickly sweet. Bloom himself was tainted with the stench, it followed after him, spoorlike. Those who smell of their own dung never seem to smell it themselves, thought Alter. One of God's small blessings.

"How much paper do you use?"

"I'm a sick man," Bloom answered in a tone that indicted his landlord for impudence, "my bowels run day and night is how much I use. I buy for a platoon, in bulk. My life is no barrel of monkeys."

"I'm sorry." *The ancient Egyptians held that when you die your soul leaves your body through your nose. Morris Bloom's soul floods away as he lives, in torrents of shit. Christ, people's lives! the exquisite forms of torture—*

"Because of my condition I had to sell the business. For

ten minutes I can't be away from the john. I'm chained to the commode. *Hurry*, will ya?"

"You put anything else in here, Mr. Bloom, besides the paper?"

Behind Alter's back, there was a shrug in Bloom's voice, the insouciance of a naughty child. "Napkins. Napkins, sometimes."

"Napkins? Dinner napkins?"

"Nah. Ladies' *diapers*, you know? They're soft, my rectum bleeds, I use 'em to wipe."

Oh *Lord*. "You mustn't, Mr. Bloom—"

"What're you telling me?"

"You can't throw those things in the toilet, they won't go down. You have to find another way to dispose of them. You understand?"

"Yeah . . . I understand. You're blaming *me*. But listen, you got no pressure up here, no water pressure at all, just a trickle like a baby's pish. It's *your* fault entirely."

"Still," Alter said, guiding the snake along twisting pipe, deep into the viscera of the building, "you cannot put . . . ladies' *diapers* in the toilet." He hit something. "This is it, I think." He grunted, forcing the snake against the obstruction; his stomach somersaulted at what must be there, an impacted swollen black mass of bloody toilet paper and sanitary pads, Bloom's death sentence. The fertile smell of refuse rose in his nostrils. The mass moved, the pipe belched. He withdrew the snake. Droplets of water beaded on its tip fell to the grey-and-white checked floor. He held the curling steel away from his body and flushed. Clear, cool water filled the bowl, then swirled away. Alter thought, foolishly, of a mountain stream. He turned.

"We're done."

The old man followed the landlord into the living room,

his slippers slapping against his heels. "And while I have you," said Bloom as Alter opened the front door, "the roof."

"Yes."

"*Yes*," Bloom said belligerently, "yes, the man says. What about *do, fix*, what about some *action*? I was in business, Alter. A business, like a building, does not run itself. You cannot let things slide, not forever."

"I am well aware of the problem," Alter replied dumbly.

"And also, the noise. When will it end?"

Bloom referred to the demolition taking place next door—another small apartment building being gutted from the inside out, finally to be renovated and restored.

"I don't know. The work has just begun."

"Some racket," Bloom complained, "all day crashing and thumping. Like donkeys copulate in my wall. By night I don't get a wink and now by day I don't get rest. Can't you make it stop?"

"No." *No, I cannot. Am I responsible for the entire world? Are you demanding, Bloom, that I accept responsibility for the whole fucking flaming bleeding world?*

Bloom wheedled. "Well, I live here, don't I? I pay rent, always on time. I am entitled to some peaceful enjoyment of the premises. Not luxuries, *peace*. Simple . . . So who else can I go to with my *tsuris*? There is only you, no one else."

"Muñoz," Alter suggested, more to himself than his tenant, "maybe I could get Muñoz to go over and talk to the demolition crew. Ask them to stop earlier. Then you could get some rest . . ."

Bloom considered it. "Angel? A nice man, but he hardly talks the language. Besides, you're the boss. The boss is the boss," he reminded him sternly.

Alter closed the door and headed for his own apartment, a man pursued.

The biographer dressed for his meeting with Chloe in a jacket of nubby brown wool, a plain white shirt, brown tie, brown trousers, his explicit intention to fade into the woodwork. Bright colors distracted, his theory went, so when conducting an interview he dressed with an eye to the drab—no inconvenience since, over time, drear had become his usual wardrobe; almost without thinking he had purged his closets and drawers of the few reds and yellows and greens he found there and replaced them with tans and beiges, bone and umber and oatmeal, a tedious palette. He wrapped an ocher-colored scarf around his neck and into the pocket of his overcoat dropped a reporter's notebook and a new Bic pen.

He left early so that he might walk in a leisurely fashion to his destination. Snow no longer fell and the temperature had plummeted, making the ground icy underfoot. Alter moved with the deliberate, gingerly steps of the recovering invalid.

Bits of shining radio antennas poked skyward, like periscopes, from automobiles entombed in sloping drifts on either side of the street. Next door, workmen from Ruggiero Demolition were back at work. A scaffolding had been erected, a canopy of wood and iron piping over the sidewalk. Two black men wearing hard hats stood at an opening on the top floor, formerly a window, pushing splintered beams, bricks, and large jagged slabs of concrete down a chute. A sink, then a toilet tank, followed. The debris hurtled with a roar into a green Dumpster at the curb. Alter watched their labor for a few moments before scuttling under the scaffold and down the block.

The bar, in a residential neighborhood, was uncrowded. Only writers, artists, bookies and others who lived in suspicious or disreputable ways frequented the place at drinking time. The bars in midtown, Alter thought with a stab of longing, would be as boisterous and lively as Rotary Club carnivals at this hour; tightly packed with businessmen, their ties and tongues loosened after a day at the office.

He himself had been a student until his twenty-ninth year, mainly because he could not imagine himself in any other role, given as he was to solitary activity. He remembered fondly his part-time job in the bowels of the university library locating research materials for those upstairs; remembered absorbing hours spent in shadowy, subterranean aisles pushing a rolling wire cart, piling up books, periodicals, folios, and sending them aloft in a dumbwaiter. He had discovered a degree of contentment in the dim basement maze, looked on himself as *an intellectual mole*, invisible, protected and warm, burrowing and taking his nourishment from a root system derived from the abundant scholarship of centuries. He felt no pressing desire to emerge into daylight. So his studies proceeded slowly (deliberately, he said), prolonging his time in the tunnels.

When at last he earned his Ph.D. in literature, he briefly considered teaching as a profession, but instead took a job as a junior advertising copywriter at a Madison Avenue firm. Alter made this experimental sally beyond the constricted circumference of academe at the urging of Grace Alter (who spoke fervently of his joining *the real world* of regular hours and paychecks, so unlike his father's). After thirteen months, Abraham Alter died and the son quit Madison

Avenue, beating a hasty retreat back into the presumed safety of the shell where he had always lived. Placid and estranged, he assumed the management of the building and began to write—a poem here, a brief critical essay there—although he was not certain, in the beginning, where precisely it would end. Even then, he was only fuzzily aware of the souls who thronged around him, hearing life in muffled sounds and perceiving images as if through smoke. His father gone, his mother dispatched to sunnier climes, he achieved not happiness but, as he thought of it, *a level of comfort*, rather like the long tepid baths he enjoyed, the water neither hot nor cold.

When he was halfway along in his first biography, Alter sensed he had found his niche—a life that could be lived largely in libraries and archives, and almost completely at second hand. All his work as a biographer might be carried on, in a sense, at one remove; whatever attachment (or resentment) his informants might conceive toward him he could ascribe to a sort of transference, in which the emotion was really directed at the subject of the biography, not the biographer. Alter had no foes that he knew of, and no particularly close companions. He told himself that this was the way he wanted things, that this was enough. Yet lately, not long after he had started on the Leibert biography, he sensed the imminence of pain, as a heaviness in the head and a scratchiness behind the eyelids announces the onset of fever. He wondered what form the pain would take. As with the decomposing building, he watched and waited for signs and manifestations with vague, uneasy anticipation, spectator at the sideshow of his own life.

The truth of his work, Alter admitted, choosing a booth near the back of the bar and slouching out of his coat, was that the days and weeks and years devoted to his typewriter and notes, with rare forays into the world outside his walls, did not strike him as labor wholly suited to a man. Men were meant to go abroad in society. To dig trenches, lay foundations, build—bridges, roads, skyscrapers; to drive locomotives, steam shovels, cranes, trucks, and tractors; to navigate vast bodies of water, the sky, ribbons of highway; to attach things to other things in a skillful and offhand manner; to rob, cheat, swindle, and connive, redirecting the flow of great rivers of wealth; to fight and die if it came to that. Sometimes Alter engaged in a peculiar voyeurism, pausing at street corners to gaze at telephone repairmen shimmying up poles; at Con Edison workers lowering themselves into hellishly steaming holes in the pavement; at policemen—they swaggered!—guns and billy clubs, handcuffs and summons books hanging from their hips. Men with tools: ripe as pregnant women and as heavy with expectation.

Only one other booth was occupied when Alter entered the bar. A young man with steel-rimmed glasses and a patchy beard, wearing blue jeans and a bulky sweater, sat silent across the aisle. Minutes later he was joined by a slim woman of his own age in similar garb. From a knapsack she produced a stack of papers, official-looking, and in a flurry of impatience slapped them on the table between them. They ordered beers.

An edict, Alter thought. Perhaps they are divorcing and these are the final documents, needing only their signatures to declare the rift irrevocable. Yet they look hardly old enough to be out of college, much less to have been married and already sweeping up the fine ash of disillusion . . . The boy particularly seemed distressed, staring fixedly into his brew as if searching for stray bits of hair in the dying foam. The girl talked on, oblivious to his lack of response—or had she grown inured to it?—turning page after page of the decree, trying to draw his attention to this paragraph or that subparagraph. But the boy would not be enlisted; he did not adjust his waxen pose or raise his troubled eyes from the glass.

Alter ordered a scotch. He glanced again at the young man and woman. Everywhere he looked, he found biography; and where a story did not suggest itself, the struggle to invent one engrossed him—an impulse as uncontrollable as a tic.

"Mr. Alter?"

He looked up. A woman in a cherry-red overcoat stared at him questioningly. It must have started to snow again; the shoulders of her coat were flecked with ice as was her thick auburn hair glinting reddish gold under an overhead light. She looked to be in her middle thirties.

"Chloe?" He half rose, his knees pinned under the table. "Raphael," he volunteered.

"Don't get up," she said, saving him. She slid onto the opposite bench, slipping her arms from the coat and leaving it there behind her, bunched up carelessly. *Or perhaps she is already preparing to run.*

"May I get you a drink?"

"A whisky sour, please."

Alter motioned for the waitress. Chloe dug in her handbag, took out cigarettes, a packet of matches. Without thinking he reached for the matches, struck one, held it out toward her. A current of air threatened the tiny flame; it flickered; she cupped her hand over his, putting the tip of the cigarette to the match. *Do I hold in my own a hand once held by Maxwell Leibert?* A shiver ran through him at the thought that the press of her fingers might connect him, in a fashion, to the life they had mutually touched. He felt a nearly irresistible desire not to let go.

"I'm trying to quit," she said, exhaling, offering an oblique and, Alter thought, nearly grudging apology for her habit. A cloud of bluish smoke settled over their heads. Chloe drew on the cigarette again. "Have you always done this kind of work?" she asked, hurrying on. He could not tell whether her tone implied a compliment or an insult.

"I started with book reviews and critical essays, that's my training. Biography came about quite by accident. I was approached by a publisher who'd seen my work, a piece I'd done on Louis Oldfield."

"Who's he?" she asked bluntly. He found it attractive that she made no attempt to bluff, to pretend to knowledge she did not possess.

"An obscure British poet and explorer. He served in one of those strange 'private armies' stationed in Cairo and Alexandria during the Second World War. His commanding officer was Evelyn Waugh. He died in Tangier in 1955 . . . No one you should know, necessarily. So, I was offered a small advance and that's how I started." He folded his arms across his chest protectively. "My story."

"Or what you wish to tell of it. There must be more." Chloe gazed at him in an open, disconcerting way.

"Really, that's it. I'm terribly dull and quiet. The days pass, I hardly know how, I look up from my work and the sun has set." *I live sealed in a secret room behind a false wall, buried alive against nameless threats.*

"You say you're 'terribly dull and quiet' but choose as your first subject an adventurer who dies in Tangier."

"Well, one explains the other. Anyway, we're not here to talk about me."

"Are you married?" she asked. He wished she would take her eyes off him. He lowered his own for an instant.

"Not now," he said, cannily equivocal. He had never been married at all.

"You live alone?"

"Yes, I do."

The waitress returned with Chloe's drink and a bowl of mixed nuts. Alter selected a large cashew and some salted almonds.

"But of course you aren't strictly *alone*," Chloe observed, discarding a maraschino cherry from the drink, "you have Max. You had Mr. Oldfield, and Mr. Jarrell. And all their friends and enemies."

She calls him "Max," not "Leibert." The intimacy of the address establishes that her familiarity is firsthand. I must go cautiously, must not let her get away.

"Yes, I have Max . . . and my other subjects, I suppose you could say." He sipped his scotch, turning watery now. "Actually, more than that. I own the building where I live, so I have my tenants too. They are in a way like family—a family of crotchety old uncles and aunts who hold me, as families will, in some disdain."

"Why?" Chloe took a healthy swallow of her drink, letting the cigarette languish in the ashtray. Alter perceived that she dwelled on him to avoid speaking of Leibert. And he allowed it, even encouraged it, hoping to break down her reticence regarding the poet.

"Because . . . I cannot do enough for them. I mean literally, I can *not*. It's impossible. The building belonged originally to my father." Alter hesitated, skidding over the sordid details of his life story, and when he opened his mouth again said, "When he died, I took it over. I probably ought to have found a buyer, because what I truly inherited from my father is the lack of a gift for business. But somehow it was difficult for me to put it into the hands of a stranger. Perhaps the building's the one thing that binds me to my dad . . . Anyway, it's a losing proposition, just hemorrhages money, and I have never been able to turn it around . . . I exist in a state of imminent disaster." *Something else I unfortunately share with Abe.*

"Join the club," she said, sighing. "The well-known human condition. But you are not, as you say, utterly alone."

"No. I guess I'm surrounded," he admitted. "And you? What are your circumstances? Married?" The question made him feel somehow ridiculously conventional.

"Never." Her tone made it clear that she did not wish to linger on the subject. Chloe tamped out her cigarette, half smoked. "How far along are you in the book?"

"Still in the research stage. I haven't begun writing yet."

"So you're of an open mind, I presume, willing to be surprised."

"I *want* to be surprised. I hope for it," Alter said eagerly. "A biography is for me a sort of pursuit, a hunt, tracking a person's path through the past, trying to ferret out the hidden truths of his life. I can't, I don't want to, know where I'll come out. It's as if I'm chasing someone, a fugitive, through a forest at night with only a flashlight to guide me. Ahead I hear the footfalls of the person I'm after, but I can only see as far as the flashlight's beam." He thought for a moment. "Then too, it's a bit of a love affair. A fragile one. You're never certain how long the infatuation may last . . . Over time you make small unpleasant discoveries that at first you try to ignore or excuse. Reality intrudes, and with it a certain useful disenchantment. Well, the affair must end if a good biography is to result . . . At the same time, though, to make my subject come alive for a reader today, I must feel with him to some extent, re-experience his thoughts and desires and struggles. I must engage the world with him. Sympathetic yet aloof, detached yet involved." He hoped he didn't sound too woefully pedantic. But Chloe seemed engaged.

"A delicate balance," she said, thoughtful. "But there's a danger, too: in becoming this other man for the purposes of your work, you risk everything. You risk yourself . . ."

"Yes. That's the danger."

She was silent for a moment. "Why biography? Why not fiction, say?"

"I suppose . . . I'm curious to know what makes other men tick." *I tick very quietly myself. Actually, I do not tick at all but hum, faintly.* "And—" He stopped himself.

"What were you going to say?" She inclined a little toward him. He tried not to notice the tops of her breasts peeking above the deep V of her dress. He thought that he blushed.

"I was, ah . . . well, I was going to say that I don't think I have the imagination for fiction. As I described just now, I live a moderate life and fiction is—immoderate, at its best."

"You're afraid of it," she announced.

He squirmed under the indictment. "Maybe so. Writing fiction you're just—out there. Alone with the work. Floundering for the story . . . But a biography gives me, I don't know, parameters—and *things*, concrete documents, real people, things I can lay my hands on." He paused. "Although I may imagine up to a point, I am prohibited from imagining the facts. You see?"

She nodded. "In fiction, one imagines what 'did not happen.' "

"Yes."

"Of course, in imagining what 'did not happen,' you've made it happen, haven't you?"

He smiled uncomfortably. She scrutinized him.

"But why Max? It seems he couldn't be less like you."

"Opposites attract," he replied unhappily, "and, well, he's more like me than Louis Oldfield." *You regard me as pale and drab like a man who never sees daylight while the Oldfields and Leiberts are vivid and bold, adventurers, fearless in meeting the world and in seeking the company of men and women.* "There is," he insisted, "an affinity between Maxwell and me—the longer I know him the more deeply I feel it."

Certainly the words "vicarious thrill" mean something to you. To be close to men who accomplished all that I will not; to lower myself into lives as a miner lowers himself into a vein of ore; to know more about these men than they knew about themselves, more than I know (or care to know) of myself . . . There's power in that—and consolation too. Alter shrugged and said aloud, "You may as well ask why two people fall in love. Tell me now, what is your connection to him?" He was unable to contain himself any longer.

Chloe looked away, shifted in her seat.

She steadies herself, locates her center, a diver on the high board flexing about with her toes before taking the plunge. Alter studied her in the ruby light of a candle on the table sheathed in a stippled red globe. The unblinking eyes were large, almond-shaped, alert and mistrustful, *like an animal who wonders whether the scrap of meat in my palm is worth the getting close.* She had smudged a line darkly at the crease on the lid and in the outer corner to create a mournful, sloe-eyed look. Her mouth was slightly too large for the small oval of her face;

the upper and lower lips did not quite meet, so that she seemed to hold them apart, about to offer something. In her cheeks and chin he saw softness, the felicity, the plasticity of a girlhood not yet relinquished.

When she lifted her drink Alter noticed that she had remarkably slender wrists from which the wrist bones protruded. *Tiny, delicate, heartbreaking.* How can it be that I am moved by a few thin bones held fast by flesh? I am singular in so many of my tastes and attitudes . . . How many times, when my father took me to the track, did I approach the allegedly carefree outing with dread?—certain that a horse would stumble, fall, and rise from the turf milling its useless mangled leg. I watched for the one that absolutely refused to run. Blindfolded, kicking, throwing gobby strings of spit, scattering its attendants until at last it was led away, scratched from competition. This was the one I rooted for, this was the beast who won my heart. Not the winner, not the loser, but the one who would not contend.

"I was his gardener." She said the words quietly, an awkward confession.

"Pardon me?"

"His gardener. I was eighteen, at college. Bennington, studying music—voice, really." It sounded like a voyage she had abandoned long ago. "I needed a job and Max had a notice up. I applied for the position. I'd never grown anything, but it was a choice between that and running a mimeograph machine. I chose the outdoors, Max's garden." She tapped another cigarette from the pack. "As it turned out I grew some nice things—a border of flowers around the house, zinnias, and a vegetable patch in back. It was quite a success. We got very attached to it."

A vision came to Alter of Chloe on her hands and knees

in the dirt, in the musky raw spring dirt, her blue-jeaned ass in the air, Maxwell Leibert towering over her, watching as his earth received bulbs and seed. He felt a thrumming in his chest.

"He loved the garden," she continued. "He'd never had luck with plants. He said he was partial to cactus—nature's survivor he called it—and showed me one he'd had for years. Kept it in the room where he worked." She started to speak more rapidly, not meeting Alter's gaze, unable to suppress her discomfort and channeling it into monologue.

The zeal of the biographer is becoming apparent to her and I must seem predatory. Or are we on the verge of an urgent engagement that she feels she must resist?

"The cactus can be left for months," he heard her say, "without water. You can leave it untended and when you come back it will be waiting for you, good as new. Max said he was a careless man and that the cactus is the plant for careless people. It can take a lot of punishment, you know."

He accepted this last as a subtle allusion to some injury she might have suffered in Leibert's society but kept the idea to himself.

"You two talked a lot . . . while gardening?"

"Well, yes . . . He was lonely. Friends didn't visit often, the drive up was long and tiring. Tamsin, his wife, hated Vermont and wanted to return to New York. They— sometimes—fought." She looked up, defensively. "It wasn't a secret, everyone at the college knew . . . One day Max said to me, 'You know how I spend my days, dear girl?— licking my wounds.' " She sighed. "He didn't care much for teaching anymore, but the college gave him a nice house, a fairly decent salary. I felt sorry for him . . . He lived like a migrant worker, moving from campus to campus with the seasons, wherever he could find work. He told me that except for his books he had only as many possessions as would fit in the trunk of a car. He said you never knew when you were going to have to pack up in the middle of the night, when the knock on the door would come, when you'd have to run, so you ought to think out beforehand exactly what must go with you if suddenly you had to be on the move. He was so uneasy . . . in his own skin. I never completely understood it." She sounded wistful, remembering the poet, as though something precious had been broken in her and she was intent on sweeping up the pieces, even those fragments too small to be purposefully saved.

"It comes partly of being a Jew," Alter murmured, "this feeling. We have a long history of being vomited out of places like poison in the gut." *Indeed we have been accused of everything—of contaminating wells, of the ritual murder of infants, of systematic attempts at economic domination, of fomenting wars and revolutions. Pseudoscientific books have been written branding us an inferior people with delusions of superiority, a treacherous race with illusions of virtue. We have been charged with falsifying the culture of nations in the guise of assimilation. So awfully chosen! In any event, after five thousand years the sense of impermanence, the impulse to flee, to go to ground (those who cower in root cellars or attics sometimes save themselves) may lurk in the genetic material, passed from generation to generation by way of preservation. The tortoise has its stony carapace, the chameleon its changing colors, the wasp its sting. Concede to the Jew his uneasy genes. . .*

Alter roused himself and leaned forward, expectant. She hadn't missed him, toying contemplatively with an unlit cigarette.

"May I ask about your letter? It was most compelling. You mentioned . . . information, about Max."

She shrank a little from him. "You're going to think me detestable, but I've decided I can't. Not just yet."

"Detestable? Never."

"I'm not certain. I wasn't certain even when I wrote the letter . . . I'm afraid . . ." There was a long pause. "I'm afraid of betraying him."

He felt the weight of her ambivalence and was powerless against it; her trouble seemed suddenly remote and personal. Her hand lay open on the table as if in invitation. Alter could hardly keep from wrapping his fingers around her wrist. It appeared to him to need hanging on to, a strong and solid hand dependably fingerlocked around those fragile bones, *the way one grabs a child to pull her to safety when the threat is unexpected and out-of-nowhere and one hasn't time to politely find the child's hand.*

"You have nothing to fear from me, I promise."

" 'I promise,' " she mimicked. "How easily you say that."

As easily as Max did? . . . and as self-servingly.

She worked her arms into her coat. "As his biographer you're in no position to promise anything, now are you?"

"Wait," he pleaded as she swiped up her handbag. "We've only begun!"

"It's time I left." She stood up, her face flushed.

"I *can* promise you . . ." Alter fumbled. His usual experience was that of passive observer; he was unfamiliar with dramas that required audience participation. ". . . honor. My honor."

She examined him ambiguously through deep, fringed lashes, serious and unstrung. "I'll call . . . after I've had time to think some more. Forgive me."

Chloe went quickly out of the bar. It had begun to snow again. Flakes splatted the plate glass window. He watched until she was swallowed up in the storm.

He knew he had made a mistake with her, had done precisely what he had not wanted to do: frightened her off. *I never should have brought up the letter but let her come to it herself.* It was a tactical error he usually did not make. Now the mistake seemed to whirl away beyond his recall in a hopeless maze of frustration. Alter picked up Chloe's package of cigarettes, abandoned beside her drink, and slipped them into his jacket pocket. He took some heart from her promise to call, perhaps a tacit grant of pardon. He would cling to that.

Passing through the lobby the biographer realized he had forgotten to pick up his mail. He backtracked to the mailroom, unlocked his box, and removed a few pieces: the expectable solicitations, flyers, and bills, a sample packet of detergent. He slit open the first letter with his thumb, from a human rights organization, and read, only half seeing the words.

". . . torturing children to obtain information—" *What passions have ravaged her?* ". . . torturing children in front of their parents by applying electric shocks to the soles of their feet—" *What insult did you suffer at his hands?* ". . . seized and driven away in military vehicles, children ages eight to seventeen—" *What secrets do you share with him that you cannot share with me?*

"There you are!" A shout. "What about my oven?"

He snapped his head at the impact of the cry. A tiny outraged presence bristled below his chin, wavering on her aluminum cane with its outsize rubber tip to prevent skids and fatal falls.

"Mrs. Pompanazzi, what about it?"

"You swore to put in another, new."

He rubbed his forehead. "Did I?" *I don't remember but I'm sure I did. It's probably on my list of the top fifty things I have sworn to repair, replace, recondition, or otherwise set to rights. Another of my feeble oaths.*

"You certainly did."

"Remind me, what's wrong with the old oven?"

"I *told* you. I light it with a match and boom! It goes up like a torch. I run for Muñoz, thank God he's here, and he puts it out. But now it's kaput, I cannot cook. For a month I'm eating cold. A woman my age can't live on cornflakes and apple juice."

"Yes. Of course you can't . . ." His eye drifted back to the letter in his hand. ". . . five-month-old infant dead after prison authorities denied it milk—"

"That's it? That's all you have to say? My stove is a fire hazard, this whole damn crazy place of yours is a hazard. Have you seen the floors? Have you observed? Tiles loose all over or no tiles, just holes. Someone's going to break their heads! But what is it to you? You have insurance and maybe you get back an apartment to rent for more money."

He looked at her. From where he stood he could see Rosalba Pompanazzi's bald spot. She was losing her hair; white whiskers grew from the top of her nose, from her chin; her chest was as flat as a boy's under her garishly flowered housecoat. *The final indignity of old age—she's turning into the opposite sex.*

"That is not my intention at all, Mrs. Pompanazzi. There are so many things to take care of . . . my resources are limited. I am only one man—"

"You know I live on a fixed income, I don't go to work

anymore. You know I cannot afford to move from here. I am your prisoner, Mr. Alter, but even a prisoner has rights."

Alter stared. "I'll . . . talk to Mr. Muñoz about the stove."

"Muñoz. *Muñoz.* There is nothing Muñoz can do," she chided. "It's on *your* conscience, mister."

He peered down at the letter in his hand: ". . . deliberately targeting children of their political opponents—" *Excuse me? What priority has your stove in speaking to my conscience? Where in the hierarchy of my moral obligations does the stove fall? I am having some difficulty keeping it straight as my conscience is pulled simultaneously in six directions at once.* ". . . taken from their homes in trucks—" *My God! I wanted to kiss her. To lean across the table, catch her unawares, and taste the illicit pleasure that comes of brushing dry startled lips!* His eye grazed more words. ". . . torture of children, a matter of the gravest urgency requiring your immediate attention—" *Children go alone, clutching the hands of strangers or the hands of other children, in trucks or trains, as other children in other wars have gone before them. For what? for the crime of being the children of their parents—*

Hold on there, Mrs. P., while I have you. Would you say, looking back, looking back over a long life, that compared with all the catastrophes of the world (and I'll include even the catastrophe of living here with me in this gulag), the catastrophe of love is minuscule? Has the barbarism, the hideous scale of slaughter, the near dissolution of human hope, so shamed us as to reduce the catastrophe of our loves to nothing?

Later that evening Alter sat in an armchair in his worn plaid robe, some of his research on the floor before him. The

Leibert project had begun to overwhelm the small apartment: stacks of books and papers occupied all corners, had
been pushed against walls in the manner of a man who
allows only enough space for himself; who has determined,
with the accretion of mild miseries and the encroachment of
age, that no life but his own will ever occupy his rooms and
so, by stages, has banished every trace of grace and hospi-
tality. He existed like someone who had once inhabited a
big house filled with people, but who—alone now and wary
of unfilled rooms—shuts off the chill of empty chambers,
confining himself to the scullery.

At arbitrary points in Alter's living room, which also
served as his office, receipts and bills related to the running
of the building were spiked or corralled in dusty in-boxes.
Cartons were stacked in alpine heaps in the small second
bedroom of the apartment, his boyhood bedroom. Occasionally, even the bathtub became a temporary archive for
some Leibert research.

On the biographer's knees, a yellow legal pad rested. He
had sat down to calculate for the fifth time in as many weeks
the things he should, but knew he would not, accomplish.
Each time, as he started to draw up his alleged plan of
action, a name and a face reminded him of another incipient
calamity: Clara Eres reminded him of the errant elevator,
Morris Bloom of the faulty plumbing, Rosalba Pompanazzi
of the cracked floor tiles in the lobby and public corridors,
Mrs. Hovanian in 3-B of a dripping showerhead (perhaps
just a washer?). His pencil faltered.

Chloe . . . Who the hell *is* she? Alter wondered, irritated
and intrigued at once. She behaves differently from my
other female sources, not at all like those other women with
whom I have dealt, the widows, ex-wives, daughters, and

lovers of famous men. Usually they come to me with open arms. Some would gladly open their legs to me too, if I asked. But I maintain the distance of the good physician, my touch impersonal and intimate at once, concerned but strictly professional. Almost without exception, each of these ladies has seen me as her sole ally in a world that turned away once the great man died or divorced or left her and she could no longer bask in his reflected light.

Although "bask" is not the correct verb, I reckon, conjuring up as it does a snooze in the sun. The writhing of the slug breaking free of the pinion of the rock better describes their condition. At last the women may emerge from the shadows to proclaim themselves as having *lived*. I am the repository not only of their documents, their bundles of correspondence and faded photographs, but of their grief and anger and privations, all their unbeheld humiliations. (And the territory of their grievances widens the longer I know them.) They have my rapt attention. I share confidences they exchanged only with the departed husband or delinquent lover. How odd this mutual monomania, how like lovers ourselves we become! Yet I cannot entirely disown my grasping motive, my overweening ambition *to have it all from them, every last drop*. What I will not do to achieve my ends! How effortlessly I slip into the other man's skin and arrange a cozy pseudodomesticity.

As in certain marriages of long standing I watch a widow adopt my mannerisms, my intonations, my brand of scotch, mirror my penchant for somber tweeds, and pick up my muddy palette in shirts and ties—until you can hardly tell us apart. At our meetings she will stroke her chin unconsciously, just as I fiddle with my beard. If we come to an impasse in our relations, a period of storm, in lieu of withholding her physical affection, she will withhold materials critical to my work, hold them against the moment when I will return, again and again, pusillanimous at first, then wheedling, cajoling, at last seductive, bearing small gifts, endearments, in a campaign to mend my fences and wrestle one more poem, a letter, a scrawl, from her trembling hands. But the enigmatic Chloe is nothing like any of these women. She seems somehow inviolate, zealously guarding some intelligence greater and more somber than I can imagine. She is the keeper of what secret gate?

Alter's gaze fell on the manila folders at his feet containing notes and typed transcripts of interviews, a pile of literary journals in which fawning necrologies and interpretive studies had appeared in the years since Leibert's death. He reached down for one slim volume amid the journals, ninety pages, a memoir of the poet by a former student, a protégé, on whom Leibert had turned, savagely and irrationally, in the last years of his life.

Leibert had accused the younger man, Edmund Hopkins, of stealing his poetry and publishing it as his own. As he had no copies of the original poem in question it was impossible to prove anything absolutely, but the claims were almost surely untrue. However, late one night Leibert took it upon himself to exact revenge, lying in ambush outside the young man's apartment. Around midnight Hopkins returned home. The poet, crouched in the vestibule of the apartment house next door, lunged, an empty beer bottle in hand. The attack sent its victim to the hospital for a week, but the young man chose not to press charges if his former mentor would enter a sanitarium for treatment. Faced with a possible prison term Leibert agreed, and was remanded by the court to a facility in New Hampshire, a fifty-acre retreat on the banks of the Connecticut River. He viewed it more as a rest cure, a short vacation, than therapy.

He befriended a psychotic patient, a veteran of the Korean War, he said, with whom he played a daily game of chess. To a friend on the outside he wrote:

> Jack is convinced he died at Heartbreak Ridge and only a very few people are able actually to see him. (He is vociferous, for instance, in his claim to be invisible to his psychiatrist.) But I apparently have "the vision." He's devised an entirely new way to play chess, new rules. The object of the match: your knights are out to murder the opposition's king, leaving the queen open to assault (rape) by the bishops. The pawns are just that—pawns, in the service of the bishops against the kings. The allegiance of a pawn, however, is never certain. One can all of a sudden and without warning change sides, turn traitor, *en passant*. In this astounding world, "castling" refers to a ploy wherein a queen may take refuge behind the turreted fortress of a rook. There, she is temporarily out of harm's way. I play poorly, Jack's insignificant epigone. The man's a screwy genius, fascinating, completely mad and ought to be permitted to stay that way.

A check of sanitarium logs disclosed no record of a patient named Jack, or John, or a Korean War veteran in residence during the period of Leibert's incarceration. Alter was secretly delighted that the entire episode might have been the poet's invention and had made a note (one among many such reminders to himself) to investigate further.

Leibert took to the pool regularly. According to staff reports, he tossed a lawn chair into the shallow end and stayed there, submerged to his neck, chatting up the serious swimmers as they paddled by his position at the three-foot marker.

On weekends he entertained on a small brick patio adjoining his room. Guests came up from New York bearing picnic hampers filled not only with roasted chickens, French bread, salads, cheeses, and cakes, but contraband quarts of gin, rum, bourbon, liters of wine. Leibert kept a bottle of vodka hidden in the tank of his toilet where, he said, "it stays pleasantly chilled."

Maxwell Leibert's stay at the White Oak sanitarium began in the spring of 1972 and lasted through that summer. During the dog days of August a summons from Leibert became, among a select group, as coveted as an invitation to the shore. There were all the amenities of a resort: acres of rolling lawn, croquet, badminton, tennis, a bowling alley, volleyball, horses for hire, and hiking trails. Leibert received the poets Philip Malcolm, Stanley Waissman, Isaac Leavy; the linguist Otto Klesl and his wife, the modern dancer Violet Tate; painters Piero Guinicelli and Maria Gutierrez; the historian Melchior Kainz; the philosopher Friedrich Schick; the classicist H. R. W. Miroslawich. Miroslawich nearly drowned one Sunday afternoon when, a nonswimmer and slightly drunk, he unwittingly floated to the deep end of the pool on an inner tube and panicked. A memorable battle occurred on the tennis court between Leibert and the literary critic Jacob Avery, when Leibert balked at continuing the game if Avery insisted on keeping score. Under a blistering noon sun the argument escalated until Avery, without regard for Leibert's precarious mental state, threw down his racket and stormed off. Violet Tate, standing courtside, remarked of Avery, "He's his own worst enemy," to which Leibert bellowed, "Not while I'm alive he isn't!"

Of his lengthening incarceration he wrote to his son Ulysses, "I haven't put a word on paper since I've been here, my brain feels burnt from the inside out—only the charred walls remain standing—and I find I repress my deepening despair in an increasingly hectic desire for company. Do come when you can." Finally in late September, when Leibert's guest list was thinning faster than the trees that ringed White Oak were denuded of leaves, he demanded to be released. A debate of several days ensued among a battery of psychiatrists until at last he was let go "against medical advice."

When Leibert returned to New York he had stopped hurling verbal rocks at his protégé but never again spoke to him, despite Hopkins' repeated attempts at reconciliation. "This was a bad sign," Alter read, scanning a page of the memoir. "Leibert's family and friends worried. For although he had ceased to identify me publicly as a plagiarist, the fact remained that he would not talk to me, would not even countenance hearing my name spoken aloud, and thus everyone deduced that, somewhere, he still harbored the conviction I had robbed him. There was no question that Max was deeply troubled—the drinking grew worse than it had been before he entered the sanitarium, and five years later he was dead."

Alter closed the book and picked up a thick folder labeled "Ulysses."

Ulysses Leibert, the poet's oldest child, was now in his forties, married and the father of three young children. He taught mathematics at Columbia University and lived in a rambling, ramshackle apartment on upper Broadway where paint peeled from the walls in sheets and naked bulbs on the ceiling were shielded with cheap Japanese paper lanterns. Bicycles crowded the foyer; a wall-mounted coatrack held so much outer gear that much of it fell to the floor and remained there. Ulysses' wife, Sheina, was a potter; each time the biographer visited, she greeted him with grey hands, clay hardening up her wrists to form little grey gloves. Evidence of her unsold work cluttered the apartment: lopsided vases and bowls, splotched and blotched glazed ashtrays, poisonous-looking mugs and pitchers.

In their living room Alter had to negotiate a minefield of Lego towers, log villages, model train tracks, building blocks, plastic telephones, scattered flash cards and dolls, to reach Ulysses at the far end of the room. Always, he was seated by the window in a high-backed chair, a prince on his throne, awaiting his father's—the king's—biographer, a steaming pot of tea by his side, and two cracked and dingy cups. There were days, especially in summer, when Alter would have preferred a cold drink, a beer or a Coke, but he never bestirred himself to disturb the rite Leibert's son had so scrupulously established. Ulysses had about him a dour quality, a plodding, overbearing aspect; he approached the examination of his father's life with clinical, almost alarming absorption. Alter supposed the son wanted his recollections of Max filtered through the haze of nothing stronger than hot water steeped in the essence of dry crushed blackberries.

At his desk, Alter leafed through some of the notes of past interviews with Ulysses, looking for a mention of that name: Chloe. Ulysses had been a grown man by the time she claimed to have entered Leibert's life, but that hardly meant that he might not have a memory of her. *Lee is nothing if not exacting in his ruminations!* Often he excused himself several times during the course of a single session to verify a fact or a date. He had insinuated several times that he would like Alter to refrain from talking to his siblings. As the firstborn and executor of his father's estate, Ulysses had taken a proprietary interest in the undertaking, indeed held the work in something of a stranglehold: on more than one occasion, the biographer discovered, Leibert's son had called in advance of Alter's meeting with an informant, to see if he might influence the substance of an interview or suppress certain recollections; and most of Maxwell Leibert's papers—Ulysses had struggled for years to lay claim to a vast trove of unpublished material—were under Ulysses' absolute control. He had grown used to Alter, even fond of him, yet still conceived of the biography, this tapestry, as his own, and looked warily at other would-be embroiderers.

He thinks he has me in his lap, a Pekinese, dependent on his largesse, Alter thought to himself, but my will in these matters is at least as strong as his. Behind my deference lies guile. I eke out my territory inches at a time, hacking my way through sometimes impenetrable jungle, a guerrilla fighter in the war to recover one man's life. I am patient, and my faith sustains me and forces me on.

Alter turned the pages in the folder, notes he hadn't yet released to his typist, Mildred, for transcription. He squinted at his scribblings but could not find Chloe's name, nor an allusion to any person that resembled her. He found an Estrelita, a Filipino woman who had cooked and cleaned for the Leiberts when Ulysses was seven; and a Becky, the daughter of a friend of the family, who had come to work one summer as a mother's helper; and a Ruth Esterhaus, Max Leibert's aunt, who had lent him five hundred dollars in 1949 when, after the publication of his first collection, *God's Guest*, the poet had found himself critically acclaimed but virtually penniless, with a wife and two small children to support.

Alter closed the folder, dropped it on the floor, and stood up to stretch. Walking around the room in aimless ambulation, he stopped before some bookshelves, three unpainted pine planks fastened to the wall over his desk. In the middle of the lowest shelf he spied a series of spiral-bound notebooks in repeating colors of yellow, red, and blue, composition books, property also of Ulysses Leibert, formerly belonging to Maxwell, on loan to Alter. Alter's hand went automatically, like a sleepwalker's, for one of the red books. Each one contained jottings, drafts of verse, ideas for essays, critical notes on literature, observations of friends, lovers, and family, in the form of a loosely kept journal. The order was chronological but months could pass between entries. Somewhere in the red book was the reference he sought. He flipped the pages rapidly and then he found it, near the end of the book, dated April 2, 1974. ". . . those zinnias, a brilliant pale around the house, and the little vegetable patch—my anxious pastoralism. In truth, the house is not mine. The things in the attic do not belong to me. Everything here is on loan. The very earth on which the house sits and in which my garden grows also is not mine." Leibert had skipped a line and written, "Naturally Freud, Marx, Einstein all end their lives far from home, in exile or as refugees." The note ended there, followed by three hasty asterisks fixed on a line below.

The trail is by no means cold! Alter sat down at his desk, took up a sheet of paper and a pen. "Dear Chloe," he began, "It was a pleasure to meet you this evening . . ."

. . .

"My dad was growing things up there, yeah, so?"

Alter turned from the window. It was morning and the sun hurt his eyes. "What sort of things, do you recall?"

"*Things*, I don't know. What difference does it make? . . . Let me think." Alter heard Ulysses bite into something, then wash it down with something else. Tea, no doubt.

"I was up to Vermont with Sheina that spring, maybe the end of March—no, April." He swallowed hard. "I'll check."

"Don't bother," Alter said quickly. "I don't need it this minute." Experience had taught him that if Ulysses went off to check he'd be left hanging on a dead line interminably.

"I'll check, no problem. I have all my datebooks. We're talking about 'seventy-four here, right?"

"Right, but—"

"—I'll look it up and get back to you," Ulysses concluded. "Anyway, I can tell you this much for sure: Sheina and I weren't married yet, so it couldn't have been May. We married in May. That's what we were there for, to tell him. So my best guess is April," Ulysses said, verifying what Alter already knew. "I do remember Dad taking me out and showing me where he'd put in some vegetables. He seemed quite pleased with himself, although nothing really'd come in yet. I remember something red, the buds of something. Tomatoes? But no, couldn't have been, they come in later, in the summer, don't they? Flowers, maybe, geraniums?"

"Zinnias," Alter said under his breath.

"What?"

"I said . . . zinnias. It was in the notebook entry."

"Oh. So what's your point, Raffi?"

"Nothing, really," Alter lied. "No real point. When I stumbled on the passage last night, it struck me, that's all. Your father didn't seem like the gardening . . . type."

"He wasn't. I don't think he had the patience." Ulysses paused. "Well, it's coming back to me. I remember thinking, and I believe I said this to him, I said he'd gone to a hell of a lot of trouble to put in a garden when the damn house wasn't even his. I mean it belonged to the college, now didn't it? He only had it while he taught there, then he had to give it back. Plus, by the time everything came in, ripened you know, he wouldn't have time to eat it. It'd be summer. He'd be gone."

"True." Alter massaged a kink in the back of his neck. He had been up until the middle of the night composing and then discarding versions of an entreaty to Chloe and had finally fallen asleep on the couch. "Let me ask you one more question, Lee."

"I've got a class to teach in twenty minutes."

"It won't take long." *Now how do I put it? Lee is perfectly capable of going after Chloe, hunting her down and scaring her off forever. He's like an animal that way, when he smells a threat, or weakness in an adversary.* "You're quite right when you say it seems like a great deal of trouble for Max, a garden and all . . . You recall if he had any help?"

"Help?"

"I mean was it your understanding that he'd done all the work himself?"

"You're referring to Tamsin, I suppose. You want to know if he enlisted her in the garden?" Ulysses sounded skeptical.

Good. You misunderstand me entirely. "Tamsin, yeah."

"No, uh-uh."

"You're sure about that."

"Positive." He bit it off like wire. "Tamsin Merrill wouldn't get her hands dirty." Ulysses called his father's second wife by her maiden name. "The woman never cooked a meal in her life—Dad called their oven a 'sterile environment'—can you see her planting squash?"

"And he mentioned no one else, no one who had anything to do with the garden?"

"It was a scrubby little patch. A few flowers, around the house. You talk like he had a farm, goddamn acres. I don't really get your interest."

"I was curious, is all. It's just a detail, somewhat out of character."

"Listen, I have to run, but when are we seeing each other? It's been a month at least. Where've you been keeping yourself?"

In my root cellar, Lee, out of harm's way. "I've been busy."

"So busy you couldn't call?"

"You don't understand. I immerse myself in my work, in this book. I . . . *lose* myself. Sometimes I go for days on end without talking to anybody. Don't take it personally." He felt mild irritation, and a desire to conclude the conversation. "Then there's this building to run."

"You have a superintendent, don't you?"

"Yes, but—"

"You need to get out more, Raffi. I'm telling you, it's not healthy the way you live . . ."

"I *manage*, Lee," Alter said coldly.

"Your trouble is, you genuinely *like* being cloistered."

"I won't argue the point."

"We're having some people over Friday after next. Why don't you come? Sheina mentioned she has someone she wants you to meet."

"Someone? . . ."

"A *girl*." He corrected himself. "A woman."

"Oh. Well, we'll see. I'll get back to you."

"Yeah, think about it," Ulysses said dryly. "You might actually have a good time."

Alter sat for a few minutes in meditative silence, thinking about it, about his cloister. He imagined himself Quasimodo, the bell ringer of Notre Dame, but his own deformities were all on the inside: a suspicion of mere affability and a distaste for useless bustle (he told himself); a love of moderation and a Midrashic inclination; and a chastising "third eye"—the Doberman, night watchdog of his spirit—that kept him cornered. These were some of the reasons, he thought, why he had turned to writing biographies: as the psychiatrist and the gynecologist found socially sanctioned outlets for their voyeurism, so the writing legitimized the *aloneness* he felt powerless to breach, and other lives filled the void. Over time, the building had become his cathedral and prison; and, like the hunchback, "living in it, sleeping in it, hardly ever leaving it, subject every hour to its mysterious impress, he came at length to resemble it, to be encrusted on it, as it were, to become an integral part of it . . . One might almost say that he had taken on its shape, as the snail takes on the shape of its shell." A few times in his life he had reached out, tentatively, awkwardly, to women, hoping for joy, completion, transfiguration, *an antidote, a counterpoison to my nausea*, but instead was rebuffed or came away from the encounters having achieved only a gruelish emotional discharge that left him feeling emptier than before—

The doorbell rang twice, urgently, then twice more. Alter rose to answer it. Angel Muñoz stood on the other side, hopping agitatedly from foot to foot.

"Leipzig fell."

The city or the man? "Not again."

"I can't liff him and he woan lemme call the wagon."

"Where?"

"Laundry room."

Alter and the superintendent proceeded to the basement. Simon Leipzig lay on the floor, twisted against a washing machine, moaning softly. Alter knelt.

"I'm sorry for the trouble," Leipzig murmured.

"No trouble," Alter lied. "You all right?"

"If you could just help me back to my place."

"Why won't you let Mr. Muñoz call the paramedics?"

"No hospital," Leipzig whispered. "I don't want to go there, don't make me go."

"You may have injured yourself." In the damp warmth of the room Alter broke into a light sweat.

"I have no pain."

"What happened exactly?"

"A little dizziness, I lose my balance."

"Did you hit your head?"

"No."

"What month is it?"

"December. Why?"

"Just checking."

"Take me upstairs, please, I want to go home."

Alter stood, nodded to Muñoz. Together they placed their hands under Simon Leipzig's perspiring armpits; Alter gagged at the wet touch. "One, two, three." They heaved.

The old man, six and a half feet, a gaunt giant, dug his fingers into Alter's forearm—a fearful clawing—as they strained to bring him up. When at last they had him on his feet, he swooned, teetered, crumpling heavily onto Alter, his hot breath rank as a dog's, in Alter's face. "I'm going *down!*"

"Hold him!" Muñoz commanded and went for a kitchen chair across the room. They eased Leipzig into the chair, into a half-seated position, bent like a bow.

Alter gasped. "I think we'd better call the ambulance."

"No," Leipzig groaned, "leave me. I'll rest."

"You can't walk. We won't leave you, not in this condition." Alter turned to Muñoz, his palms open in supplication.

The super crooked an index finger on his lips, assessing the situation. He delivered his verdict: "We carry him."

"You're not serious."

"We carry him," Muñoz insisted, "on the chair."

"That's crazy. We'll never make it."

"We make it. From here to the elevator, from the elevator to his door, not so bad."

"C'mere a minute." Alter beckoned Muñoz to the bank of clothes dryers, out of his tenant's earshot. A load of sheets tumbled; Alter's nostrils filled with the powdery scent of fabric softener. "You stay with him, I'll go upstairs and make the call."

"He say already that's not what he wants."

"I know what he says but it's too bad. I'm sorry—"

"He got no family, no one to watch out for him—"

"Yes, exactly. I'm not running a nursing home here. In the hospital he'll get care—"

"*No,*" Muñoz interrupted. "In the hospital he go in but he's afraid he doan come out."

"So if it's his time, then it's his *time,*" Alter barked. "I mean for crying out loud!"

"He live here twenny years, pay his rent, a good tenant.

He doan ask much. Maybe he die, could be. He jus' wanna die in his home."

"Damn it, Angel—that's *not* my responsibility."

Muñoz raised his brows significantly. "Whose then?"

Alter shook his head, slowly, speechless.

Back in his apartment Simon Leipzig asked to be laid on the sofa in his living room. Alter nestled throw pillows in the small of his back; he draped a moth-eaten crocheted coverlet over his knees. "What else can I do for you?"

"Nothing. Thanks." Leipzig considered. "Well . . . the TV?"

Alter turned on a floor-model color television set, an old Motorola, the hues all purples and greens like random runny watercolors. "Any particular station?"

"The news, the cable news."

Ah good, keep in touch—with the world, with breaking developments; a balm for the lonely and the old, a lifeline, an anchor— the little figures and nattering heads that have all but annihilated surprise and spoon out our "news" in small anesthetic doses as we adjust and grow numb to the new order, and distracted from the throbbing ache of the inflamed and tender organ of memory—

"The sound, up a little?" the man on the couch requested.

"Anything else?"

Leipzig straightened his large body on the pillows, repositioned the quilt over his enormous feet. "Perhaps if it wouldn't be trouble, a drop of cognac? Over the sink there's a bottle and glasses. Take for yourself too."

In the kitchen Alter found the brandy, a discount brand, and two small snifters. In the open cupboard beside them he saw a tin of sardines, an old bottle of mustard, the condiment hardened to a crust around the lid, a box of Saltine crackers, Smucker's grape jelly, and three jars of baby food—peas, green beans, tapioca. Nosy, he opened the refrigerator: on the top shelf sat a half-pint of heavy cream, a jar of green olives, an almost empty bottle of Pepto-Bismol, a greying onion.

He poured only one drink. In the living room he handed the snifter to Leipzig. "Cheers."

Leipzig kept his eyes on the television, a noon report from Wall Street. "Thanks. Don't let me keep you."

Alter stood watching the commentator and Simon Leipzig's intent regard of the screen. "You in the market?"

"I used to have a little in, not much. Had to sell it all when my wife was sick, insurance ran out." Leipzig sipped the brandy with a shaking hand, barely able to bring the glass to his mouth.

Alter remembered the last years of Miriam Leipzig's life. On sunny days even in winter, bundled in coats and hats and scarves, she and her husband sat on folding beach chairs in front of the building; he remembered the perplexed, uncertain gaze of her senility, as if she found her condition curious, to say the least. Leipzig had cared for her until the end when she lapsed into a coma, was taken to the hospital, and died there a few days later.

"When is the last time you ate?"

"Oh I don't know," Leipzig said softly. "Look, IBM up two and seven-eighths."

"You really don't know?"

Leipzig shrugged. "I'm getting *famisht,* foggy. Maybe a blessing. Fog is peaceful. Beyond, I don't want to know."

"When?" Alter demanded. "When did you eat?"

"Five, six? Yesterday. Food don't interest me. I lose my taste years ago, everything tastes the same."

"What did you eat?"

"What's it to you?" Leipzig snapped, his sallow face defiant. "Lipton's tea, crackers, jelly. It's enough."

"It is not enough," Alter insisted. "Perhaps this is why you keep passing out. You're starving yourself to death." He pulled a chair close to the sofa and sat. "You hear me?"

Leipzig turned his head slightly from the TV and looked at Alter with cloudy blue eyes. "I hear you loud and clear. But listen to me: malnutrition is not my worry. I don't *want*. Not food, not anything. Nothing, *nada* . . . When Miriam was alive, for forty years, I drag along, went on, for her. She puts a plate in front of me, some meat, potatoes, I eat, I make believe I enjoy. I make believe I want." Leipzig bared horsey yellow teeth in an oddly beatific grin. "Now she is gone I have no longer to make believe. I am free, unencumbered by desire. I float."

"Look, I cannot keep picking you off the floor, Mr. Leipzig. Have a little pity, for God's sake. *Eat* something."

Leipzig returned his attention to the miniature events unfolding on the television, young boys and women hurling rocks at soldiers in riot gear who fired back exploding cannisters of gas.

"Pity? For you? No, sorry, I am past it. I wasn't always, but suffer enough and a person becomes capable of many transgressions against his own true nature." Leipzig stared unseeing at the screen, seeming to maintain the dialogue only out of the smallest obligation to courtesy. "You know how I earned a living? You remember?"

Alter pondered for a moment. "Upholstery? . . . I think you did a chair once, for my mother."

Leipzig nodded. "I take people's furniture to my shop, ruined, strip it down to the bones and re-cover it. Make it exactly—no, better than—new. I was good, the best . . .

Re-cover." He said it bitterly, like two words. "For other people I can heal the wounds, make like perfect, but not for myself . . . I work with nails in my mouth. All my life my mouth is full of upholstery nails . . . Sometimes I have the fantasy to swallow them. Swallow all the nails"—miming it, he inhaled sharply—"like that."

Alter rose and moved away, apprehensive.

The room was almost impassable with clubfooted antique furniture covered in faded chintzes and cabbage roses, dust trapped like sediment in the whorls and curlicues of its ornamentation. Ashtrays filled with blackish brown cigar butts overflowed onto tables sticky with the rings left by glasses; cellophane wrappers from the cigars were crumpled on the seat cushions of armchairs; empty matchbooks and spent matches littered the bubbled shellac on top of the television set where they had been dropped while still hot. On a knickknack shelf three houseplants in hand-painted pots had perished, their sere leaves blanketing the floor. A breakfront held a collection of Jewish religious objects: a large silver menorah and silver Shabbat candlesticks, challah plates, a row of tiny kiddush cups in brass and rose glass. On the walls were family portraits also filmed in dust, stiffly posed photographs from an earlier time.

Alter paused before one that hung at eye level. Probably taken in the 1930s, it showed a handsome woman wearing a formal high-necked black dress and three pensive dark-eyed children. One, an infant, sat on her lap; a boy of about six in a sailor suit and high-button black shoes stood at her right; a younger girl in a low-waisted white dress and a matching white ribbon in her long curling hair stood at her left. The baby had jug ears and the wizened face of an old man. Alter thought he recognized the woman, the widow's peak of her hairline, the deep-set eyes. "Mrs. Leipzig?" He turned. Simon Leipzig looked up, his gaze bland and aloof. "I wasn't aware . . . you have children?" Leipzig did not reply. "Perhaps we ought to give them a call, let them know what their father is doing to himself."

"Can't."

Belligerence overtook Alter the way a wave in the ocean overtakes a swimmer. "Sure we can. Give me their phone numbers. Maybe they can talk some sense into you."

The mountain of a man stared, his eyes savage. "Can't. They're gone."

"Gone?"

"Dead."

Alter's heart heaved and blood rushed to his ears in a roar. He edged nearer the front door. There were some things he preferred not to hear.

"Dachau."

"Ohhh . . ."

Leipzig spoke in low dry tones. "With my own hands . . . with my paternal love . . . I ground their bones to dust. Still warm from the ovens what did not burn we were forced to pound with rocks, crush on giant slabs the bones until they were powder. And every day we carry the powder in sacks to the river to dump it in. Back and forth, back and forth, like factory work."

Alter returned from the door and sank into the nearest chair, letting all the air out of his body. There was no strength left in his limbs.

"Picture it, Alter. Sometimes the wind blows scattering the ash and I wonder to myself: is this the bones of my children? I think of their bodies when I would bathe them, so thin, so fragile, flawless, the bodies of angels . . . In your worst nightmare you never dreamed such pain . . . In Berlin they play the great winter cycle of Beethoven as usual, and in the Palm Garden of the Hotel Eden on the Budapesterstrasse the five o'clock *thé dansant* goes on as always."

Alter lowered his head to his hands. Leipzig's voice grew raspy.

"When my wife and I come here after, I say, No more children. Enough. Miriam's a religious woman, says we must start again, through children the wine is blessed, the bread sanctified, is what she believes. Every Friday all these years, without fail, I go through the motions, for her, the two of us alone. She lights the candles, I make the kiddush, the *broches* before the meals . . . But I am a selfish man. I will give no more children to God, no more fodder for His inferno. I will burden no more sons, no more daughters, with the doom of my love. My wife begs me, but I swear to you, I dry up. Not a drop comes out from me. I am like a desert inside, I dry up. Maybe I hold it in . . . I have known hell, Alter. It is here, aboveground. *Here.*" His tone went icy. "*He* is responsible. I hold *Him* to account. It began with Him, *His* word, 'Let there be . . .' Before Dachau, I never pray. But after—you'll say I'm crazy—I lay tefillin every day, I daven—blasphemies. 'This time You go too far,' I say, 'too far! Curse the Lord,' I pray. 'This time You go too far! The children of men do *not* take refuge in the shadow of Thy wings! They do not have their fill of the choice food of Thy house, and Thou dost not give them drink of thy stream of delights! Even as I cover myself with the tallith in this world, I pray that You should rot and putrefy and stink in the universe forever.' "

Alter sat there, paralyzed, unable to answer Simon Leipzig's terrible gaze. He heard his voice.

"Those who died? . . . They're better off dead."

Alter's eyes strained in their sockets, at the threadbare Persian rug beneath his feet. There was a long excruciating silence in the room. Suddenly he heard a strangled moan, followed by another silence, then pillow-muffled weeping, racking wails. Those wails. He knew the sound, had known it all his life, had run from it, until now, here in the blighted building, it had begun to catch up to him . . .

Somewhere on the other side of Leipzig's wall a load of debris from the renovation next door crashed thunderously. The entire edifice shuddered. The shaking verified the colossal weight of the structure, the immensity of brick and concrete and steel containing and hanging over all their lives, that could crush them.

Like miners we are trapped, hope of rescue fading. We take short shallow breaths and wait for the last of the air to give out.

That night, he dreamed. Of a stripper he had seen long ago, Raven de la Croix. Nailed to a rough wooden cross, nude, she sang in his dream with a symphony orchestra at Carnegie Hall. Alter sat in the black-tie audience. Without being told he recognized this as a benefit gathering for the Friends of the Library, Chums Night.

The orchestra, on bleachers on the brightly lit stage behind Raven, was led by Leonard Bernstein. Alter could not see Bernstein's face but knew the maestro by the white silk scarf draped raffishly over his shoulders and by the cigarette he smoked while conducting, flicking the ashes into a silver podium ashtray by his side that sparkled brilliantly in the way that stage props—glasses, coffee urns, cigarette lighters—gleam under the white heat of stage lights.

Raven de la Croix, joined by an invisible chorus, sang the Kyrie from a requiem mass. "Kyrie eleison!" Raven beseeched in a high clear soprano. She kept her eyes closed. Blood dripped from the wounds in her hands and feet.

Alter, in the dream, glanced about him, embarrassed, aware that he was aroused by her performance even as she endured her Passion.

"Kyrie! Eleison!" The dream-hall quaked with the cry of her heart.

Lord, have mercy.

THREE

"I am as low in spirit as I have been for some time," Maxwell Leibert wrote his editor, Sam Pintchik, in 1963; he had just turned fifty.

Another wasted morning has passed. All I'm able to do is compose a letter to you. And hardly that. I'm running out of time, Sam. Those moments of aphrodisiacal elation that come when the words and ideas flow easily are too few and far between. I have abandoned the long waits for inspiration, for the muse to pay a call, and dutifully labor on . . . But when I cannot work, as now, or work badly, I feel like a man who has lost his honorable place in the world. Positively gelded. No—I would be satisfied with even a dishonorable place: I feel as though I have lost my way home. The Almighty, or whoever is in charge, should take away my bed, my desk, my chair, my pens, paper, food and drink, and suspend me on wires somewhere. I am unworthy. I have no claim to floor space.

It's a lonely frightening panicky life, Sam. And when I am in this condition I am more prey than ever to the

seductions of Lady Hypochondria and her evil twin
Dyspepsia—to that nebulous collection of somatic complaints that migrate in no apparent pattern from one part
of my body to another. Today, in addition to depression
and a kind of nervous anxiety that keeps popping me out
of my seat, I have a searing pain over my left eye. Aspirin
doesn't help. I haven't had a drink all day (it's noon) and
last night limited myself to a can of beer and a couple of
wines. So I doubt it's a hangover. Possibly I am devel-
oping migraines. Possibly I *want* to develop them. Migraines would periodically send me to bed in a darkened
room and I would feel less guilty about so many nonpro-
ductive days. I could visit a Dr. but like many of Lady
H's most ardent suitors, I am desperately afraid of them.
A doctor's waiting room is, to me, the anteroom to Pur-
gatory. For the last several weeks I have been bothered by
(in no special order): a bum knee; intermittent stabbing
in lower groin; sciatica; earache; a dull pain, barely discernible at times, in my right chest wall. TB? Pleurisy?
Cancer?

My poor Edythe. (I am reminded of her by her absence: *I don't hear the vacuum anymore!*—she attacks dust-
balls as mortal enemies, finds them where no one else
can, or she's running the dishwasher, polishing candlesticks and silver, reorganizing closets. For years, to me,
she's given off the faint disagreeable smell of ammonia,
Comet, Clorox. Until I married I had no idea dailiness
was so—*dirty.*) I imagine her outside this attic workroom
pressing her ear to the door, listening for signs of life. She
hears the typewriter's intermittent clack and believes I
am creating—something, anything!—to put food in our
mouths, pay our children's tuitions (the best we have

been able to do with Lee and Ben is partial scholarships
so I am very much still on the hook), and most important
to elevate her to the station in life she feels she deserves.
Who's to say she doesn't? I'm 50 now, she's 47 and sorely
lacks all she desires. Exempting this house, for which her
parents years ago made the down payment, we don't own
a hell of a lot else. If it was up to me, we'd own even less,
but here's the inventory: two secondhand automobiles; an
electric lawn mower bought from neighbors; one television set, also secondhand, a gift from Edythe's brother
Tom; a spinet piano (none of the kids has learned to
play), also from the maternal grandparents. We have
lived largely on hand-me-downs, cast-offs, grudging
charity masked as "loans." She wants more. She wants
the house painted, the floors stripped, sanded and waxed;
she wants the kitchen remodeled and pretty wooden shut-
ters on all the windows. She wants a new car. She wants
to entertain more—although who in the world will drive
all the way to Peekskill for a not-great homecooked meal?
She wants vacations. Worst, she wants *me*—which has
become, tormentingly, out of the question.

We have, the two of us, less and less together, less and
less in common. The children remain the one good, real
and true thing we share. But they are mostly grown and
what I do not comprehend is her refusal to go out and
seek employment. She's not a dim-witted woman, but
there's very little here these days to keep her occupied.
Except me. I understand her reluctance only insofar as such
a change in circumstance would alter our relations, shift
the balance, tip something in this marriage she doesn't
want tipped. Upend it. I can see that from her point of
view: it's precarious enough as it is. I sometimes think

she is just holding out for the moment when the kids begin to marry, have kids of their own, get divorced—and then, she hopes, we will have their marriages and kids and divorces on which to collaborate, and deflect us (or me, at any rate) from the truth: we shouldn't be married at all . . . Among Edythe's needs, indeed her paramount need, as far as I can make out, is for me to believe she cannot—will not—go on without me. I must believe absolutely that she needs *me* in order to survive. She's by no means a weak woman but wants to live in a state of utter dependency. Trouble is, I can't support it much longer. I mean, *how many years have I got left?!*

I sometimes wish we were both committing adultery (although at present I haven't got anyone, probably accounts at least partly for my mood). The terms might relax a little. But I'm not sure who would have her. That's sad. She's hardened with the years. Her attractiveness recedes, her features flatten and I don't think it's necessarily the result of age. No, I used to like her face and it seems she's gone and changed it out of spite.

She keeps her hair short now, swept off her brow in a mannishly *efficient* style; she dresses efficiently too, in olive drabs and khakis, slacks and vests, as if she's prepared to go to war. (I suppose she is.) At social occasions she follows me with her eyes and, catching me in conversation with anyone in skirts, swoops like a vulture—she smiles pleasantly enough, but her talons show. The only softness left is in her voice. When I close my eyes I can hear the girlishness. It hasn't deepened or coarsened as some women's do. Otherwise, I hardly recognize her.

Don't you say it, I will: I am not without blame. She has had to defend against me. She says my writing is anti-Edythe. She's right—it's anti-Edythe, antifamily, antieveryone.

I look back, eighteen or so years ago, just married, living in that tiny apartment on Sullivan Street, tapping out my poems at night on this very Olympia portable then perched precariously atop two orange crates, running the Theatre De Lys box office by night—it seemed all right then, what I was supposed to be doing. I had my first affair the year after Ulysses' birth and developed a taste for betrayal—a taste that grew into a calling, a vocation. Young actress I met at the theater. I have always been drawn to actors, they are so abundantly edgy, so tingling with an energy unavailable to the rest of us mortals; they have a sort of dumb, dazzling courage. Have you ever sat in one of those late-night restaurants near the theaters when the cast members come in after the show? Even offstage they glow like bulbs, ignited by numinous currents.

This rambling concerns you, I know. I should be writing. You are a good friend, but have lost confidence, I fear, in my ability to deliver more work. I simply long to produce something fine, and rich, and cannot do that anymore, not here, not in this house. I have been toying therefore with the notion of finding myself a small apartment in town, a pied à terre, a place to write and spend the occasional overnight should Fate and opportunity conspire to put someone lovely in my bed. If not, I should still be grateful for such an island of solitude. It won't please my wife, who will resent (with some justification) that I insist on spending our limited resources on "a room of my own." She won't believe me when I say it's for the sake of work, for the sake of my sanity, that it's time for a change of venue, and in the long run for the good of all of us. In fact, though, Edythe has it right: it's mostly for the good of me.

I feel today as Voltaire must have when he announced to his father that he was going to be a man of letters. To which the old man replied "In other words, you want to be useless to society, a charge on your family and eventually to die of hunger."

The letter stopped there. Alter replaced the pages in a manila folder. Leibert never mailed it, never finished it, and it turned up many years later among some of his personal papers.

The letter was dated February 4; by the spring of that year he had sublet a one-room apartment with a bath and Pullman kitchen on the ground floor of a brownstone on Cornelia Street in Greenwich Village. In one of his journals from that time the poet exulted:

My first day here and already I am intoxicated—even by the soot that films my windowsill and mantelpiece, scuffed up from the street outside. Cinder rains from heaven and settles here, safe from Edythe's rags and cleansers! From my desk—which I have arranged facing the west wall (the temptation to stare out is irresistible)—I can hear snatches of street life. Mothers scolding children, lovers' quarrels, the hoots and whistles of workingmen across the way as girls pass. The weather is warm and I think I ought to purchase an air conditioner but would hate to erase these sounds after the deadening quiet of Peekskill. I am entranced by the gnashing gears of a downshifting truck, the squeal of airbrakes, taxi horns, the rattle of jackhammers, the scream of police cars—prefer them infinitely to birdsong. I am city-bred and these are the potent sounds of the summer city, reminding me of my youth when I walked freely and happily among them, drenched in the cacophony, feeling immune to the possibility of misfortune. They make me come alive again, inspire in me the hope that I still have some promise and the strength of character to fulfill it.

Alter read on to the next day's entry:

Back home, Peekskill. Attic-bound. Have yet to dredge up the nerve to tell E my intention to spend some over-nights in NY. She still thinks it's only an office. Before I caught the 7:14 home went on a shopping spree, stock-ing up on provisions for Cornelia St.: booze, black olives, pickled herring, clam juice, instant mashed potatoes, a saucepan, canned gravy, small jar mayo, mustard, liver-wurst, rye bread, tomatoes, Bermuda onion, corned beef hash, ketchup, two Hershey chocolate bars with almonds, can of coffee, milk, club soda, paper plates, plastic uten-sils, Ajax, toilet brush, sponge, bar soap. Came back and made a liverwurst sandwich. Swabbed toilet and sink. Exhilarating, the therapy of these everyday tasks! (I begin—almost—to understand E's compulsion.)

Alter flipped the page to an entry dated two days later:

11 A.M. Peekskill. Monster hangover. Last night beer vodka then wine. Saw my wife's unhappiness. She has caught the idea that I am liking my new circumstances too much. She's pregnant with unease, tumid with the

sense of impending calamity—it actually seems to be weighing her down: her movements are lethargic and she sighs constantly, as I remember her doing when she carried our children and had trouble catching her breath in those last months. She's not wrong to be afraid: I *am* drifting away, I feel it. Tried to be sympathetic, nonchalant, but my pleasure in my new digs (even gloating, I'm ashamed to say) is unmistakable. I have made a move into the future, she has not. One minute I experience her unhappiness as if it were my own, and the next am consumed with feelings best described as . . . *unpacific*: hostile, bloody-minded, truculent. Long, difficult, tense evening. Much saber-rattling. Up half the night brooding and thinking after E, exhausted, finally went to sleep. Want nothing so much now as a good long nap. Must try to work, resist the siren call of the bed, navigate away to avoid wrecking on its pillowy shoals.

Three hastily drawn asterisks followed—his usual punctuation—then Leibert continued:

Interrupted by a call from Pintchik who requests the pleasure of my company at lunch tomorrow. I accepted readily, eagerly, greedily. Any excuse to get out of the house! Pintchik's stodgy and occasionally prosaic but a good soul, a sort who's going out of style—loyalty's first with him, not money, he sticks with his friends and his writers through thick and thin. With me, although it's been thin lately, he stays in touch and keeps me in print. Always on my best behavior when we meet. Struggle into suit and tie and polished shoes, slickback hair, watch my language, sit up straight, laugh at his jokes, use the correct forks and knives—a proper schoolboy.

A few days later Leibert noted:

Pintchik informed me at lunch he's received a query from the New School. They'd like me to teach this summer and possibly the fall semester as well. I'm gratified with the offer. Besides the money which I need desperately, two classes a week will give me an excuse to use my place regularly, ease into it, give E a chance to accustom herself to my absence . . . After lunch spent a couple of hours browsing secondhand bookshops ending at the Strand. Emboldened by a touch too much luncheon wine, buoyed by my good fortune in landing the teaching position, I hit on a coed with the pale oval face of a Byzantine madonna I found in the Philosophy aisle. A pathetic and clumsy attempt. She scampered off, unnerved. Returned to my apartment emptyhanded, read a review of D's latest novel in which his prose is excoriated as being "so dull, so wizened with hoary clichés, that the words seem literally to turn to dust and crumble before our eyes." Can't say I disagree; nevertheless a chill ran through me.

Called E prepared to say I was spending the night in NY. When I heard her hurt little-girl voice—anticipating yet another blow—I blurted "I'm taking the 6:10." That night tried to make love to her, make it all up. A half-hearted attempt, coldly rebuffed: "You don't mean it anymore." More and more I see my wife as an enemy to be subdued. The effort is too exhausting. I've become depleted and dysphoric, caught in

this bramble patch of a marriage. Our arms have turned
thorny, like vines.

God, how I pine for the golden dazzle of love!

An entry a week later read, "Regarding immediately
above, I amend: I've been writing in circles, getting nowhere, my trashbasket needs emptying every hour. What I
pine for more than love is The Book That Writes Itself.
Every writer deserves one in a lifetime, a gift of God, and as
my life is more than half over I think it's my turn."

The end of the following year saw the publication of
Leibert's fourth collection of poems, *elegy*. It had been six
years since the last, *The Planets*. In March of 1966, after *elegy*
received a National Book Award, Max and Edythe were
divorced.

The telephone trilled three times. Alter, in the kitchen, ran
to answer.

"It's Chloe."

He tried to sound at ease. "How are you?"

"I got your letter. I've thought about it and I'm ready to
meet again if you'd like."

"Where and when?"

"Isn't that from an old song?"

She sounded to Alter's wishful ear almost flirtatious. He
recalled the refrain and, astonished, he realized he was singing aloud. Alarm zipped down his spine and detonated in an
explosion of goose bumps on his buttocks.

"Hello?" *Damn! I've done it again, frightened her. She thinks
I'm mad.* "Jeez. Sorry. I don't know what came over me."
Both of us doomed to monosyllables, shy as adolescents. No wonder

I resort to song. Though one other thought does occur: brain tumor. Early symptoms include bizarre unprovoked behavior.

"It's all right . . . You have a nice voice."

"A little rusty."

"Maybe you ought to use it more. Where is that song from, anyhow?"

"Babes in Arms."

"I wasn't sure."

"I have a few years on you." *A few? Who're you kidding? Ten, fifteen at least.* Last month I go to a doctor, Chloe, about a crick in my neck because I can't turn around, I can't do this . . . (He did it, unthinkingly, a jerk of the head to the right.) The doctor, McCrae of Park Avenue, takes X-rays and tells me something is degenerating in there. A piece of my spine is flicking away, my vertebrae are flaking like paint off a house. Just to be sure, he sends me for tests. Cost me three large to collect the information that I'm not getting any younger and that I can look forward to further steady deterioration in these and other vital parts. Now a tumor proclaims itself in an outburst of old show tunes crooned to you, whom I barely know. However, thankfully, I did not suddenly go blind on a city bus or unleash a volley of obscenities in front of Nick the Mailman on whom I so inanely depend . . . I have not yet started to drool, Chloe, or to spill food around my plate and under my chair—

"Raphael? Are you there?"

Her voice came to him as from the bottom of an ashcan.

"Yes."

"I said, how's Saturday?"

"What about it?"

"To see you. Would Saturday be good?"

"Let me look at my book." He riffled the blank pages of

the calendar on his desk. "Saturday would be . . . good. Fine. Wonderful."

"I could come to your place, if that's okay."

Alter felt faint. "Oh . . . kay."

"You won't feel too—invaded?"

Invaded? Surely not. No more than if the Seventh Panzer elected to use my living room for field maneuvers. "I'm looking forward to it. See you then. About seven, say? It's apartment one-A. My name's on the buzzer."

Alter replaced the receiver and shuffled through some notes he had made outlining a possible first chapter. He could not focus; these were bits and pieces, vagrant thoughts, discrete, like stones on a beach, and they made less sense to him than stones. Inhaling deeply he smelled a noxious odor. No, something worse, far more deadly: *fumes.* He breathed in again. Testing the air with the nose of a stranger, he sorted through an exotic, pungent bouquet: greasy kreplach creeping like mustard gas through the duct-work from Miss Eres's on the floor above; mothballs; garlic; cigar smoke; rotting garbage . . . *diesel fuel?* The tumor has probably impaired my senses. I smell and taste things that aren't really there. Metal on the palate, burning rubber in the nostrils. I have read about these signs and warnings of the distressed brain.

Alter swiveled in his chair, contemplating the living room with a surgical eye. With Chloe's eye. The furniture had not been cleaned or reupholstered in a decade. The paisley of an armchair had faded almost away in all the places where his body had rested—the seat cushion, arms, the back; anemic impressions of a pattern remained. The white Haitian cotton of the sofa had darkened in patches to brown. Scotch tape mended the cracked corner of a glass coffee table. A water stain blemished the floor where a potted tree once stood. Everything in the room cringed against walls that had turned, it seemed to him, the color of undercooked pork. He turned to the windows: fossilized rain specks were entombed in a veil of grime. This will never do! You ought to have woken up sooner, opened your eyes. Now it's too late . . .

He rose, laboriously, an aging grizzly, crept to the bedroom and curled up on his bed. He groped for the radio, snapped it on. Over the air came the oleaginous tones of a man calling himself "Uncle Fred," who invited his "radio family" to unburden themselves of dilemmas ranging from "affairs of the pocketbook to affairs of the heart."

Hello, you're on the air.

Uncle Fred? Thank you for taking my call . . . My name is Raphael, from Manhattan. Where to begin? With the pocketbook? The head? The heart? I have been suffering for the longest time, from . . . how to explain? Like this: *implosion*. A violent collapse inward, as of a rapidly evacuated vessel.

Alter dozed.

"Come on in, I was just fixing myself a drink."

Al Bruno, fiftyish with a florid face, minced away from the door, leaving it ajar. He smelled unnaturally of some sweet funereal flower. Alter blinked in the semidark of the entranceway and came into the apartment.

"Join me." Bruno flourished a glass.

"No, thanks."

"The rent, I know. Give me a minute, checkbook's in the bedroom."

Alter watched Bruno, three hundred pounds in a dragon-red kimono, swish past the television playing "The People's Court."

"I love this show," Bruno called over his shoulder. "Everyone's dead serious, even though it's not real."

"I thought it was," Alter said guardedly. Behind Bruno's geniality he sensed another adversary lurking.

"Well it is and it isn't. The judge's decisions are final. But the litigants all get paid from a common fund—so if you win, you win, and if you lose, you win. Still, everybody wants to win. They've got some girl on now, says her permanent wave went bad, hair burned up. Wants her money back and five hundred more for pain and suffering. I'm with her—the hairdresser's a stupid son of a bitch."

Alter looked at the screen. The plaintiff's platinum hair was shorn to within a half-inch of her scalp. Over the image he heard a man yelling and the furious rapping of a judge's gavel.

"I agree," Alter said, wanting nothing more than to leave the apartment. "She should get her money back."

Bruno pored over a collection of liquor bottles on a wicker trolley. "What're you having?"

"Nothing. Just the check, thanks."

"You'll get your rent. Come *on.*" Bruno rattled the bottles. "By the by, I slipped on something in the incinerator room, felt like a banana peel. Nearly crowned myself. Light's out in there."

"I'll see Mr. Muñoz puts in a new one."

"It could've been serious."

"I'll get Muñoz on it first thing. Or I'll do it."

"God, not you!" Bruno laughed. "You'll kill yourself."

"I didn't know you cared."

"Oh but I do," Bruno said lightly, "although I have half a mind to sue."

"Nothing happened." A twinge of anxiety seized Alter. "Only teasing."

"The humor escaped me. In my position, lawsuits are no joke." A sharper retort came to his lips, but he stifled it just in time. *What have I got to prove? The man's a little off, that's all.*

"But by way of making it up to me, and in the spirit of the season, you'll have a drink." It was in the nature of a command. Bruno turned with two short glasses in his hand.

Reluctantly Alter accepted the glass. He sniffed. Bourbon. "Just a quick one. I have four more apartments to visit."

He folded himself into the far end of the sofa and looked around the room. Bruno had decorated entirely in shades of red: crimson flocked wallpaper, tangerine tasseled lampshades, shirred vermilion slipcovers. The room had a frenzied, overheated aura.

"Tell me, why do you do it?" Bruno asked, sinking onto the sofa with a loud, contented groan. He placed his drink on a small table where it would be easily retrievable and rested his swollen, bare feet on a scarlet footstool. Alter saw that his tenant extended to his body the small attentions of the very overweight or chronically ill, courtesies and accommodations more ordinarily due to the *other*, the thing apart.

"Do what?"

"Collect the rents this way. It's positively Victorian. I feel like I live in a widow-lady's boarding house. Why not do it by mail? Or, for a modest monthly fee you hire a management company. They collect and disburse, they deal with Muñoz, your hands never touch dirty water."

"I collect the way my father did, it's tradition." Alter paused. "He didn't know from sending bills. He conducted all his business out of his pants pocket . . . Anyway, I *am* management. I don't need a company."

"Management manages—you cope, just barely . . . Sometimes I think you're an apparition, a figment of my dream life. When you enter a room, it's like someone has just left. It's occurred to me that you doubt your own existence, and that this might explain the miserable condition of the premises—you live here but you're not really *here*." Alter shrank from Bruno's aggressive gaze. "You ever notice how this place concentrates despair, the way a mirror if you hold it in the right position, gathers heat from the sun?"

"Spare me," Alter said laconically. "The whole planet is going up in flames."

"But here," Bruno said, pointing down into the building, "it starts with you."

"Me? You want to hold *me* accountable?" There was no sidestepping them; every apartment held a new prosecutor.

"It's your place. You set the tone."

"Look, I run a building, not an asylum."

"Buildings *are* asylums, ports in a storm . . ."

"I do what I can, Al, but don't hold me to blame." Anger welled in him; he could not tell against whom it was directed, himself or Bruno, and so it went up crazily, a missile off course, and exploded, showering them both with sparks. "What do you want? That I should make over the world?—all your sorry lives? Who do you think that I am?"

He was startled by the cruelty of his outburst; the frenzied redness of the room seemed to close in on him. Bruno looked at the landlord with an expression that caused him to shudder—the patience of the lion, so sure of its prey that it lies down on the veldt, to rest. Alter lowered his voice. "Why should it matter to me? I don't ask for these intimacies—all your complaints, your sad stories, your endless threnodies of woe . . . what makes you think I *care?*"

"It's in those hungry, hungry eyes of yours," Bruno said placidly, "and because you could so easily stay away from us. But you choose to engage. In your way . . . Sometimes, just when I think you're dozing, I look again and see something stir within, a breeze blows."

Alter checked his watch. "I've still got those four apartments, Al. Maybe we could continue this next month."

"A moment more of your time."

"You want—what?" Alter asked tersely, anxiety rising in him at the thought of another unattainable request. "Wall-to-wall carpeting? A microwave? Dishwasher? Go on, speak right up, everyone else does."

"No. Dishwashers, carpeting, microwaves, these are simple, Alter, unimportant amenities. What I want from you, what I want . . ." Bruno flushed suddenly. "Well look, I have something to tell you. I'm getting a roommate. My friend, Henry Arnold, is moving in next week . . . Ten years we've been together, and finally he's decided to risk it all with me." Bruno's eyes, stranded deep in the cement fleshiness of his face, appeared to moisten. "Actually, Henry's not well. He needs my care."

Alter sensed Bruno was treating him to some divine privilege and was calling upon him to sanctify it, but his tongue went to lead on the floor of his mouth.

"You must do better than silence," Bruno pleaded, an impassioned entreaty. "Congratulations? Mazel tov? Your blessings on whatever future may be left to Henry and me?"

"Blessings?" Alter intoned helplessly. "I'm only . . . the landlord."

The fat man inclined across the sofa as far as his bulk would allow. "Ah, but in spite of yourself, our burdens *are* yours. Like the biographer you are, you animate the dead of this place—you imagine us to life." Bruno's eyes glistened. "A word, please. 'Luck' will do. I have no one else . . ."

"Good luck," Alter gasped. It came out sounding like "gluck," the quack of a goose.

Bruno settled back, relieved. "Thank you. I know you mean it . . . The extraordinary thing is that, even in the face of Henry's illness, you find me in a state of happiness. Oddly, genuinely joyful. And I haven't been before, not for the longest time. Henry is a very attractive man. He was always going off, leaving me for others, coming back. I waited for him. I was in love. Besides, look at me: what choice did I have? . . . Now *he* needs *me*, and I'll take him any way I can get him. But it isn't only need; we have discovered each other in some transcendent way. We will spend all our days together now, share completely whatever time we have left. And I tell you—I *have* hope. For Henry. For me. For us together. Like grass splits the concrete, so hope blooms. In the unlikeliest situations, and against all the odds."

"Yesss . . ." Alter felt dizzy. "Well, I wish you the best. Both of you."

He stood up, placing his untouched drink on a red lacquered sideboard and taking his receipt book and pen from his breast pocket. "I must be going."

" 'Hello, I must be going!' " Bruno sang, pushing himself up off the sofa. "It could be your theme song." The garish kimono fell away, exposing his skinny splayed legs. Alter was startled by them, grotesque in relation to the enormity of the torso to which they were attached. Bruno made for the bedroom, the gown billowing in silken drifts.

"Back in a jiff." A moment later he reappeared. "Seems I'm fresh out of checks. What with this new life, I've been buying like a bride. Pots, pans, stemware, new sheets and towels. I want everything *perfect*. So you'll extend a little credit?"

Alter closed the receipt book slowly.

Roslyn DeAngelis waddled from the living room, leaving Alter alone with her sister, Loretta. "Wait there," she called. "I'll get our rent." The women were in their late forties, Alter guessed, and had the same large, slightly hooked noses and liquid, semiconscious eyes. Although not twins—Roslyn was a couple of years older and fuller of hip and face—they dressed exactly alike, their brownish hair that seemed sapped of pigment was clipped in the same Buster Brown style, and both worked for the telephone company as information operators. They came and went together every day, and it occurred to him, standing there, that he had never seen them apart, ever.

The blinds in the room were tightly drawn; two lamps with brown paper shades stood at either end of a beige sofa and cast the place in a dingy light. The sisters' apartment was the antithesis of Bruno's. No spot of color disturbed the eye, except for a cheap chrome étagère against one wall that held a score of glass and ceramic unicorns. In a corner Alter spied tall stacks of tabloids: the *Enquirer*, the *Globe*, the *National Star*. A black headline on the *World Weekly News* sounded the alarm: SPACE ALIENS KIDNAP 10,000 HUMANS A YEAR FOR SLAVE LABOR. It was all the news, he thought, the sisters needed or wanted, confirming for them the frangibility of life.

He recalled the one time he had been allowed to set foot deeper into their apartment, when the women reported having seen a mouse in the bedroom. He remembered the unwrinkled twin beds placed side-by-side, two matching pine dressers, each set with a small mirrored tray on which rested a lipstick, a powder compact, and a hairbrush. Over their beds two small wood crucifixes floated on the wall. There were no frills, no touch of whimsy, no smell of perfume, unguents, or scented soaps, those evanescent yet potent essences of women. The decor, Alter reflected, could only be described as apprehensive.

"Here you go." Roslyn rejoined her sister. "I had to find my pockabook." She spoke nasally, handing over a money order.

Alter scribbled a receipt hastily. The women threatened him with drowsiness; he feared he might nod off on the spot.

"Any problems?" he asked, then wondered with a jolt why he had laid himself open. He cursed Al Bruno for throwing him off his stride.

"No," Loretta said.

"Well . . ." Roslyn said.

"Now Roz, it's really nothing."

"Speak to me," Alter said, still writing.

"It's the sink," Roslyn said quickly.

"The bathroom sink," Loretta supplied.

"It drips, you see," Roslyn said. "And drips. We can't make it stop."

"It's just . . . it keeps us awake," Loretta chimed in apologetically, "and we need our sleep. We have to be at work by eight."

Signing the receipt, he looked up and was astounded to

see Roslyn and Loretta gazing at him with what he appre-
hended as a sort of shameful, scourged longing. For an
instant he saw them as though evaginated, and contemplated the deep bruises on their spirits.

"I'll see what I can do . . . about the sink."

He fled.

Hours later, in his armchair, Alter woke. For a moment he
couldn't recall where he was. The apartment was dark, but
a thick beam of light from the kitchen dimly lit the foyer.
On the radio, to which he had fallen asleep, he heard a
silky-voiced woman announce tomorrow's weather conditions. He looked at his watch, moving his wrist back and
forth before his face to find the distance that would allow
him to read its illuminated dial: midnight. He sighed. It
seemed a bitter paradox that, with the passage of time, as
life grew shorter, instead of being able to do things more
quickly and easily, even simple tasks got harder and took so
much longer. Longer for the eyes to focus on a watch dial
and for the urine to flow, to sit down and stand up again.
There were the once familiar names that took forever to
dislodge themselves from the crevices of the brain, as though
the synapses were gorged with glue. And the time spent
worrying about one's health—mentally tinkering with those
inner mechanisms that maintained a tenuous equilibrium—
occupied hours, as the prospect of serious illness loomed.
Nothing *hurried*, except time itself, which flew faster and
faster. He got up to close the window.

Outside snow fell again, swirling in the peach glow of a
street lamp. A young black man wearing only a hooded
sweatshirt, jeans, and basketball sneakers raced past the

window, down the middle of the silent, wet street, on a skateboard. Pumping rhythmically, kicking the pavement, elbows cocked like pistons, his face glinted as he whizzed under the lamp: he had the high chiseled cheekbones, the shapely lips of a mannequin and a look as hard as diamonds. In a flash he was gone, the wheels of the board hissing on the snow-slick asphalt. Something in the boy's solitary, thin, underclad figure, propelled helplessly through the night on ferocious tidal bursts of testosterone, suggested to Alter pain on a scale unlike his own and yet he felt kinship with him. Briefly, he tried to summon the distant sensation of youth. He was forty-eight. Forty-eight was not old . . . but he was old. Sometimes the midnight darkness made his predicament, his self-imposed isolation, tolerable for a while; and in these moments he was able to convince himself that his ways were set and he had no need for change. But tonight was different.

Behind him, the silky-voiced woman forecast frost.

Alter lay on his back in bed making his customary morning appraisal of the day. Were there notes to be transcribed by Mildred the Typist? (Mildred the Typist, Nick the Mailman, Angel the Super—a place for everyone and everyone in his place.) Did he have an interview scheduled? What part of the rotting building demanded the most immediate attention? (Al Bruno. Incinerator room. Bulb. DeAngelis sisters. Bathroom. Drip.) Were groceries required, a trip to the market, or could he get away with staying in all day? (Groceries required! Chloe will be here soon!) Then it came to him, with force. *Chloe*, the *name*—a boat's white sail on the horizon on a bright summer day, like out of nowhere.

But how? In a dream? He could not remember dreaming, only blackness, a dead sleep.

Alter got up from bed and padded to the living room in his undershorts, where he perused again the shelf of spiral-bound notebooks over his desk. In which one had he come across the clue? But it hadn't registered then because it was B.C. (Before Chloe) and there was nothing—or no one—with which to connect it. He pulled out a blue notebook. Ulysses had carefully marked them all; this one had 1970–71 etched on its cover. Too early. He ran his fingers along their wire spines and selected another, yellow, farther down the line. 1973–74. The Bennington years. Alter sat at the desk and turned the opening pages. He was reminded anew of the mordant quality running through many of these later journals as the poet, nearing sixty, raked over the coals of past infatuations and affairs, sounding disquietingly sour notes. He leafed rapidly, but paused now and then to read a snatch of doggerel, crude snatches of thoughts, mostly about women, which Leibert may have hoped contained the embryo of a poem:

> . . . I grow weary of her & troubled lest she make sleeping here / a regular thing . . . Restless till 12, / When she calls to say she has the curse and isn't coming. Liar. / I keep track. / She's been with someone else, who brought roses, / And what else? . . . Angry that I did not telephone, she screws without zest / Then cries all night, weeps she has no friends now, / And cannot leave me. / Such is the tragedy of desire— . . . There's this about copulation & affection: / It's the one act that convinces her she still matters . . . I've tired of my various girls & / long for a new love. / For T. I have no more interest / Than in a wooden table.

He moved deeper into the notebook, then saw it, an entry dated February 14, 1974. "I've fallen for C. And hard. Tamsin senses and complains, asks if I won't refrain? She fears I'll bring her to this bed and says 'I want one room where I do not find the traces of other women.' " Another entry, dated a week later, read:

> She tends my little garden, putting in bulbs and tubers and seedlings for the spring and we talk. Or *I* talk, she listens, rarely meeting my eye. She understands & sympathizes with my necessities and lacks, dismisses aggressive & vain male youth, caring more for weight & age, grey hairs, intelligence and force . . . She's adorable, worthy of worship, has a lovely form, soft & softly rounded, hair halfway 'tween brown & gold. Beautiful hands. Likes good books & poems. Gifted with poise— though I rattle her sometimes (she's uncertain what I want of her, can't believe I want what she *thinks* I want, is flattered & unstrung by my attentions)—and natural intuition . . .

A month passed without an entry, and the next time Leibert put pen to paper in his journal he wrote, "Made my move at last and—success. O *God!* This child will preserve my puny soul from daily living death! I will no longer dream unhappy dreams of failure! I'll write for *her*, fuck her to exhaustion, then—*feed her soup.*

> *"Asleep! O sleep a little while, white pearl!*
> *And let me kneel, and let me pray to thee,*
> *And let me call Heaven's blessing on thine eyes,*
> *And let me breathe into the happy air,*
> *That doth enfold and touch thee all about,*

Vows of my slavery, my giving up,
My sudden adoration, my great love!"

The entry ended with the lines of Keats.

Chloe? It seemed beyond doubt. Alter closed his eyes, conjuring an image of her in her cherry overcoat, her hair *halfway 'tween brown & gold* glistening with crystals of melted snow. He felt a stirring in his groin and sensed a door opening into the intense light of an unknown room.

FOUR

The following morning Alter was roused from sleep at day-break by a call from Ulysses Leibert.

"Too early for you, Raffi?"

"No, uh-uh," Alter mumbled, cradling the telephone receiver on the pillow.

"I've got an eight-thirty tutorial and I didn't want to wait to tell you. Remember my Uncle Irving?"

"Max's brother, yes."

"I have good news."

He's come back to life and I can talk to him.

"His daughter, my cousin Esther, has decided to sell Irving's factory in Hackensack. He manufactured textiles, you know. So Esther and her husband were going through some storerooms in the back and they found another carton of Dad's papers. The box arrived yesterday. I was up half the night going through it."

Alter's heart leapt: a fresh cache! He raised himself on an elbow, ran a hand over his narrow, hairy, naked chest. What day is it? Where am I? God, I'm freezing! "What *time* is it, Lee?"

"Six-thirty. I thought you said you were up."

"I was, am, sort of."

"I think I found a mention of that garden you were curious about. It's just a few lines. You want to write this down? You got a notebook there?"

Oh yeah, right here, under the blanket. I sleep with my notes, Lee, instead of girls. "Uh, no, I'm afraid I'm in the wrong—room."

Ulysses sighed, a tremendous gust of disapproval, a veritable typhoon of displeasure. Alter knew what he was thinking: *Why* was Alter in the wrong room? Why was he not in the right room, where he ought to be—the Work Room—at his *desk*, for crying out loud? This man would be the author of the first major book on his father's life, *so what was he doing in the wrong room?*

"All right, then you just listen now and you can look at it later. It's from a poem called 'Damned' he never finished, apparently. There're two drafts. One's handwritten on the back of a menu from"—he paused—"Villa d'Este, some Italian place in Jersey. The other's typed. He made revisions, but the relevant lines are the same in both versions." Ulysses took a deep breath.

Alter shivered, wanting desperately to slip into his bathrobe, but it lay out of reach, draped over a chair. He pulled on the receiver cord, testing; it wouldn't stretch.

"You ready?"

"Breathless with anticipation." And my cock is shriveled like a gherkin with the cold—get on with it!

"Don't mock me, Raffi."

"I'm not . . . I don't." I *do*, but never mind.

"I'm just trying to help."

"I know."

"So listen: 'We put in rows of lettuce, / zucchini & zinnias, / On our knees together.' " Ulysses paused, then continued conversationally. "It goes on, blah-blah-blah, some obscene references to vegetables, carrots and cucumbers, I won't bore you with, this isn't his best work, you'll read it yourself, and then, oh here—'In the dead of night, like a wolf, / I bury the secret of those wild hours. / And from the mulchy grave spring vines, / Bearing fruit as ripe as her breasts.' " He stopped. "Not great, huh? But interesting." He seemed to want Alter to refute his estimation or in some degree to temper it.

"He'd done much better. He could do better," Alter conceded. "When is it dated?"

"Nineteen seventy-five, right after Bennington, about two years before he died. He was in such bad straits then, living in that cruddy little place on Jane Street, he was storing his shit all over. I suppose he left this box with Irving . . . Well, there's your garden, anyway . . . What do you make of the burying business? Secrets? Wild hours?"

"Allusion, metaphor . . . melodrama. I don't know. I'll have to study it," Alter said cagily, drawing the blanket over one shoulder. "What else did you find?"

"Letters, some papers he wrote in college, photographs . . . Oh, and you'll enjoy this: a couple of checkbooks with the registers still inside. You oughta have hours of fun with those."

"So when do I get a peek?"

"When?" Ulysses grew distinctly querulous. "I remind you that when last we spoke, you were going to get back to me. But here we are again, as usual, with me getting back to you. Now I have something you may need and suddenly you want to see me."

He talks like a spurned lover. "I apologize, Lee." I know, sometimes I have all the grace of a thug, but I want what I want and need what I need. So give me the damn box and evaporate. Scram, beat it, get lost for a while. Leave me to work in peace.

"You know, when I agreed to let you have access to Dad's stuff, I thought we were sort of in this together. Collaborators, kind of."

Well, you were wrong, sweet boy.

"I'm starting to feel pretty iced out," Ulysses concluded.

"I'm sorry to hear that. But you've got to understand: it *is* my book. In the end, I'm the one doing it, not you. You trusted me as your father's biographer."

There was great good fortune in writing the life of a person while those who knew and were close to him were still alive. But at some moments with Ulysses, Alter wished he had chosen to chronicle a man who had breathed his last in 1700. Long and safely dead—and all his wives and children too.

"Sure, I know." Ulysses sounded dejected. "I just thought . . . I thought . . . you were my good friend."

No you didn't. You thought I was your father, your second, unflawed father. "I am, Lee, I'm your good friend."

"Okay, I don't mean to bug you, Raffi. I know you're doing a terrific job. Forgive me?"

Alter lay down flat. *Crisis averted.* "Hmmm?"

"Do you?"

"Do I what?"

"Forgive me."

"There's nothing to forgive."

Ulysses, the neglected son, tugged at Alter's trouser leg, begging for attention, for respect, for more of the biographer's time and affection. He would do almost anything to gain admittance, even pretend to discover documents belonging to his father that Alter suspected had been at his fingertips all along. He wondered if this wasn't the case now. As Alter saw it, Ulysses did not want their mutual enterprise to end, not ever, if that were possible. For then he would lose Alter and, in a way, he'd lose his father— again. Sometimes the biographer found himself worrying for Ulysses toward the inevitable day of the book's publication. What then? Annihilation? He smiled inwardly. No, at least not before a flurry of joint appearances on "Bookchat," "Bookmark," "Bookworm" with Lee hogging all the air time.

"You were right in the first place." Alter took up the thread of their conversation. "I'm preoccupied and I forget. I really meant to call you. I'm the one who should be forgiven."

"So next week," Ulysses replied more cheerily, "you'll come over, we'll have tea, we'll go through the box. We'll go through the box together."

Alter felt himself drifting off. "Together, yes."

Alter lowered his head, a contemplative pose. *Shower-monk.* Steam billowed, fogging the shower stall's glass door. With his index finger he drew her name in block letters on the glass: C-H-L-O-E. Hot water sluiced over his limp penis. He gazed at it. He hadn't had on swimming trunks in years but their impression remained: below his navel the skin turned a ghastly white and his organ seemed to him somehow foreign, small and frail, vulnerable to assault, nesting in its rain forest of hair. He watched the shimmering beads of water collect in the pubic patch then fall away, cascading off his cock in streams.

A vision of her flashed behind his eyes and he blinked, dismayed, as he stiffened.

"Damn," he whispered. *Be still, you wretched fool.*

Toweling off, Alter calculated. Today was Friday; tomorrow, Saturday, would be the day of her visit. He had forty-eight hours to prepare. Battles had been fought, won and lost, governments had toppled, the fates of entire nations decided, in less time than was left to him.

He stood there nude, unraveling a long thread from the hem of his bath towel and wrapping it around his index finger tight, tighter, until the tip of the finger turned blue.

The air was clear and cold as Alter emerged from the building and started down the block. Overflowing ashcans, cigarette butts and bits of paper littering the gutter, the Dumpster filled with debris from the next-door demolition—busted-up window frames, toilet tanks, old linoleum tiles—all of it seemed appealing in the play of morning sun and shadow. Two young mothers wheeling their toddlers in strollers passed Alter, conversing animatedly. Their voices wafted over, then enveloped him. He was almost convinced he might make it easily through this day.

Alter stood next to Pete, owner of the neighborhood liquor emporium, a peaceful place of burnished woods and classical music. The store was nearly empty on this weekday morning. Along the walls from floor to ceiling hundreds of bottles gleamed tantalizingly under spotlights, like a stage set. His eyes took in the crystal clarity of the vodkas and gins, the brown and amber hues of the whiskies, the minty and melony greens and burnt oranges of aperitifs and cordials. A festival of booze.

"That's six bottles of red, six of white—I'll give ya a break on the case—a fifth of Stoly, a fifth of Chivas, one dry vermouth, one sweet, fifth of Tanqueray, liter of Remy—"

Pete looked up from his order pad. He had a rosy, well-rested complexion and his steady, even gaze gave him a comforting air of calm. Here is a man, Alter thought, who sleeps the whole night through, a person of supreme confidence who makes other men feel small beside him; a man who knows all there is to know about his business, and feels no one else could run the place as competently as himself. He fears neither stickup artists nor discount chains: either one, he'll stare down all comers and prevail. He commands loyalty and respect because he does not want to be doing anything else than what he does, and does not wish to be anywhere else but where he is right now. A lucky man—

"Will that be it?"

"Well no, not exactly." Alter paused. *I buy a hundred dollars worth of booze in order to ask a simple question.*

"Speak to me," Pete encouraged.

"How does one make a whisky sour?"

"Nothing to it. Bourbon. A little sugar. A squeeze of fresh lemon juice—really oughta be fresh not bottled. And a maraschino cherry, if you want."

Sugar. Cherries. A lemon. Alter added these to his mental shopping list. ". . . Throw in a bottle of bourbon, I'm low."

"Any particular brand?"

"Whatever you recommend."

"Good." Pete scratched hieroglyphics on his pad. "So we deliver at five tomorrow?"

"Yes . . . by five, you're sure?"

"Trust me."

I do, Pete, I trust you. You're one of the most trustworthy men I know. I'd trust you with my life, with my wife if I had one, with the lives of my children if I had any. You, Nick, Angel—I love you guys. "Will you take a personal check?"

"I'll take whatever you got."

And you trust me.

Alter rested on his mop, perspiring. It was hopeless. Ludicrous. The kitchen linoleum was permanently grey. He'd have to replace it completely, or sandblast it, to reclaim its original pristine white. He propped the mop diagonally across the doorframe and lumbered toward the bathroom.

I'll just keep Chloe out of the kitchen. Surely there's no reason a guest needs to visit the kitchen. Of course it's been so long since I've had guests, what would I know of their behavior? Don't they follow you around, trying to make themselves useful? Visitors are a species as foreign to me as the aardvark . . . He entered the bathroom and examined the bathtub. He'd removed the cartons of research materials and saw with a thrill of disgust that a dark turquoise ring circled the drain, soap scum streaked the walls, the faucets were caked with it too. The soap dish had cracked off a year ago and he had failed to ask Muñoz to replace it. Where the porcelain dish used to hang, at knee level, was a square hole filled with crumbly grit. He snapped the shower curtain shut. *She won't be bathing.*

He picked up a can of cleanser and a brush and scoured the toilet in slow strokes. A line of Max Leibert's occurred to him, from a letter he'd written to Ulysses in the weeks before his death: "Lee," he mourned, "I have lived for too much time in a state of self-imposed autism . . ."

All day Alter worked in the apartment, getting it ready.

On his hands and knees with a brush, he scrubbed the bathroom floor. He found himself enjoying the work—the feel of the stiff bristles on the cool tiles, the slosh of the water. He cleaned the stove inside and out, even scraping off the hardened drippings in the oven. Unaccustomed to harsh detergents, his throat and nose grew raw, and flecks of dirt settled in his hair. He filled plastic bags with garbage and carried them to the curb. Muñoz, bringing the building's trash barrels out for collection, stared at him curiously, offered a hand. Alter waved him away. The superintendent's expression turned from curiosity to guardian concern. Alter caught the look and it gave them an intimacy neither man was certain he wished to accommodate. Late in the afternoon Alter approached Muñoz in the basement, as he was preparing to leave for the day. Proferring a twenty and a ten, he asked if Muñoz would return the following morning, his day off, to wash the windows in his apartment. Angel nodded, solemn, and pocketed the cash.

By six o'clock Alter was rearranging furniture. Couch in front of the window? Uh-uh, looks like a dance floor. Couch in front of the mantel? No good, blocks the fireplace. Should I build a fire? But I haven't tried, not in years. I could burn the place down. There may be rats in the flue. Dead rats, decomposing. He reminded himself to speak to Muñoz: *Fire. Flue. Rats.*

Tired beyond exhaustion, lightheaded, he sank onto the couch in a purifying sweat.

That evening Alter read further from Leibert's letter to Ulysses in which he bemoaned his "self-imposed autism . . . After a long life," he went on in a sloping, unsteady hand,

> (but not long enough, never long enough) I still cannot answer the question posed by a character of James's who asks, after an encounter with a woman, whether "it is better to cultivate art than to cultivate a passion." James answered it for himself: thirty books—novels, stories, criticism, travel writing, autobiographical works, thousands of letters, plays. . . . I find myself thinking of the early hermits who abandoned the pagan world to live apart, seeking salvation in the deserts of Egypt, Palestine, Arabia and Persia. They regarded society as a shipwreck from which a man had to swim for his life. As I grow older, I wonder if I would have lived more contentedly, productively, *safely*, if I had simply committed myself, body and soul, to an ascetic existence—the existence of an Essene, my days as strictly regulated as theirs: prayers in the morning followed by work in the fields; midday washings and a common meal; afterwards, more work; and again in the evening a common meal. (Rx for a writer.)
>
> How many lives I have manhandled and destroyed!—I

do not speak here of my own (except insofar as I regret all the time wasted, the work I did not do), but yours, your cherished sister and brothers, your mother, and others. I sit now, alone, and ask: What is love, after all, but a squall in the heart? It comes suddenly, passes just as quickly, and leaves devastation in its wake.

Muñoz's legs, in green work pants and scuffed lace-up boots, dangled inside Alter's living room as he worked on the outside of a window. His nephew, Ramon, a round mahogany-colored seven-year-old, played with a basketball on the sidewalk. Alter heard the slap of the ball against the outer wall and the child's exultant cries as he scored again and again. Muñoz finished the window and slithered in, lithe as a panther.

"All finish."

"Thanks, Angel. They look great." Sunshine flooded the apartment, bathing it in light, for the first time in as long as Alter could remember.

"Shoun't wait so long between washings. Takes a lotta elbow grease."

"My fault." Guilty, Alter dug in his pocket for his wallet. Muñoz held up a hand.

"No. Thirty's good." He lifted his bucket, rags, placed a squeegee in the dirty water. "I'll jus' clean up and me and Ramon'll be on our way."

The superintendent passed through the room. Alter observed him taking it in; his appraisal was surreptitious but his astonishment palpable. He'd never seen it as neat and clean. Nearly virginal, the room seemed to hold its breath, in wait. The silent, bemused inspection discomfited Alter; he worried that his efforts would be found lacking. Muñoz lingered over a bouquet of yellow daisies Alter had plunked in a vase on the coffee table.

"I'm having company this evening and I thought, well, flowers . . ." He faltered, keeping the rest to himself.

Abruptly Muñoz set down the bucket and parted the blooms, his meaty fingers working expertly among the stems. "You got 'em bunched too close, gotta give 'em room, they live longer." Muñoz looked up with an inquisitive yet secluded expression. He had his secrets too; they gave him an air of quiet self-containment. But Alter recognized he wanted more. It was disarming.

"A . . . woman."

"Woman." Muñoz nodded gravely. "Man needs a woman, someone to lean on, keep him warm . . . It's a col' world." Muñoz lifted the bucket, rags, uneasy even with this minimal exchange of information. From the street came the sound of the basketball on the wall and Ramon's shrill chortling. "Four feet, jus' up to my waist, thinks he's Magic. Some 'magination, that kid." His voice held layers of feeling: humor, wonderment, pride.

Muñoz disappeared into the kitchen. Alter listened to the running water and the clank of the bucket in the sink, to the relentless thwack-thunk, thwack-thunk of Ramon's ball. There seemed some music in it, the plash of water onto metal, the clang of metal against sink, set to the beat of the ball. He smiled, a barely perceptible creasing at the corners of his mouth.

Martin Aswith entered the landlord's apartment unbidden, trailed by his sad-eyed five-year-old daughter, Marion. Her sandy hair was tortured into two lopsided pigtails. Her pink overalls were stained with chocolate, like a wound on her little chest, and dried egg yolk clung to her cheek. She pulled a wooden dog behind her on a string; it clacked loudly with each tug. Her father's flannel shirt hung out of his pants; his hair, the same sandy color as his daughter's, stood away from his head in harried tufts. The laces of his sneakers were coming untied. His left thumb was heavily, professionally bandaged.

"How's it going, Martin?" Alter, realizing the absurdity of the question, regretted it as soon as the words left his lips. Aswith's wife had deserted him three months ago for another man, cleaning out their bank account, and leaving him with Marion.

"We're coping," Aswith replied wearily. He seemed worn away, whitened as if dropped in bleach, abraded to the point of transparency. "I'm here with the rent. Sorry I wasn't around, I kept the store open late. Then I had to pick Marion up from day care." He took a breath. The litany was almost too much for him. "Then I'm cutting us bagels and I slice my finger instead. Ten stitches. We were in the emergency room till midnight and they tell me I cut a nerve. I may need surgery."

"God, Martin."

"Ever since Catherine . . . well, it's been one disaster after another. I fell getting off the bus, tore my Achilles tendon. I beaned myself pushing Marion on a swing. I slipped in the shower, dislocated my shoulder . . . It's gotten dangerous to be *me*." He lowered his voice. "Then yesterday I get a call from Catherine, in Miami, she's thinking she wants custody, after *she* runs off! Christ. Says Marion would be better off without me. I haven't got the dough to fight her in court. I swear, if she goes through with it I'll take the kid and run, I swear I will. Marion's all I've got."

"Don't do anything drastic, Martin."

"Sometimes drastic measures are necessary. I'm not sure you'd understand. I mean no insult, but I get the feeling you've never made a drastic move in your life."

"I simply live tranquilly," Alter replied, faintly irritated by one more tenant's unsolicited evaluation of him. He glanced at his watch. Six-thirty. Chloe was due soon. "Anyway I'd . . . miss you, you and Marion. Not that it's a real consideration."

Aswith brightened. "Would you?"

Alter shrugged. "Sure." It was an inconsequential lie. And perhaps he would, he wasn't certain. Things were shifting around within him so rapidly, rearranging and reorganizing themselves, he felt he was living on some internal fault line in which nothing was sure, nothing held fast.

"How's the book coming?"

"It's coming," Alter said. "Slowly, the way books come, mine anyway."

Aswith looked at Marion, hiding behind his legs. "Marion, give Mr. Alter the check." She made no move, watching Alter hypnotically. "The check, baby, that piece of paper I gave you to hold for us. Pay the man."

The little girl took her thumb from her mouth, stuck the hand into the breast pocket of her overalls and handed over a bit of folded blue, now damp with drool. Alter took it with two fingers.

"I'll write you a receipt."

"Don't bother, I'll only lose it. My head's not screwed on right these days. C'mon, sweetie, dinnertime. Spaghetti and meatballs."

Marion straggled to the front door, the wooden dog clacking like a duck.

"How's she taking it?" Alter asked, sotto voce, as he saw them out.

"She misses her mother, but it's hard to tell. She never actually says, not a word, but I see it in her eyes. There's resentment, and fear. She's keeping it all inside and one day it's going to come spilling out. I lie in bed at night, terrified." Martin Aswith gazed fixedly at the top of Marion's head as though he were trying to bore through her skull and read something there. "Catherine used to dress her in these beautiful dresses, with bows in her hair. You remember? People would stop and smile . . . We had a decent life, maybe not ideal but decent. I don't understand what happened, what went wrong." His voice quivered with anger. "It's like milk gone sour. Suddenly she just couldn't stand the taste of me . . ."

Maybe she fell in love, Martin. People do crazy things when they're in love. They leave their lives. "Some things," Alter faltered, "are beyond explanation."

Aswith started over the threshold, then stopped and turned. "I almost forgot. Since I signed a new lease on the apartment, I believe I'm entitled to a paint job. It's been at least four years." He spoke like a man who was not at all convinced of his entitlement, to anything.

"Indeed a paint job is due." *Although under what rock I'll find the money to pay for it, I haven't the faintest idea.*

"Can we set something up?"

Alter looked away. "I'll call the painters, get back to you with some dates."

The landlord's averted eyes might have made Aswith suspect stalling, but he was in no condition to get into it, only sighed, a tremolo of grief. "Sometimes I think a man's troubles settle in his walls. Maybe some fresh paint . . . maybe white . . ."

. . .

Alter followed Chloe closely, like a hound, on the scent of her perfume: sweet as vanilla mingled with the trace of wildflowers. He thought he had never smelled anything so complex, so intoxicating.

"All this is yours?" she asked. "The whole building?"

"Every last lousy brick and leaking faucet. Every stove that does not cook, window that does not close, radiator that does not heat."

"Are you overstating the case?" she asked solicitously. "It seems solid enough to me."

"Illusion, completely. It's near collapse."

"But worth saving, surely?"

"Saving," Alter repeated dully. The idea had never occurred to him quite that way. Not to *restore*, that was never his plan, only to keep the physical plant operating somehow, just barely, at a simmer, a pan of water on a low flame. "Something to drink?"

"A glass of white wine, if you have some."

Pete, as good as his word, has supplied me with enough for a wedding reception, or a wake. "Got it." At the makeshift bar he had set up on his desk, Alter poured wine for her and a scotch for himself.

"Buildings remind me of monasteries," she observed, while he worked at the bar.

The whole human race, seeking sanctuary!

"I mean in their extended, unfolding dramas," she continued, "they hold mysteries. Each has its own rituals, its own secret music, its own ceremonies of light and darkness."

"And I," Alter turned with their drinks in hand, "I suppose I remind you of the monk in the monastery."

"Perhaps, a little."

An Essene. She's got me pegged. No—"A stylite, that's me," he said aloud, self-mockingly.

"A what?"

It was not the conversation he intended to have on this evening, with this woman; nevertheless, he went on with it.

"Saint Simeon Stylites, a hermit of the fifth century A.D." Alter passed Chloe a goblet and took a seat on the other side of the coffee table, facing her. "He spent the last forty years of his life living on top of a tall pillar—a column—in Antioch. He didn't expect to be widely imitated but stylitism spread, and Simeon gained disciples." He gave a half smile. "And so we read of 'monks, hermits and stylites . . .'"

"It's a peculiar paradox, though," she said, regarding Alter seriously, "to create a hermitage on top of a pillar."

"Well, yes."

"It's making a spectacle of oneself."

"That's the point," he replied quietly. "There are those who enter cloistered orders, take vows of silence, shun normal human intercourse as a way of bearing witness to the shame of the world . . . But the stylites cloistered themselves thirty feet in the air in the public square. You see?"

She raised her glass and smiled. "Here's to column-dwelling prophets."

Enough of monks and monasteries! Unnerved, he pushed a platter of melting Brie toward his guest. "Cheese?" He had surrounded the wedge with a fan of small breads, and felt like a third-rate caterer.

She spread a knifeful of Brie on a slice of pumpernickel and ate it, more out of comity, it appeared to Alter, than hunger. She scanned the table, searching. He followed her eyes and recognized immediately what was missing from his carefully laid tableau of cheese, stuffed grape leaves, potato chips, onion dip, peanuts. Some caterer . . .

"I'll get them."

Alter returned from the kitchen with a stack of black and yellow cocktail napkins deployed in alternating bands of color. He set them on the table and frowned. The scheme was hideous. Whatever had possessed him? These were dismal hues, shades of bumblebees, killer wasps; railroad crossings, road signs: MEN AT WORK. SLOW—CHILDREN. DANGER FALLING ROCK ZONE.

"Does it work?" Chloe asked, gesturing at the fireplace. Three dusty logs rested in a pyramid on the grate.

"No . . . Well, I'm not sure." He hadn't remembered to check it out with Muñoz. Visions of disaster flooded in: plumes of smoke, funneling, billowing blackly. Asphyxiation. Garments in flames. "It ought to, it's supposed to, but I haven't used it in so long I'm afraid it may not anymore." The words traveled in an endless loop. *I'm not sure . . . afraid . . . haven't used it in so long.* Decorative . . . like my dick. He felt something wet—a tear?—sting the corner of his eye. He swatted at it.

"It's chilly in here." She wrapped her arms around herself. "Don't you think so?"

The night might be winding down disastrously before it had hardly begun. "Furnace needs work." He looked at her. Chloe wore a blue sheath dress of some silky material that displayed, subtly, the curves of her figure. *Soft & softly rounded.* "Let me find you a sweater."

"No, let's try it. Let's make a fire!" She seemed as pleased by the notion as a child.

Before he could stop her, Chloe was crouched on her haunches at the hearth. She removed the protective screen

and craned her head into the chimney. Alter heard a scraping as she moved a lever.

"Have you got any old newspapers?" Her voice echoed.

"Let me get you the sweater. Please, Chloe, forget this."
He could already smell it: roasted mouse.

"Just find me the newspapers."

From his bedroom Alter hauled most of the previous
Sunday's edition of the *New York Times*.

"I'm warning you—God only knows what may be up
there."

"It's for Him to know and us to find out." She crumpled
sheets of paper into wads and packed them under the logs.
"Give me a match. There should be some in my bag."

Alter picked up her purse from the floor beside the sofa.
Inside he discovered a book of matches lost among lipsticks,
a keychain, a wallet, a tampon. He gave her the matches.
She struck one and touched it to the balled-up papers.
Flame curled their edges. The bark of the dry wood ignited
slowly. A draft coaxed the smoke up the chimney.

Alter, amazed, extended his hand to Chloe and, as if
asking for the first dance, helped her to her feet.

"My flue," Alter murmured, "you opened my flue."

"It wasn't that hard to open," she said, amused.

"It works!"

"It has always worked, you just didn't know it. You
never tried."

They sat for a while in silence on the sofa, listening to
the crackle and hiss of the burning wood. Alter stole looks
at her when she was unaware of it. Her hair fell in waves
grazing her shoulders; the glow of the flames gilded her
face. *I could stay this way forever with her, two floaters on a
lake.* He was astonished by the thought, having never con-

sidered staying with anyone for a full week, much less forever.

"What do you know about me?" she said suddenly.

Chloe shook him from his reverie.

"How do you mean?"

"I mean, as Max's biographer it's conceivable that you know things about me that he . . ." She trailed off.

"If I am to honestly answer your question," Alter said gently, "it won't work."

"I don't understand."

"If I told you, for instance, about something that Max had written about you, it would color whatever else you have to tell me. Or," he ventured, "if I were to tell you that I know nothing, that he never mentioned your name . . . how would you feel then?" She turned to him, her eyes disconsolate. "You see? So you go first." Chloe stared back into the fire, unmoving.

I'll tease it out of her, he thought, then blurted indelicately, "You were—involved with Max? May I assume that?" He found himself dreading the confirming reply, seeing her astride the poet, her naked belly against his, a languorous rhythm established.

"You may assume that," she answered dryly, "although 'involved' does not quite characterize . . . what?—" Her tone became tinged with bitterness. "My thralldom? . . . Yes, I was in his thrall, engulfed. It's like I drowned there and have yet to fully surface. I lived through Max, and for him, and thought of my life in terms of him. Oh God, I was *flayed*, defenseless . . ." She took a shuddering breath. "I'm ashamed. Even after it's so over, after all these years, and his death, I still . . . wait. Enchanted. As if . . . I have been given orders not to move."

Stunned by the severity of her words, he kept silent for a moment, to assure himself that her outburst had ended. "What finally happened?" he asked.

"I ended it," Chloe murmured. She seemed beyond solace, inconsolable.

"Why?" Her succinct reply only heightened the mystery he found so alluring.

"There was *more* than enough reason. I could not go on."

"Tamsin?" Alter pressed.

". . . Yes, in part." Her tone still hinted at evasion. She stood up abruptly. He noticed she trembled.

"What is it, Chloe?"

"I want . . . I want very much to trust you."

Alter rose. "You can."

She moved toward him, her face blurring in his sight. Impulsively, he took her hand, cold as ice. He felt a wall begin to crumble inside.

"I don't know."

He put his arms around her, surprised at how naturally the embrace came to him and how easily she permitted it. Her breasts made warm impressions in his chest. His chin rested in the hollow of her neck; he smelled her hair, vanilla, wildflowers, a slight tinge of smoke from the fire.

"Try me."

"Look, Raphael," she whispered, "I have unfinished business with Max."

"I'll help you finish. That's why you wrote to me, isn't it? So you could—move away from him. And move on."

"It's ugly. Something horrendous . . . I'm sure you cannot imagine. Are you certain you want to know?"

". . . Yes," he said, uncertainly.

"Then you'll come with me."

"Where? Where will we go?"

"Vermont. Bennington. Unless you see it with your own eyes, you'll think me mad."

"No, I'd never think you mad." *Would I?*

"I'll call. As soon as I've made the arrangements."

Hours afterward, unable to be still, the apartment barren without her, Alter walked down Broadway to Columbus Circle to buy the early edition of the Sunday paper. His skin felt porous, pregnable, an altogether new sensation but not unpleasant.

As he neared the Circle he saw twenty or so charter buses parked fender to fender along the curbs. He recognized the buses: they were bound for Attica, the maximum security penitentiary in upstate New York. Their giant engines idled, scenting the winter air with acid fumes. The lines bore incongruously cheerful names: Sunshine, Bluebird, Peter Pan, Happy Trails. Standing in groups on the sidewalk were families huddled in clots against the cold. Mostly women, many children—the mothers, wives, girlfriends, sisters, and offspring of convicts—hovered protectively over little mountains of plastic supermarket bags filled with food, disposable diapers, clothing. Babies slumbered on the shoulders of adults. Older children played tag, laughing and shouting as if it were noontime in July. A few women hung by the open doors of the buses, prohibited for some reason from entering. Alter heard them questioning the drivers in loud, uncomprehending tones.

The caravan left routinely at midnight. At dawn on Sunday morning the vehicles would pull into a rest stop several miles from the prison walls. There, all passengers disembarked. The women would crowd into large public bathrooms to change their clothes and apply makeup in anticipation of reunion with their men.

Alter thought of these wives and mothers and lovers, summoning images of them pouchy-eyed from lack of sleep, wrestling mewling babies and cranky toddlers; pulling on pantyhose, daubing on lipstick and rouge and eyeshadows; balancing cigarettes and coffee containers on the rounded edges of washbasins. In his mind's eye he concentrated on one woman especially, a woman he did not know: she stood bent over a toilet, its seat raised, her son's infant cock in her hand, directing the jet of his pee into the bowl. Silently, in the public john, in the overheated overbright tumultuous public john, on the side of the grey ribbon of superhighway that stretched for her like a nightmare from midnight to morning, a nightmare from which she would not soon awaken (*having received orders not to move*), she cursed: *His daddy should be doing this for him.*

Alter passed through the knots of women on the sidewalk and bought the *Times.* He started back. The wind whipped his thinning hair. He felt thin-skinned too, his nerve endings exposed, but the feeling somehow made him hopeful. It is said of burn victims that they must suffer to survive. It is said, he reminded himself, that only after they have endured unendurable pain can the healing begin.

"Some men," Alter read that night from one of Maxwell Leibert's journals,

are given to casual infidelities. But many, myself included, indulge in no such easy diversions. I go in for *entanglements.*

The husband so entangled (I know from experience)

operates from a false premise: he makes love as if the connection were permanent, and he himself a permanent partner in it. I have worked away at my affairs until it always came down, at last, to "Leave your wife and come with me." I believe that impossible demand to have been my objective. If they had been the sorts of affairs that had not led to this denouement, they would have been too shallow to hold me. Those minor infidelities, I quickly jettisoned as a waste of time . . .

Alter turned back a page to where the entry began, and verified the date again: March 2, 1974. It had been written in the months before Leibert's Bennington tenure ended. He continued reading.

She thinks rather less of herself than I think of her, and the affair has the stimulation to me of urgency. First, I believe I am helping to raise her in her own eyes (she has told me as much), and perhaps there's some good in that. Second, she gives me the illusion that I am loved wildly and hopelessly and forever (or *is* it illusion?). In any event, not something I can expect from T. But knowing that it's unlikely I will leave my wife, I bring to the affair foreknowledge of its doom. I know the time of *choice* must come. And when it does, and I choose Tamsin (if choice it can be called, and not some form of pre-morbid rigor mortis), I know, too, that my lover will then vanish. And I live with that peril in my mind.

During these days I have watched intently for evidence of her ardor waning or turning elsewhere: I pounce on a name murmured in conversation, an unexplained bracelet dangling from her wrist, an odd turn of phrase

apparently borrowed from someone else's vocabulary—
not mine . . . We lie in bed and I tell her I want her to
dress like a whore. No, a nun! She's confused. She asks
me what I mean, she asks me why. She's very young. I
tell her: You *know* what I mean, you know why. While
she is mine she must be wholly mine; I try to fill our time
together with a concentration of devotion as dense and
sharp as tincture of iodine, as though to compensate for
the years of non-love and no-connection that surely lurk
for us not far off.

And throughout all this moody business, self-
knowledge is of absolutely no use. The patterns at work
in my psyche and in my heart are not foreign to me, I
have spent a lifetime studying them in others. I know,
also, the primary lie of this affair, the one on which it is
founded: that it is not Tamsin to whom I am profoundly
unfaithful but to her, to this darling precious girl. It is
on *her* dreams that I have laid doom.

And yet I cannot let it go at that. For, truthfully, I
sometimes think love is better without the promise of
home, fidelity and future. The very impermanence of my
passion gives our relations not only extra life but extra
dimension. In such a love I posture, invent and act, and
thus the dimension of art enriches my kisses. It's a mud-
dled head and heart (and yes, inveterate liar) who brings
her these kisses, but also an artist. I believe I create for
myself, and for my lover, a beauty beyond truth, beyond
the future, beyond reality.

Leibert had skipped two lines and below the entry, in a
different pen, had lightly scrawled, "Despite the foregoing,
I could make a fine case for our marrying!—and living
happily ever after (?)."

. . .

Monday, noon. No call from Chloe. Alter glanced at her telephone number—she had given him that much—but he hesitated to use it for fear of pushing too hard and driving her away. He made his pilgrimage into the lobby for the mail. Maybe she had written him a note. Nick the Mailman seemed to bow a little at his approach and tenderly placed a bundle of mail in Alter's hands. He noted the postmark on the top envelope. December 14. Christmas was around the corner. Nick's holiday tip was due, if not overdue, considering the date and the biographer's dependency on him. Walking back to his apartment, he recalled the ardent, if largely epistolary, affair of Gustave Flaubert with his mistress, Louise Colet. In a letter Flaubert recounted his own slavish devotion to the mail carrier: "I was waiting for the postman on the quay, looking unconcerned and smoking my pipe. I love that postman! I've left orders in the kitchen that he's to have a glass of wine to refresh him. He likes this house and is very punctual. Yesterday he brought me nothing and so he gets nothing."

Alter vowed to take himself to the bank for crisp new bills, then to the stationery store for a packet of envelopes, especially for gratuities, bearing "Season's Greetings" or "Happy Holidays" imprinted in gold leaf. He would go all out, do it right. Perhaps an increase was in order this year?—fifty dollars? He owed Nick something more, something special. After all, it was the postman who had brought him Chloe's pink letter. A quick shuffle of the day's envelopes and magazines produced no more pink, however.

At his desk Alter opened the latest issue of *Publishers Weekly* and read the author interview. It was a conversation

with a novelist, a writer to whom Alter had been introduced
once or twice at literary convocations. The man had recently
published a novel about the dissolution of a marriage. His
own, Alter was convinced; rather, the fervently, devoutly,
richly imagined end of his own—for the couple, he knew,
went on living together. Alter had read the book in a single
sitting. Only one hundred and thirty pages long, it was as
thin as a chapbook, as brutal as a kick in the stomach. The
novel detailed myriad small sexual deceits, and one more
serious affair that preoccupied the narrator's attention and
ran, a leitmotif, through the story: an "entanglement," in
Max Leibert's word. The novelist practically cried out in the
pages with feverish, unrestrained longing for . . . a renovated life. There was also dread, and self-loathing; nonetheless, the work stood as an engraved invitation to his wife
to pack her bags. The writer maintained in the interview
that he had composed a "brave" book.

Brave? Alter asked himself. Or cruel? Was it necessary to
bludgeon the woman with his candor? He had no answer,
actually deeming his own question impertinent: Who am I
to render judgment on the claims of art and love? What do
I know of betrayal, save what I have gleaned, secondhand,
reflecting on the lives of others? Perhaps the man *is* coura-
geous. At least he has lived, and loved. While I, alone on
my column or secluded in my cathedral, *a bystander*, have
hardly lived, and never dared to love at all.

FIVE

"Max and Edythe were married twenty-five years. It was twenty-five, wasn't it, Raphael?"

Max Leibert's editor, Sam Pintchik, picked an invisible speck of lint from the lapel of his navy suit. Pinstripes as delicate as rainwashed chalk ran through the expensive weave. Pintchik, in his late seventies, had a wreath of white hair; his broad face, prosperously florid, was hooded by flamboyant grey eyebrows. A double chin partly obscured the knot in his silk tie.

Pintchik had never married, dedicating his life instead to his stable of writers and the care and feeding of a wraith named Hal. Very few people knew Hal's last name, or how he spent his days, but it was common knowledge that the two men had lived quietly together for over thirty years, gentlemen bachelors. The arrangement recalled to Alter another, sweeter time, when such attachments were referred to as "passionate friendships." Pintchik was born a Jew, raised in Brooklyn, but one would not have guessed it—save for his name. He had veiled his origins in patrician mannerisms both awesome and pathetic.

"Raphael? Are you with me?"

Alter, startled, looked up from his coffee. "Twenty-six years, actually."

They were having lunch at a downtown men's club to which Sam Pintchik belonged, a faded establishment—threadbare, hushed, and eternal—where ancient members were sometimes found dead in their armchairs and out-of-town members passed away in their beds in the small up-stairs rooms. Genteel decay hung over the place, even to the food served in the dining room, in which Alter detected a mustiness reminiscent of shuttered attics and mildewed cellars.

Pintchik went on at interminable, ponderous length dur-ing their luncheons, and seemed to Alter to have been born without a sense of humor. But the editor had turned over to him hundreds of letters and other documents and was the repository of voluminous anecdotal lore concerning the poet Leibert, which made these meals as inevitable as they were sometimes excruciating.

Alter looked at the clock on the wall with relief: ten to three. Pintchik worked only half days now and at three o'clock on the dot Hal would pull up in front of the club to collect Sam for the drive to their home in the country. The men owned a house in Bucks County that Alter had heard via the publishing grapevine was a riot of paisley and chintz, "a regular shrine to Laura Ashley."

Pintchik patted the corners of his mouth and examined the napkin intently, as if for blood. "Of course," he said, "Max was traveling back and forth so much in that last year of their marriage it's hard to pinpoint when the break came. The physical rupture, I mean. I don't think even Edythe's quite certain."

"No, she's not," Alter replied. He played with his spoon in a dish of tapioca pudding. "He had the apartment on Cornelia Street but kept most of his clothes in Peekskill and went up every few days for his mail and things. He was home most weekends."

"When is the last time you saw Edythe?" Pintchik asked.

"Couple of weeks ago. We've been meeting about once a month."

"I really must give her a call." Pintchik's tone suggested unenthusiasm for the task.

"She's been most cooperative, and really quite generous with her time."

"You cannot take her at her word." Pintchik cautioned.

"Why not?"

"Well," he sniffed, "the wives do tend to be somewhat— unreliable." Pintchik raised an eyebrow, defying Alter to contradict him. "They cast it all in such a rosy light, after the fact. Or otherwise, far too darkly."

Alter had suspected for some time that Sam Pintchik had been a little bit in love with Leibert and, even after his death, carried a torch.

"I think Edythe's been fair, and pretty straight with me."

"Ahh . . ." Pintchik could not conceal his disappointment. "I suppose, considering the circumstances of the marriage, one must give her credit." He signaled for the check with a barely perceptible flick of his index finger. "I was best man at their wedding, you know."

"I know."

"I warned her. I said, 'Edythe, you're marrying the most ungovernable man in the world. He has a wild and restive spirit and you'll never have a moment's peace of mind.' She didn't care, I guess. Not then, anyway."

"That spirit may be exactly what she loved about him."

"Perhaps . . . In my opinion, though, Maxwell ought never to have married. God knows what possessed him to do it twice."

"I have come to think that there was a part of him that needed the marriages. They anchored him to . . . something."

An elderly waiter tottered up with the bill. Pintchik examined it cursorily and signed his name with a Victorian flourish.

"We've never talked much about Tamsin," Alter said. "What did you think of her?"

"Coldish, distant. Tough. But she had a certain superficial sort of glamour that attracted Maxwell. Tamsin was a world traveler, had never married or had children—very unlike Edythe in that respect."

"How did she support herself before she married Max?"

"I was under the impression she had a small inheritance to see her through the lean times. And she worked for a number of years at a woman's fashion magazine, in Europe. British *Vogue*, I think, or maybe one of the French magazines—she spoke passable French. I don't remember precisely. We were not particularly friendly. She also took photographs."

"Ulysses has mentioned it."

"She sold some prints, from time to time. I recall a show she had at a small gallery downtown." Pintchik paused, apparently unhappy with his next recollection. "I attended the opening and bought a print. Picture of Maxwell, actually. The show was called 'Sleepers,' I believe. She'd gone around the world taking photographs of people *sleeping*," the editor said disdainfully. "Maori tribesmen, Yves Montand,

Bess Truman. I bought the print out of courtesy, naturally, and also to take it off the market. It was horrid. Maxwell didn't look as though he were asleep, he looked really rather *dead*. Nearly embalmed. I didn't like the whole idea, actually. Sleep. Such a private act, I didn't appreciate the notion of one of our most important poets *exposed* that way . . . Although I expect that was her point."

"Did you ever discover, by the way, where Tamsin went after she left him?"

Pintchik folded his napkin in a square on the table and stood up. Alter followed.

"No, it's as much a mystery as ever. She upped and got out of Vermont and as far as I know, that's the last anyone heard of her . . . Although now that I think of it, you may be on to something when you say Maxwell needed to be married. Because I can tell you that after Tamsin left him, he was never quite the same."

They made their way across the dining room and through the shabby lounge, where club members favored Pintchik's regal presence with deferential nods.

"How do you mean 'never the same'?"

"Just that." Pintchik put down two one-dollar bills at the cloakroom, and the attendant helped him into his tan cashmere coat. "He was never the same. In all the years I had known him, even at his worst, Maxwell retained an ebullience, a joie de vivre, that would assert itself even when he was at his lowest ebb. When he returned to the city at the end of his year at Bennington it seemed to me that the life had been sucked out of him. He was somehow— reduced. Frightened. And as you know, he soon came completely unraveled." Pintchik's face clouded.

They proceeded out the front door. At the curb an old Ford station wagon waited, reliable Hal at the wheel. He raised a gnarled hand to Alter in greeting. In the biting afternoon air, a stream of exhaust from the car's tailpipe enfolded the automobile in billows of whitish fog.

"Even after he attacked that boy with the beer bottle and was sent off to White Oak," Pintchik went on, "he didn't completely lose his zest. Or perhaps . . ." He paused. "Perhaps I mistook mania for a revival in his spirits . . . In any event, two years later, when he came back from Vermont and moved into the flat on Jane Street, it was just down and down until the end." The editor pulled on black leather gloves and motioned to Hal that he was on his way. "We had dinner together a few weeks before Max was struck by that wretched taxi. He said to me something chilling. He said, 'I killed her, Sam. I murdered her soul.' "

"Whose soul?" Alter urged, "whose?"

Pintchik strolled to the curb and got into the Ford. "I'm sure I have no idea. We were both, frankly, quite drunk, and I was afraid to ask. Edythe? Tamsin? Every woman he ever knew? Take your pick." He slammed the door. "Good to see you. Get some rest. You look peaked, if you don't mind my saying. Maybe you're working too hard." Pintchik gave the biographer a long look. "You know how much I want to see you do this book, Raphael, but I sometimes think to allow the grave to keep certain of its secrets might be better all around."

"Yet there's a need," the biographer countered, "for—resolution. For a beginning, a middle . . . and an end."

Alter slept fitfully, disturbed during the night by a shrieking chorus of sirens that grew uncontainably strident and seemed to stop at his window.

Early the next morning he found Muñoz hosing down the

sidewalk. He noticed a wide, deep red stain on the pavement near the curb.

"What's that?"

"Blood," Muñoz answered, directing the spray patiently from left to right, right to left.

"What happened?" Alter asked, a chill seizing him. Had Martin Aswith cut himself again, this time deeply, fatally?

"Guy stab another guy. You could follow the trail alla way t'Broadway. This's where he drop."

Alter looked. The "trail"—many stains of dried blood—extended in a zigzag path, the gait of the staggering victim, along the sidewalk as far as he could see. Muñoz turned off the hose and stood over the red blot he was trying to eradicate, examining his work. Shaking his head he took a few steps back, turned on the hose again, and directed the water against a cluster of smaller stains.

"Goddamn stuff like memories, doan wash out. You jus' gotta let 'em fade."

But they don't.

Alter set a stack of index cards on his desk, an oak dining table. He required a desk larger than most writers, since his work space rapidly proliferated books and manuscripts, certificates of birth and death, photos, deeds, wills, letters, testimonials, notebooks, diaries, journals, check stubs, bank statements, news clippings, all of it strewn about as if a maniacal second-story man had, willy-nilly, flung the contents of an entire life—dozens of drawers, trunks, and a couple of attics—on the desk in a vain search for valuables.

But what *was* valuable? The death of the owner leveled his effects into enigma. Who was to say that this letter, or that one, was truly written in love or in the simulation of it? The writer was gone; in many instances so was his correspondent. So the force of the words, what it had meant to receive them, was lost to history. Essences impalpable surrounded these palpable objects.

Alter surveyed the desk, the hillocks descending into valleys of Leibert material and memorabilia, filled with rationalizations and pretenses, exaggerations, outright falsehoods and wishful thinking, compassion, ruthlessness, magnanimity, pettiness, and catalogues of daily banality. He had entered a labyrinth, a hall of mirrors, the exit to which he felt far from discovering.

From the next-door building renovation, he heard pounding, a sledgehammer on plaster. He turned his head in the direction of the sound and noticed for the first time a hairline crack running the length of his living room wall, from floor to ceiling. With a frisson of alarm, he wondered how long it had been there.

The dean's office was hot; a steam radiator, unseen behind waist-high stacks of books, hissed. Alter loosened his tie.

He had come downtown to New York University to interview Dean Norman Halliwell, chairman of the Department of English during the time when Maxwell Leibert had taught The Craft of Poetry there. After quadruple heart bypass surgery Halliwell had taken the previous year to recuperate. He had returned after his absence to these cramped quarters in the basement.

"I retain my former title the way ex-presidents are called 'Mr. President' until they die," Dean Halliwell explained mournfully, "but I am despised as an anomaly, half on, half off the faculty. Consigned to limbo, if you will, neither heaven nor hell." He nudged little round black-framed spectacles up his nose; immediately they slid down the perspiring slope, coming to rest on its bulbous tip. He had a walrus mustache that did not completely conceal a drooping lower lip. His still-black hair dipped over one eye. He looked to Alter like Leon Trotsky after a few too many. "By virtue of my age and recent misfortune," Halliwell continued, "I have become a lesser dean . . . One doesn't expect it, that it will happen to *you* . . . No way to prepare . . . that people will grow intolerant and impatient." He reached for his crotch, feeling for his testicles. "Where were we?"

"The winter of 1972," Alter said quickly, "right before Christmas."

Halliwell resumed where he had left off moments earlier. "Sometime in early December, yes. Leibert came to my office." He paused, adding wistfully, "In those days, you know, I overlooked Washington Square Park. Well, never mind . . . Leibert arrived and announced he would keep his class going through Christmas and New Year's. Apparently it didn't occur to him that students have families, they might prefer to go home."

"Did Max say why he wanted to stay with it?"

"No, but I supposed he was lonely, what with his wife—what was her name?"

"Tamsin."

". . . Tamsin, off on one of her jaunts. As far as I knew, he was alone, and really, he had nowhere else to go. When he'd finished his day's writing, if he worked at all, it was either come over here or visit a bar. If he came here, it meant a walk from his apartment, a class or meetings with students, the occasional faculty conference. That postponed the heavy drinking until nighttime. He knew he had a problem. I think he was genuinely scared about what would happen to him during the holidays if he did not teach."

The dean folded his hands over his ample stomach. Alter saw that his shirt gaped where a button was missing; through the small portal he was able to see Halliwell's cavernous navel. He looked away. The dark hole seemed taboo.

"Do you recall your response to his request to teach?"

"I told him it was out of the question. I explained the practical considerations, that many buildings would be closed in those weeks, only a skeletal maintenance staff would remain, possibly no heat. And physically, he didn't look well to me, puffy and pale, shambling about in clothes that looked like they hadn't been changed in weeks. I suggested he should have a vacation, like everyone else."

"But he did, in any case, end up holding classes?"

"In his apartment, he did indeed. He buttonholed me a few days later and said he'd decided to give an off-campus seminar for whoever wanted to attend."

"What did you say?"

"What could I say? I agreed. He proposed to conduct an intensive course, five days a week instead of his usual two. I told him that students wanting to participate were free to do so . . . And I wished him a happy New Year." Halliwell opened a desk drawer and removed a meerschaum pipe and a leather pouch. He unfurled the pouch, extracted several large pinches of the hairlike leaves and tamped them into the pipe's bowl. "That was the genesis of the unfortunate plagiarism scandal. The young man he accused, as you know, was a student in that holiday seminar."

"Edmund Hopkins. How did Max's accusations come to your attention?"

Halliwell looked up from his pipe. "Why, he made the

allegations to me himself. Appeared in my office not a week after the winter break, shut the door, and in sepulchral tones whispered that Hopkins had stolen work—right out of his apartment—during the seminar weeks, and was copying it almost verbatim and palming it off as his own."

"What evidence did he offer?"

"None, really. It seemed off the wall. Hopkins had had a short poem accepted in the school's literary review, and Leibert suggested that several stanzas had been lifted. There *was* a reminiscent flavor. But as he had no copies of the original work, it was impossible to prove. And then, a few days later, I discovered that Hopkins's poem had been submitted months before the seminar took place."

"But were you inclined to accept his story, right then?" Alter asked.

"I had a soft place in my heart for Leibert, always did, always will, and he seemed deeply distraught." Halliwell took a silver lighter from the drawer. "You don't mind, do you?" Alter shook his head. "I can't do this at home, drives my wife mad, after my illness." He wetly sucked the pipe to life; the room was suffused with the scent of cherry tobacco. Alter inhaled the aroma. Halliwell released a mouthful of smoke. "But no, I was not inclined to take his charge seriously. My suspicion was that the work in question must have existed and that Leibert, in an increasingly confused state, had mislaid it. He translated the loss into thievery. Then too, I knew Hopkins."

"What did you think of him?"

"He seemed a pleasant young man, quiet and unassuming." Halliwell smiled. "I'll never forget his hair—bright carrot red. He idolized Leibert, and I cannot imagine to this day that he would do anything so grotesque as to brazenly pilfer the man's poetry. Even if he *had*, Leibert's reaction was . . . grossly inappropriate."

Alter took a handkerchief from his hip pocket and ran it across his damp brow and behind his neck.

"I apologize about the climatic conditions in here," Halliwell said, "the window's been painted shut. Apparently I'm also off-limits to the janitorial staff. They're trying to sweat me out."

"Tell me what you remember of the attack itself," Alter said, replacing the handkerchief in his pocket.

"A week or so after our meeting, Leibert sidled up to me in a coffee shop on University Place, and said he'd hired a private detective to shadow Hopkins. He wanted the man to break into Hopkins's rooms and give them a thorough going-over. By this time I had no doubt that Leibert had gone around the bend. I tried to talk sense to him but he was absolutely unreachable.

"It must have been a few days later that he broke the bottle over the boy's head. Hopkins had no relatives in town. I was the one called to the hospital, St. Vincent's." Halliwell chewed on the stem of his pipe. "Such a brutal assault, the force of the blow . . . I held his hand while they closed the wound. I can see the scene to this day . . . Blood everywhere—on the doctors, the nurses, on Hopkins, on me. And then he refused to press charges, if Leibert would enter the sanitarium. Rather graceful, I thought, under the circumstances."

"Did you see Max again?"

"Of course the university dismissed him, and before he left for White Oak he turned his class records over to me. And then I saw him once more . . . my wife and I visited him up there."

"What do you recall of the visit?"

Halliwell reddened a little. "Truthfully, we had a lovely time. We drove up with Tamsin—she'd returned by then—and a few colleagues from the department, Jimmy Arthur, and Norma Kilgrew and her husband. When we arrived we found Leibert with another guest. It was rather odd . . . he'd invited the policeman who had arrested him on the night of the attack. As it turned out, he'd been attending night school—auditing literature courses—and was acquainted with Leibert's work, a fan in fact. Well, when this cop realized who he was taking into custody, he construed it as a sort of honor. Treated Leibert with kid gloves. During the twenty-four hours Max spent in jail while we put together the bail, this young fellow brought him a change of clothes, food, cigarettes . . . At White Oak, we discovered Leibert and the policeman deep in conversation, talking of mass murder. Leibert had become fixated on those ghastly Manson murders out in Los Angeles. He was expounding on a grisly theory of his that serial killing would become a dominant form of self-expression in late twentieth-century America."

Alter scribbled a note. "How did Max seem to you that day?"

"Remarkably well, I thought. He appeared more fit, he'd lost some weight, some of the bloat. He was perhaps a touch overwound but not alarmingly so . . . I'll admit I was envious of the policeman. Leibert was far more interested in him than in any of us. But the weather was delightful, we had a long walk in the woods . . . All in all I remember a most agreeable afternoon."

Halliwell touched the flame of the lighter to his pipe. "I was disappointed," he said between puffs, "never to have been invited back."

. . .

As Alter was leaving, with silent thanks, the humid basement office, Dean Halliwell said, "Now I have a question
for you."

Alter turned sharply.

"Have you ever tried your hand at a biography of someone who is still alive? I'm just curious."

Alter smiled slightly. "Oh, no. I stick strictly to the
dead. With a dead man, there's some hope of ultimate
discovery, of final understanding. I mean, one never truly
does, but with the living . . ." He felt himself grimace.
"The wounds still bleed, the blood has not dried, the blows
still ache." He thought of Leipzig, of the dying Morris
Bloom, the cuckolded Aswith, the lovelorn Al Bruno, the
DeAngelis sisters in their tiny cell. "There's a kind of peace
in dealing with the dead. What's done has been done."

And it diverts one, in a way, from more proximate ag-
onies . . .

That evening, Alter attended a cocktail party at the home
of his publisher, Ralph Shimmerlinck. The occasion was
the publication of *Maximilian Braunszweig, The Annotated
Diaries: Vienna 1922–1938*, the first of an annotated four
volumes.

The door of Shimmerlinck's town house on Manhattan's
Upper East Side was answered by the houseman, a stooped,
angry Belgian who pretended to speak no English. Glow-
ering, he collected Alter's topcoat and waved him up the
stairs leading to the main floor of the house. Alter climbed
slowly, uneasy at the prospect of sociability, toward the
sound of voices. Over the general din he heard Shimmer-

linck boom, "That's not going to be an easy piece of taffy to chew up, as my old grandmother used to say!" When Alter entered the vast living room, he spied his publisher talking to the head of another house. Shimmerlinck, also Maxwell Leibert's publisher and friend for thirty years, had been instrumental in engaging Alter as the poet's biographer; like Sam Pintchik, like Ulysses Leibert, he took an oppressive personal interest in the work. Unready to face him before he had had a drink, Alter slipped into the crowd unremarked.

As he moved among the party guests, his impression was of a churning sea of women. Upon closer inspection he realized he knew many of them, at least by reputation: the Company of Widows, literary widows, gathered this evening to honor the most recently published of their group, Braunszweig's widow, Hilde, who had served as consulting editor of his diaries.

Alter approached the bar and observed standing nearby, in the beam cast by a light recessed in the ceiling, the widows, respectively, of a dissident Argentinian playwright and an American theater critic. Alter ordered a scotch and soda and edged closer to the women to listen. Eavesdropping had evolved in him to something approaching an art.

". . . I made a deal with Ralph just last month for Richard's papers from the fifties," said the critic's wife, Joan, who had pulled her jet black hair into a ponytail secured with a large rhinestone clasp in the shape of a butterfly.

"Celso dint date all his. I have a hell of a time to figure out what is what." Barely five feet tall, nut brown, the Argentinian woman was as wrinkled as an old grocery sack. "And from prison, all those years, he use-ed, how you say? code. I can't crack it."

"It's not *up* to you to crack it, Dalia," the critic's widow replied airily. "You're new at this, let me take you under my wing. We'll get you a publisher. Tomorrow morning, I'll call Ralph at his office. He positively relishes these things. He may take it on himself. Or he'll put out feelers." She frowned. "Better yet, we'll see about finding you a biographer, make it a sort of package deal: the papers, the plays, the authorized life. Celso doesn't have a biographer yet, does he?" Alter took a step away.

Dalia shook her head sadly. "He's only gone a year, Joan. It's too soon, no?"

"No. In this country writers are commodities, like it or not, and they're *peddled*, like soap." Joan sipped her wine. "Didn't I read that someone's putting on a new production of *Gorilla Gorilla*?"

"I have talks with Joe Patt."

"Papp . . . Well, you see?—interest is *there*. One strikes while the iron is hot. Where are his papers, his letters?"

"Home. Buenos Aires."

"You get back there as soon as you can, my dear, and bring them to me."

Dalia's eyes widened. "All of dem?"

"Not *all*, sweetie, naturally not. A few, a handful, maybe that little code-thing you mentioned, enough to tickle the fancy. You'll allow fuller access, of course, to whomever you finally choose as Celso's biographer. Then, later, you can begin to let the original material, the actual stuff, the letters and whatnot, filter out in dribs and drabs, over years . . . *decades*. See Meredith, the one who's wolfing down caviar as if there were no tomorrow?" Joan gestured at a heavyset woman on the other side of the long buffet table. "Meredith's already squeezed a biography and three collections out of Otto's meager output, and she's got enough left over for more."

"You tell me to keep Celso's things hidden?" Dalia inquired conspiratorially.

"Not hidden, one withholds judiciously, so to speak. There's a difference . . . Everything that was his, every scratch and doodle, now belongs to you. You want to sell it outright, in bulk?—that's not *my* style, but you're free to do it." Joan reached out and pinched a smoked salmon canapé from the table. "Ah listen, who needs to know that I have Richard's life neatly catalogued from beginning to end, in fireproof filing cabinets in the basement?—two entire *walls* of them. Whose business is it that my husband spent the last three years of his life compulsively arranging and tidying up for the biographers? Who has to know his dirty little secret?—that he built a necropolis to himself."

Joan bit into the canapé and helped it down with a swig of white wine. "Oh, but can you blame him, really? We live in obscenely self-conscious times . . . I shouldn't joke. He made my work much easier, though some of the fun is missing now. I mean, the subjects have totally anticipated their pursuers! Richard actually made photocopies of every letter he ever wrote, *and* the replies, and it's all filed together, then collated according to year, correspondent, and I-don't-know-what . . . Where's the thrill of the chase? Well, that's not my problem. I'm the solution, dearest, as you will be too—for your Celso. And I can tell you, I've done a damn sight better financially since Richard's death than in all the years we were married.

"Poor darling, he's worth more dead than alive," Joan mulled aloud. "His posthumous papers alone have brought in as much money as everything he ever published in his lifetime. This country has a positive *appetite* for corpses. It's

sad in a way, because more people are bound to know that
Richard had a drinking problem, or a little 'thing' for black
girls, or suffered from curvature of the spine, than will ever
have read a word he wrote." She paused, suddenly wistful.
"A shame, because at his best, he was quite good."

Joan chewed her bottom lip, thinking. Bits of coral lipstick stuck to the edges of her upper teeth. "Listen, did
Celso keep a journal?"

"In prison, yes."

"Prison!—of course. Exquisite. Bring me a few pages of
that too."

"I . . ." The tiny Argentinian seemed to grow smaller. "I
cannot . . . his childrens have them—"

"Children?!" Joan shrilled.

"From the first marriage."

"Dalia, get them *back* for God's sake. *Angel*, you're his
widow." She lowered her voice and inclined her head. Alter
strained to hear. *"And no one but no one can take that away from
you."*

Alter pressed on through the living room and library.
Dreamlike, he began to see them everywhere . . . There,
on a love seat, two more widows, lifting their goblets,
toasting he imagined, the barter for dollars of some juicy
chunk of one of their husbands' lives . . . And next to the
fireplace, the round woman in green sequins with buck-
teeth and very little chin, laughing raucously with Sam
Pintchik . . . At Pintchik's back, another widow, a striking redhead, who, Alter knew, would still be hooking in
Rome had not her late husband, an art historian, picked
her up on the Via di Porta Latina in front of the Little
Oratory of S. Giovanni, where Saint John the Evangelist
emerged unscathed, it was said, from a cauldron of boil-
ing oil . . . In the corner Ralph Shimmerlinck flirted with

the widow of a novelist whose last work he would publish in the spring; *she* might still be selling shoes on Madison Avenue if her deceased spouse had not stumbled in out of the rain to purchase from her a pair of Wellington boots. The woman accompanied him home to demonstrate their uses in situations other than inclement weather. The novelist was smitten.

Alter continued to work his way around the fringes of the crowd, a huge, writhing wriggling mass, a hundred-headed entity that had taken on an independent life quite apart from the individual celebrants. He caught sight of the widow of a British essayist and cabinet minister. Six feet tall, gangly, with shoulders the size of a linebacker's, she stood alone, disconsolate, seeming in the grip of some paralyzing, despondent intoxication, clutching a flute of champagne to her chest. Her husband, Alter recalled, had been a gnome, five-five, with a weak heart. At the time of his death a few months earlier, there was cynically amused speculation about the circumstances surrounding his last, fatal attack; his wife had fueled the fire by stubbornly refusing to discuss the details. Alter wondered: Had the diminutive essayist expired while trying valiantly one more time to scale her greatness? Had he, like a luckless mountaineer, at last given up the struggle, laid himself down and perished, right below her summit?

Alter made a circuit of both rooms again, stopping to exchange greetings with a few acquaintances, until he found himself back at the buffet groaning with hors d'oeuvres. He surveyed his choices and selected a little hot dog on a toothpick. Next he ate a cracker and cheese, then a carrot stick and a zucchini strip with sour cream dip.

". . . We're twinny. Like this . . ." Shimmerlinck's

voice wafted across the expanse of white linen tablecloth. "Terribly *intermezzo.*" Alter glanced up from a chafing dish of Swedish meatballs. Shimmerlinck had his arm slung over the shoulder of Hilde Braunszweig, the guest of honor, a woman in her fifties with slightly crossed eyes. Seeing them together reminded him of the gossip that Maximilian's widow had been one of Shimmerlinck's many extramarital liaisons. *Did anyone stay in his own bed anymore?*

He swallowed the meatball as the publisher's voice reasserted itself, slicing through the bedlam.

". . . Just keep in mind, dearie, I may be a prick but I am *the* prick, the one on top . . ." "Been twisting a few arms over the Feyder deal and I think I'm starting to hear a crack . . ." Shimmerlinck's words faded in and out on one subject and another, as though somebody were shifting the volume on a radio. "Internal rate of return on a discounted cash flow basis." . . . "I'm sorry to put these clouds in front of your sun, but Walter's in Billings waiting for his mummy to die." . . . "Who the fuck told you that?—I had his *balls* for breakfast, on toast . . ."

The crush of bodies forced Alter further down the length of the table until he stood before a platter of cherry tomatoes filled with swirled green goo. He ate three and was about to go for a fourth.

"Raffi!" Shimmerlinck had somehow crept around the table. He clamped a large hot hand on the back of the biographer's neck.

Alter turned. "Ralph. Thanks for having me."

The publisher shrugged. "Your name came up on the Rolodex, old boy."

Ralph Shimmerlinck sported a head of wavy white hair and a large, aristocratic nose. *The better to look down on you.*

He wore a black suit with wide lapels, a grey silk tie, a red carnation in his buttonhole.

He's looking more and more like a gangster all the time. "Great party."

"So how's the Leibert epic coming?" Shimmerlinck massaged the smaller man's neck with powerful fingers. Alter saw stars.

He wants to remind me he can ruin me if I displease. He could have me killed. He could do it himself, with his bare hands. "Good, Ralph, very well, in fact."

"When are you gonna bite the bullet, baby? I'd like to see some pages before I die."

"Not too long. I'm making notes for a first chapter."

Shimmerlinck squeezed Alter's neck hard, grinning malevolently. "Beware, Raphael. I'm losing my Peter Pan ability to believe."

If I were a canary I'd be dead by now.

Leaving the party Alter was waylaid by another widow, a woman he knew in passing.

"Raphael!" she beckoned urgently.

"Kate?"

"Come over here." She drew him into an alcove near the stairs leading to the ground floor of the house.

"Are you all right, Kate?" Alter noticed she wore a dress too small for her, the buttons at the bodice straining, tight around the hips, the sleeves ending far above her wrists. The longer he dwelled on it the more clear it became: the garment belonged to someone else, a hand-me-down, or a thrift-shop purchase.

"I need a favor," she said, abashed and harried.

Another importuner. "What can I do?" What, indeed—
that was the question. He flinched.

But Kate did not see it, hardly meeting his eyes. "You
taught at Georgetown University, didn't you?"

"Ages ago."

"Do you think you could interest them in taking Aaron's
papers? His manuscripts, you know, his worksheets and
things? I'm having a devil of a time . . . I've tried everywhere . . . It's his alma mater and even they don't seem to
want them." She clasped and unclasped her hands nervously.
"The fact is, Aaron left a horrible mess. The IRS is all over
me. I've had to sell the house, the furniture . . . I'm staying
with friends. I'm desperate."

Alter studied her; in the ill-fitting dress, Kate seemed to
have gained weight but also to have withered. Familiar with
her late husband's writing, he did not have the heart to tell
her the truth—that the man had been, at best, second rate,
and Kate could count herself fortunate if a community college would take the papers off her hands.

"I thought if you put in a good word," she continued
quietly, "maybe Georgetown would reconsider."

"I'll make a call, see what I can do." His tone promised
more than he could possibly deliver.

Kate lowered her head abjectly. "Thank you . . . thank
you."

"Don't thank me yet, I haven't done anything."

"It's not Aaron's fault, you know. My predicament . . ."

*Of course it is. If not his, then whose? Who's the culprit here,
who's to blame for this one?* "Uh-huh," he murmured non-
committally.

"He didn't mean to do this to me, he was never any good
with money."

Yeah. He spent like a drunken sailor. "Aaron was . . . generous to a fault."

"I loved him, Raffi. And sometimes I try to see it all as a big cosmic joke, and I laugh." She smiled wanly. "It isn't easy, though."

"A wise woman once observed that life's a comedy, Kate, and so is love, as long as you're not playing one of the roles." Alter kissed her lightly. The skin of her cheek felt hard, dry, reptilian to his lips. "Take care of yourself," he said, hearing its hollowness, knowing she could not.

Later that night, unable to sleep, Alter lay in bed reading the letters of Gustave Flaubert to Louise Colet. ". . . when you love a person completely you love him just as he is, with all his faults and his monstrousnesses; you adore even his scabs and the hump on his back; you love *to inhale the breath that poisons you.*" He turned to the choleric dispatch Flaubert had sent her upon the dissolution of their affair: "Madame: I was told you took the trouble to come here and see me three times last evening. *I was not in.* And, fearing lest persistence expose you to humiliation, I am bound by the rules of politeness to warn you that *I shall never be in.*" Colet's reply was succinct; over the blue stationery on which her lover wrote those words, she had scrawled: "*Lâche, couard et canaille.*" Poltroon. Coward. Cur.

He placed the book face down on the night table beside him. Perhaps his next work ought not to be a biography. He'd do something simpler, drawing on past research and personal experience. A memoir of sorts, it would be shorter, more intimate and contemplative than anything he'd thus far attempted. He knew what he wanted to write about, and he knew exactly what to call it.

Wives of the Poets.

The next day's mail brought several letters sent by Maxwell Leibert to an old friend, confidant, and classmate, Linus Wagner; they had attended Evander Childs High School in the Bronx together and kept closely in touch through the years. Wagner, an aspiring poet as a teenager, had gone into the insurance business and lost his life in a cable car accident in 1976 while on vacation in San Francisco. The letters came in a bundle from his daughter, in response to Alter's advertisement.

Standing at the kitchen counter, eating a Swiss cheese and onion sandwich, Alter read from one dated January 6, 1953.

". . . A predilection, a predisposition to poverty runs in my line, I think," wrote Leibert, in a strong and clean hand that showed no sign of the deterioration that would characterize it in later years.

With my clan, conventional wisdom works entirely backwards: the harder we strive, the poorer we become; we have some natural inclination, as a plant grows toward the sun, to destitution. It was this way with my father and, as I understand, his father before him—a minute and mysterious collocation of genetic inheritance that I've come to believe has had a shaping effect on my history.

The end of the month will mark, at long last, the publication of my second book, *Everybody Steals From Everybody* (a line *I* stole from a con man whom I once knew through my father). And on this, the eve of what ought to be a joyful event in my life, I make a trip to the bank to discover that I am more overdrawn than usual! Irony, all is irony. The teller rudely refused to cash my check, so I am left with twenty dollars and change with which to feed and entertain my family until next week. I promised Ulysses and Ben a movie (*Bambi*), and Edythe dinner out. I have no idea, now, how I'll manage. But here it is: all week I'm on my feet ticketing passengers at Idlewild, a job that pays better, but I enjoy less, than my stint at the De Lys box office. Nights, I write. And I have recently taken a position at the YMCA teaching poetry writing to taxi drivers and housewives, Thursday evenings, 7 to 9. (An earnest and industrious group, but they naively believe I can help them—turn them into publishable poets.) Still, I'm strapped. I don't know where the money goes, honestly I don't.

I'm angry, Linus, violently so. It's radicalized me. Dynamite, I fantasize—*this* is the stuff! Plug a few pounds into a pipe, stop up the ends, insert a cap with a fuse. Then smuggle it into the neighborhood of a lot of rich men who live by the sweat of other men's brows and light the fuse. A most gratifying event will follow. It can be used against persons or things, but I'd employ it against the former instead of against masonry or brick. A genuine boon to the disinherited, dynamite—striking terror in the guilty, who fear the wrath of an outraged population, the duped and swindled.

Edythe is quick to point out that I have all the qualities of, in her words, a "child-man." I whine and complain, throw fits, race from the room when company not to my liking appears, get drunk, fly into rages if I am criticized the least little bit, and sit for hours in silence (bacon frying in my own fat) as our boys, mesmerized and drooling, once sat as infants on the living room floor, tearing up the colored pages of Edythe's discarded *Vogues* and *Harper's Bazaars*. She also remarks that I pout and occasionally weep, and, when I am not engaged in any of the above, spend inordinate amounts of time pouring into her ears tales of how the world abuses and misunderstands me. Well, it's true: both what she says *and* that I am abused and misunderstood.

Edythe reminds me that in my case even praise is "dangerous," for then I only "want more." Translation: I am megalomaniacal and vain—characterizations that I cannot entirely disown. Yet I only wish to be invited to the banquet—literary and financial—to taste of some of the sweet fruits on which others, far less gifted than myself, have *gorged*. My wife does not have a great deal of patience with me—she's made of sturdier stuff than I—a Connecticut Yankee and more stoical than this agonizing Jew (that's at least partly why I married her).

As I await publication of *Everybody Steals* I am especially on edge. What will the reviews say? What if I am set upon by a pack of wolves?—they're out there, you know, absolute butchers. I have no defenses. (To steady my nerves I remind myself: for poets it's a triumph to be reviewed *at all*.)

Last week I exploded when Edythe informed me that her parents had agreed to make the down payment for us on a large house in Peekskill. First, I resist Peekskill, a community for which my wife has an indecipherable affection; second, I resist my in-laws' charity, knowing they disapprove of me, were opposed to our marriage from the outset, and want the house for their daughter and grandchildren. I'm just along for the ride. (Which reminds me: Edythe thinks she's pregnant again. Every child's a blessing, but this is also a ride I feel I'm just along for . . .)

I have developed a genius these last months for getting into minor scrapes. Yesterday, for example: I entered our building, rode the elevator to what I believed to be our floor, and found myself trying to force my house key into Mrs. Milton's lock on 5. We live on 6. Even when she came to the door—all ninety pounds of her—I refused to accept facts. For an instant I entertained the notion, admittedly crazy, that she was in the apartment with the intention of murdering my wife and eating my offspring, or something like that. Suffice it to say that my irrational panic gave way to hostility. Two Sundays ago, I borrowed an automobile to drive to Stonington with the family to visit Edythe's folks. My mind must have been wandering. Somewhere around Norwalk we ended up on George Herman's front lawn. I know his name because I had to write him a check for one hundred dollars to cover the cost of some rose bushes I destroyed. (Was I unconsciously trying to kill us all?)

My sons are baffled by me, poor things. They have no idea, really, what it is I do that distracts me and makes me odd, so unlike the fathers of their playmates; only that, whatever it is (I have overheard Benjamin describe me as a "typist"), it seems rarely to occasion much joy in their dad. Or, when it *does*, the emotion is more akin to hysteria than to ordinary happiness. A few lines I consider good, that's enough to set me off, and it's all I can do to concentrate on a skinned knee, or a bedtime story, or the broken tricycle they want fixed *immediately*. (And now it looks like I'm about to bring another soul into this mess!) I take them to the playground, busy myself on a bench with paper and pen, and forget where I am—any pederast could make off with my boys and I wouldn't look up until it was too late. They, all of them—Edythe too—have every right to expect more of me. Yet, too often the smallest, dimmest part of myself is all that's available. My family's the *scrim* against, or behind which, I play the scenes of my life.

Dear Ulysses has been particularly solicitous lately. He acts wisely, without knowing what he does. A few mornings ago, having been absent from school with a cold, he brought me a note to his teacher. He had composed the little letter all by himself, and asked only that I sign it! I was moved by his perception, and heartbroken. Self-absorbed I may be, unconscious I am not.

I can't tell you how much, strangely, I envy you your life. You have told me that your work seems trivial to you, but you earn a respectable and steady income and injure no one in the process. You are apparently able to enjoy a contentment that eludes me. I am unable even to suffer, as Dr. Freud put it, common human misery. I cannot break free of this need, Linus, this burning to be great (a fire that sears anyone who gets close and will eventually, I'm convinced, incinerate me). That need gives birth to my *uncommon unhappiness* and is the accomplice of my unspeakable anguish . . . Histrionic, I know. But I sometimes wish I could be satisfied to put on a suit and tie and live an ordinary, unremarkable life. It's unfortunately true, Flaubert's lament, that "Art, like the God of the Jews, feasts on holocausts."

My love to you and Nancy, and to your beautiful little Sophie. When you're next in town, let's all get together, wives and kids and all. Happiest of New Year's. Max.

Before leaving the kitchen, Alter folded the letter slowly and replaced it in its envelope.

At his desk, the biographer read from still another letter to Wagner, this one dated June 10, 1953.

Yesterday I attended a rally in support of the Rosenbergs. *Attend* is perhaps the wrong word. I was in a queer, agitated state & my brain wasn't working at all, so I took a long walk. I spied the crowd & worked myself into the middle of it, staying for the duration. It's fruitless of course, they're going to be executed.

Last night I had an odd dream, one word, *Solidism*. In the dream I understood this to be the study of existence: the reliability, the soundness of people, objects and ideas. It was clear that the Solidists are out to prove that the things of life are well nailed down: that if you can touch or taste it, or talk about it, it's *there*. In this dreamscape objectivism, an explanation exists for every phenomenon, no mystery cannot be solved. Then there's the other camp, of which I am a member, whose motto is "All That Is Solid Melts into Air." Our emblem is the rolled-up umbrella used, symbolically, for poking and prodding to reveal durability, stoutness, in short, *substantiality*, as almost always counterfeit concepts. We anti-Solidists are sure only that nothing is sure, no one wholly trustworthy (what distinguishes man from the animals is his ability to betray), and that the air can be let out of *any* balloon. That's my dream; as far as I can recall, unadulterated by actors or event. Just Solidism all the way. Around and around in my brain it went until I was awakened at dawn, exhausted, by Benjamin pulling on my pajama top asking for cereal.

Perhaps the dream was inspired by the Rosenberg rally earlier in the day, which deeply affected me; or, more likely, by the fact that since the publication of *Everybody Steals* I have been writing and throwing away, writing and throwing away. The wastebasket has become my best friend. I have done four poems. Only one can I say is alright. (I'll send it to you soon. You're still my best first reader.)

As you know, the book was generally greeted affirmatively, but I am more uncertain than ever. Rather than bolstering my confidence, I am consumed with doubt. I sit on the edge of my chair in the House of Literature like a Jew in church; worse, like a felon: fugitive, a fraud— frightened that God (the merry prankster) will rip the seat from under me and I'll go crashing to the floor. Unmasked! (God's agent, the parish priest, passes silently along the aisles of this House, eyeing the stranger in his pew pretending to a novena; indeed, I've started one, to Sabbatai Zevi, false messiah to the Jews, patron saint of impostors.)

However: thanks to the modest success of *Steals,* life has changed drastically. In the fall, I'll quit the airport. I've accepted an appointment for one year at Barnard College on the English faculty. Two classes, fifty students, and four public lectures. (I think I'd almost have preferred a chaste, all-male establishment where temptation is not so omnipresent. A seminary. Fordham.)

Edythe and I are suddenly asked to gatherings at which a year ago we'd never have been guests. Last week we were invited to a Sunday "open house" at the home of the critic and editor Robin Wicks. Opened the door to his glorious Riverside Drive flat to find a crush of two hundred! Among them Wicks, stripped to the waist, a bright red Xmas scarf wound about his neck, nursing the flu with hot rum toddies. I haven't the foggiest notion why he entertained half-naked, although someone mentioned he had a rather high fever. But doesn't fever give one chills? Anyway, a most extraordinary afternoon. Guests included Lowell, Delmore, Wystan Auden, Thornton Wilder, Beatrice Lillie, Bennett Cerf, Cleanth Brooks and others I'm ashamed to admit I don't remember because I stayed too long and drank too much.

My opinion on matters literary is now actively solicited. At my bedside are five volumes (at last count) sent to me by various periodicals for review. I have my choice! I also did three readings recently. Two at the University of Connecticut and one at Yale. $650 in honorariums added to the family fortune. Edythe saw me off on the bus and said I looked more like a trembling child being sent to a new school than a celebrated poet. (I disappoint, and disappoint . . . but somehow the acclaim attendant to this one short book has a touch of the absurd. I haven't *done* anything yet in my own estimation and the old fears persist: will I ever be good *enough*? And now, I am saddled with RENOWN, my God!) It could drive a man to drink—which is where I'm off to as soon as I finish this letter. The post office is, conveniently, in a direct line between the apartment and my neighborhood tavern. The children are racing loudly about; and my wife, in the middle of packing, interrupts every two minutes to ask, Should we take this to the country?—or that? . . . I'll welcome the disengaged congeniality of the bar. Then I'll return and go back to work, mindful of the words of Horace: "No poems can please for long or live that are written by water-drinkers."

Edythe's in her sixth month, by the way, and looks like she's in her tenth. The doctor hears one strong heart-beat or I'd swear we were having triplets. We move to Peekskill next week. I'll miss the city but intend to throw myself wholeheartedly into suburban life: lawn-mowing, leaf raking, barbecues on Sunday and softball in the yard. Up last weekend to move in a few things, met some of our neighbors. Very WASPish, cool and complacent—backbone of the Solidism movement.

Oh, that I were able to believe faith alone sufficient to ensure salvation!

Yours, Max.

The letter underneath this one, dated December 18, 1953, was unsettling; it jolted Alter more than the others. "Linus, my gratitude is boundless. Thank you for the money. You have saved me from the worst disaster.

"I turned to you because I knew I could rely on your discretion, that you would not ask why? or what for? I find the episode painful even to think about, but perhaps some-time in the future when I have put it behind me, I'll tell you everything. In the meantime, I renew my pledge to repay you as soon as I am able. Very soon, I hope. Ever thine, Max."

. . .

In a blue notebook, one that covered the last months of 1953 and the early months of 1954, Alter tracked down:

12/21/53. I have not written here in weeks. Black days, much ado. But LW came thru as I expected he would. Thank heaven for old friends! I am profoundly ashamed and saddened and from now on resolve to Be Good. No more larking about. How I'll make restitution on LW's loan of two grand, though, remains to be seen. All my college salary goes into the domestic exchequer. Shimmerlinck has agreed to an advance of $5000 on my next book. He's under the impression I'm halfway there. I'll let him believe it until I can't anymore. There's work to be done on this house, and I'd hate to dip too deeply into the first $2500. A token $250 might convince LW of my honorable intent.

Received an invitation to give some readings in London this spring. The dates correspond to the Easter break at the college and I'd dearly love to go. They *pay*, first of all. Even so, E's against it. Now we are five and she doesn't want to be left alone with Lee, Ben and Jonathan. Her mother isn't well, it's not anticipated that she'll get much better, E doesn't care to travel. But that's not the entire story. My wife fears I'd go for flattery and the sort of undemanding affection I do not receive at home. She's said as much. Hurt me. Because it cut too close. Why couldn't she have said I'd go for "appreciation" instead? And left unsaid was "and for girls." Well, the adulteries are certainly easier far from family. Logistics simpler, and, when away, I am Alice on the other side of the looking glass or down the rabbit hole—in a world divorced from reality & home. But no, I'm finished with all that. I've learned my lesson.

Alter looked up and frowned. *Yeah. Sure.* He went on reading.

This weekend took Lee and Ben and baby Jonathan to the Bronx Zoo, giving E the day to herself. Weighed down with stroller, diapers, toys, snacks, formula, felt like Admiral Peary on his way to the Pole (freezing weather conspired in this). Saw there a solenodon, mammal of the order Insectivora. Resembles a rat, with an elongated snout. Naked, scaly tail; long, coarse, rusty brown hair. Besides insects, eats lizards and frogs. Mainly nocturnal. Of considerable zoological interest as solenodons are thought to be survivors of a sunken continent. Threatened with extinction. Reminded me of me.

Alter closed Leibert's notebook.

I sometimes run out of patience with you, Max, exasperated by your obtuseness and obsessive pain. With what artful diligence and purposeless guilt you pursue your women (your Muse?), you high priest of art, while on your altar you sacrifice precious lives— Edythe, Tamsin, Chloe, your kids and God-knows-who-else. Sniveling, puling, puerile, self-pitying, self-aggrandizing boor . . . bore . . . bastard.

Sometimes Alter was almost grateful to be released from the book for a while by the chores of the building. At one o'clock he walked through Martin Aswith's apartment with the painter, Nathaniel Law, proprietor of Masters of Illusion on Amsterdam Avenue.

Law, solemn and taciturn in white overalls, went slowly through the small rooms, absorbed in hermetic calculations. The landlord almost heard him think: how much spackle? how many gallons of paint? how many days?

"It's not in such bad shape," Alter remarked, as if saying that would make it so. His voice echoed in the tile chamber of Aswith's bathroom.

"Hmmm." Law ran his hand around the showerhead. Bits of moist grout flaked off on his fingers and fell into the old, pitted tub. "Hmmm."

Law stood in the middle of the living room, evaluating the ceiling. "Leak."

Alter followed the painter's gaze. In the corner, directly over Aswith's nondescript boxy couch, was a deep brownish-yellow stain, the paint bubbled and cracked on the ceiling.

"Can't you spackle and paint over?"

"Do anything you want."

"That's what I want."

"But it's on'y gonna come back."

"How long?"

"Three, mebbe six months. Tops."

"Good enough."

"Gotta get yourself a plumber, get into that wall."

"I can't afford it. Do the best you can."

Law kept his eyes on the ceiling. "Whatever you say, but these things they on'y get worse. I can't make no guarantees."

"I'm not asking for guarantees."

Law coughed, and pulled a crushed pack of Newports from his back pocket.

He lit one. The mentholated smoke seemed to ease the spasm. He turned to Alter. Caked with paint and plaster, aged by them, his black skin had gone ashy; he looked like a ghost.

"Inside alla closets?"

"I suppose," Alter replied regretfully.

"Cabinets?"

"Yes."

Law walked into the kitchen. Alter trailed on his heels and leaned against the kitchen counter to await the verdict.

"Okay if I help myself to a glassa water?" Alter nodded. The painter removed a glass from the drainboard and filled it to the brim with tap water. He took tiny, delicate sips, pondering the extent of the job.

Aswith had left the dinner and breakfast dishes unwashed in the sink: on plain white plates rested dried chicken bones, leftover potato and three-bean salad; a half-empty mug of cold coffee, a tumbler of soda, and another with orange pulp clinging to its sides stood beside two flowered porcelain cereal bowls in which the soggy remains of Cheerios floated in puddles of milk. Knives, forks, and spoons were heaped in a jumble in a saucepan of soapy water.

Two children's books, *Curious George* and *Ferdinand the Bull*, lay on the little round kitchen table; next to them, Marion's Barbie doll on her back, in a poodle skirt, nude from the waist up. The doll's platinum hair sprang out in savagely matted tufts, her arms twisted up and over her head in a posture reminiscent of terror. One leg was crooked to the left in an unnatural angle; her jutting plastic breasts had been defaced with a ballpoint pen. She looked to Alter like the victim of an assault, left there to die. On the floor near the oven he caught sight of a pair of Marion's white cotton underpants, slightly discolored in the crotch. The landlord felt an unwilling witness in the lonely, deserted rooms. And the guilt of the silent witness, not unlike the guilt of the survivor, nagged him. But his remorse was of no more use to Aswith than Leibert's had been to Edythe, or Ulysses, or any of them . . . He wanted to close his eyes, to get out of there as fast as possible, the tangible distress of the absent tenants more than he could bear.

Nathaniel Law cleared his throat. "You're looking at one other man and myself, three days. I can do it for fifteen hundred."

"That's your best offer?"

Law set down the water glass. "Yep. And that's reasonable."

"The apartment's not large," Alter said, pointing out the obvious.

"Big job, lotta work. Plastering alone's gonna take us a day." He dragged on the cigarette and exhaled; smoke poured from his nostrils. "You wanna forget the closets, I'll take off a couple of hundred."

Alter thought. He eyed the little girl's discarded panties. "No. Do the closets. Let's set a date."

Law put the cigarette between his lips and lifted a battered black notebook from a pocket on the leg of his overalls. "I think I got open right after New Year's."

On his way out of Aswith's apartment, Alter spied a brown paper Sloan's grocery bag outside Mrs. Hovanian's door. He let Nathaniel Law go on alone and detoured to investigate. The bag was filled with garbage.

What the hell does she think this is—a hotel? Soon they'll be leaving me their shoes to shine. Alter was about to ring her bell, then thought better of it. Mrs. Hovanian had a disease of the lungs that required regular deliveries of oxygen. Every so often Alter ran into men from the hospital supply company, burly blacks and Hispanics, wheeling in or out a scarred and beaten tank. A couple of times a year Mrs. Hovanian, wan and bony underneath bluish skin translucent as waxed paper, was loaded into an Ambulette parked at the curb outside the building and driven away. She stayed in the hospital several weeks while the doctors cobbled her, if not back to health, then to a degree of function that allowed her to return and get on with her dying at home. For over a decade this had been going on. Alter remembered a time when she had been ambulatory, coming and going as any normal woman. Now she remained indoors always, hanging on to life. But sometimes I think she'll outlive me by sheer tenacity of will, Alter thought, picking up the bag and carrying it downstairs to the garbage room at the far end of the lobby.

Tenants' refuse cluttered the floor of the room. Three small empty cardboard cartons of a nutritional supplement, SupliCal, addressed to Etty Hovanian, were stacked against the wall. Jeremiah Crust, her downstairs neighbor, suffered a disorder that caused him to need intravenous infusions of sodium chloride solution. Alter noted the empty plastic bottles, their heavy-gauge needles and tubing still attached, tucked into shopping bags where Crust's visiting nurse left them. A stack of newspapers was piled beside the bag in the corner. On top, a page from the *New York Times* Neediest Cases was exposed. He glanced at the headlines, a pornographic catalogue of affliction: FATAL ILLNESS FUELS FAMILY'S GRIEF . . . CANCER-STRICKEN MOTHER SEEKS

AGENCY'S HELP . . . SOUP KITCHENS AND WINTRY EVE-
NINGS: THE BATTLE TO ENDURE . . . REMEMBER THE
NEEDIEST!

A windfall of small papers littered the floor around the
incinerator chute. Alter set down the grocery bag and bent
to collect them. They were notes in the spidery hand of
Morris Bloom. Before his bowels turned against him, Bloom
had owned a menswear concern; the jottings Alter held in
his hand were on the backs of old invoices imprinted "In
Account of Morris Bloom, Maker of Fine Somerset Clothes,
498 Broadway." Alter squatted and began working patiently to fit the disconnected scraps together like a jigsaw
puzzle. Where others might see only trash he saw a gift, art,
found biography. It was a hopeless addiction, he mused.
And soon enough Bloom's notes told the tale: he was looking for a home attendant. Mae Taylor asked seven dollars an
hour. Chantal's rate was much steeper, fifteen dollars an
hour. But the tasks she would agree to undertake were far
more various and loathsome. "Bathing. ToiLET. CAthe-
ter," Bloom had written torturously next to her name. He
had called the United Jewish Appeal for financial assistance,
as well as the Jewish Poverty Coordinating Council, Jewish
Services for the Aged, and the Bureau of Medical Assistance. And then his search had grown profoundly desperate,
for at the bottom of one scrap he had inscribed in large
gnarled letters, "Cath. ChariTIES" and a telephone number.

Alter read another crumpled bit, torn off in the middle.
"DR. YANoff," it went, "I develope terr. thirst. Cont.
drink water. Why do I drINK so much? Can YanOFF help
with—" The tear in the paper precluded further discoveries.

Folding the pieces, Alter got to his feet. He opened the
incinerator chute and let them fly. Catching the currents in
the shaft, they stalled, hovering for an instant in the close,

fetid air. Then with a rush they were sucked down to the basement, where, Alter knew, Angel Muñoz tended the inferno.

Leaving the building at five-thirty for an interview, Alter passed Al Bruno in the lobby. Arm in arm with him was a thin man with haunted, purple-ringed eyes, and grooves carved in his sunken cheeks. They were dressed for the outdoors.

"Alter," Bruno summoned, "permit me to introduce Henry Arnold. Henry, Raphael Alter, who owns our venerable building."

"Pleased to meet you." Arnold greeted him hoarsely, each word an effort. Extending a gloved hand, he laid it in Alter's palm, the grasp barely discernible.

"We're on our way to the flicks," Bruno broke in with forced gaiety. "Henry hasn't been out since day before yesterday but he's feeling a little stronger today. Aren't you, Henry?" Bruno peered anxiously under the peak of his companion's plaid cap.

Arnold's face strained. "A little," he managed to say.

"There's a double bill, *Jezebel* and *Mr. Skeffington*. Bette Davis," Bruno said to Alter, "then it's on for Chinese."

Alter walked ahead and held wide the front door. "You have a good time . . . Be careful, the streets are icy."

"Thanks." Bruno and his companion passed over the threshold. Suddenly Henry Arnold pulled up short and half turned.

"Your name . . . Raphael," he wheezed, "you know what it means?" Alter looked puzzled. "Healing . . . means healing."

The two men crept into the frigid death-damp night.

. . .

"Come . . . sit." Dr. Erich Sallinger motioned to the biographer from behind his desk. Alter entered the consulting room.

Sallinger, Viennese by birth, was the court-appointed psychiatrist who had recommended Maxwell Leibert's committal to the sanitarium, White Oak. He had continued to treat the poet until the end of his life. Now nearing ninety, Sallinger still practiced four days a week in his grand limestone townhouse on East Sixty-ninth Street. Sallinger, who had himself been analyzed by Anna Freud, had consented to cooperate with Leibert's biographer. They had met three times so far, convening in the evening after Sallinger's last patient of the day. The psychiatrist allotted the customary analytic fifty minutes to their sessions. He also charged his customary rate for his time.

Alter removed his coat and laid it on the analyst's couch. He crossed the room and took his place in a low-slung modern chair that cowered several inches below Sallinger's own thronelike seat, an overstuffed cradle of tufted black leather. The psychiatrist, a small man, attenuated almost to childishness, seemed to Alter to have dwindled even further since their last meeting; the collar of his shirt swam about his neck, the cuffs of his suit jacket fell over his wrists, the vest beneath the jacket ballooned over his chest. Sallinger had no hair to speak of and wore glasses with magnifying lenses; his eyes appeared disconcertingly froglike. He fixed Alter with his usual fallaciously avuncular stare, silent and intimidating.

"How have you been?" Alter asked, opening a notebook, in part to scan his notes from their previous encounter, but also because he could find nothing in his repertoire with which to answer the gaze.

"A stroke," Sallinger answered in heavily German-inflected English. "I have had a mild stroke."

Alter looked up, concerned.

"Nothing to speak of." Sallinger waved an arm. "An annoying inconvenience."

"You're recovering, I hope?"

"A slight weakness on the right side. I lost some sight in the right eye as well but it seems to come back a little now."

"Are you certain you're up for this? I could come back—"

"No, no. Let's get on with it," Sallinger snapped, by way of reply.

Momentarily flustered, Alter consulted his notes again. "When we stopped last time you were speaking about Max's drinking, toward the end of his life. You used the word 'excessive.' "

"Barbarous is more accurate," Sallinger said. "As if he were trying to poison something within himself."

"You were also prescribing medications."

"Tranquilizers."

"Reading his diaries I have come across references to amphetamines—he mentions Dexamyl and Dexedrine, and sleeping pills too, Seconal . . . May I assume he got these drugs from other sources?"

Erich Sallinger retreated a little into his leathery crib. "I could not be with him twenty-four hours a day, Mr. Alter, and there are always sycophants, even physicians, who will procure for a man like Maxwell whatever he wants. He cultivated these types, especially at the end, when so many others had lost patience and deserted him." Sallinger rubbed his eyes behind the glasses. "Maxwell always found someone. He was most charming, most seductive, when he chose to be. As you must be aware by now."

"May I ask . . . did you feel that you yourself were seduced by him?"

The psychiatrist considered his response for a moment.

"I was . . . probably more drawn to Leibert than to some other patients. This is natural, after all. But it is often predictive of a better outcome to treat patients who interest one less. One sometimes loses perspective, doesn't see or hear as clearly as one might."

"You believe your treatment was affected by your . . . rapport with Max?"

Sallinger regarded Alter stonily. "I believe then and believe now that I was the best man for him. I did as well as anyone could have done, given the circumstances of his final years."

But you could not save him.

As if Sallinger had heard Alter's accusation he went on, "Yet Maxwell died too young, in an accident with suicidal overtones, this I won't deny. It's a burden on me."

"You mean, you believe he walked in front of the cab deliberately," Alter prompted.

"As you know, no charges were filed against the driver. He claimed that Maxwell stepped into the street so suddenly that he didn't have a chance to apply his brakes. The police confirmed this, they found no skid marks. But whether Maxwell acted willfully, bent on self-destruction, or whether he lost his footing and drunkenly fell, we will never know. It was late at night. There were no witnesses, save for the driver. So, as I say: 'an accident with suicidal overtones.' " Sallinger regarded Alter testily. "You wish me to be more conclusive on this point, I see, but I cannot . . .

Life is not tidy, Mr. Alter, it does not offer us so many absolute answers."

Alter looked down at the notes in his lap, acquiescing to Sallinger's veiled condemnation. "Yes, well of course, naturally not." After this flimsy, mumbled attempt at exculpation, he quickly changed the subject.

"I'm curious, to go back a little, did you see him at all during his months at White Oak?"

"I had only just begun treating him at that time, as you know. I was in touch with his physicians there. I went up once . . . It was not, strictly speaking, a professional visit. I was not managing his care, only consulting with the White Oak staff. Maxwell expressed a desire to see me independently, and after speaking to his doctors, we agreed it would be beneficial. I didn't see him, though, in an analytic setting."

Before Sallinger could continue there was a knock on the door and his wife, Frieda, came in with a pot of coffee and plateful of desserts on a silver tray. A handsome, full-bosomed woman in her eighties, she set the food on the desk.

"Good evening, Mr. Alter," she said, "so nice to see you again. Let me explain what treats I have for you tonight. These are cheese strudel and those next to them are poppy seed." She passed her hand above the confections. "This is a piece of Kugelhopf left from yesterday but still very fresh and light as a feather. Here are some Linzer tortes, and I saved just for you this lovely Krapfen. If you have never had it, it is a cousin to your jelly doughnut."

"Frieda!" Sallinger barked. "*Enough* with the food! Can't you see we're busy here?"

The old woman jumped as though punched. Tears welled in her pale blue eyes. "I was only . . . I'm sorry,

Erich. Goodbye, Mr. Alter." She fled from the office. Sallinger made no move to excuse his outburst but Alter heard him mutter under his breath, "God help me." He reached out to pour the coffee. "What was I saying?"

"White Oak," Alter supplied.

"Yes . . . Maxwell exhibited some mild agitation after I arrived. He wanted me to arrange for his release. I refused."

"Do you remember any other details of the day?"

"To be completely candid, Maxwell convinced me to play a game of table tennis. I should never have acquiesced."

"Because it violated the therapeutic relationship?" Alter eyed the Kugelhopf covetously.

The psychiatrist reddened. "So to speak . . . I had, I had a violent countertransference reaction."

"To Ping-Pong? . . . I don't understand."

Sallinger selected a Linzer torte from the plate and put it on a paper napkin. "Maxwell refused to keep score. For reasons at first unclear, this angered me. I concealed my feelings, of course, and consented to play by his rules—or lack of them. But later I became withdrawn, hostile and anxious. I cut short the visit. Maxwell was disturbed by my abrupt departure and I could not explain my actions to him." Sallinger bit off a piece of Linzer torte; powdered sugar sprayed over his suit front. Alter's mouth watered.

"Several days later a childhood memory crystallized for me what had happened: as a small boy I had played a game of miniature golf with my father in the Prater. He cheated. It was a warm summer day, a long match, and in the middle I excused myself to go to the public toilet. When I returned I discovered my father had moved my ball." A vein throbbed on Sallinger's naked scalp.

This man is ninety years old . . . "You were mistaken, surely."

Sallinger's expression hardened. "No mistake. Papa had moved . . . my . . . ball. I had left it precisely at the drawbridge of the fairy castle. A light tap would have propelled it across the moat through to the other side and I would have been ahead. But I found it yards away, near the windmill . . . I had blocked the entire incident and only after playing Ping-Pong with Maxwell was I able to recall it. As a child I had been confused and furious at my father's deceit. I had connected his cheating with my trip to the restroom. At last I was able to untangle my feelings and to understand that I had suppressed a desire to urinate on my father. And so you see, I was responding to Maxwell's disinclination to keep score with a profound wish to urinate on *him*. I repressed this urge, hence the anger and anxiety," Sallinger concluded, triumphant.

Maybe if you had just whipped out your dick and pissed all over him . . . Alter felt a bubble of laughter tickle his throat. He burped and went for the Kugelhopf, which he suspected would have been Frieda's choice for him.

"Indigestion? Then I suggest you refrain from my wife's baking. She has never been accused of having a dainty touch in the kitchen."

Sallinger struggled from his chair. He moved slowly, his right foot dragging, to a large black-lacquered Oriental cabinet with glass doors. "I published a short paper years ago about my experience with Maxwell." He rustled in a drawer of the cabinet and came up with a few sheets of paper, stapled together. "Here it is."

Crossing back, he dropped the article in Alter's lap. Alter glanced at the title: "Keeping Score: A Study in Counter-transference."

"You may have it."

"Thank you." Alter folded the pages in half and stuck

them in his jacket pocket. "Let me ask you about something we haven't really touched on yet, the last years, after Bennington, and Tamsin."

"Bennington?" Sallinger, sitting down with effort, appeared to resist it.

"The college, Vermont." The psychiatrist nodded, but offered no answer. Alter took another tack. "Max returned to New York and you continued to treat him." Sallinger nodded again. "And it's common knowledge that he was in as bad shape as he had ever been."

"Indeed." It could have been a question or a corroboration.

"How much of his steady deterioration do you attribute to the failure of his marriage, to Tamsin leaving?"

"Tamsin . . . Certainly this caused him distress," Sallinger said tightly.

"Did he . . . did Max ever mention another woman, that another woman might have been implicated in their breakup?"

"A woman? . . . Well, there were always women, you know. A man like Maxwell . . ." He hurried on. "But there were also delusions."

"What sort?"

"It has been a long time, and questions of confidentiality still remain." Sallinger fell silent; outside the wind gusted and a tree at the level of the window scraped its branches against the pane. "There were . . . paranoid fantasies: sinister men who followed Maxwell around the city, who stole things from him, telephone calls being monitored by government agents . . . And another sort of delusion. I remember he thought he had a child."

"He had four," Alter reminded Sallinger.

"A fifth, I mean. Illegitimately."

Alter moved forward in his seat. "When did he tell you about this illegitimate child?"

"It became something of a preoccupation, during the last year or so."

"You didn't believe him?"

"After years of alcoholism, and the drugs . . ." Sallinger put out his hands, palms up. "Of course, the fantasy had its emotional roots: Maxwell felt deficient as a father toward his real, his natural children and—projected if you will—another, phantom child, one he had abandoned." Alter saw Sallinger grip the lip of his desk with his fingertips.

"How old would the child have been?"

"There *was* no child." He looked at his watch, seeming disquieted. "I'm afraid our time is up."

"But how old?—just hypothetically."

Sallinger hesitated. "Maxwell believed she had been conceived many years earlier."

"You say 'she'?" Some dim signal went off in the biographer's brain.

"He believed the child to be female. That, anyway, is my recollection . . . We really must stop now, Mr. Alter. I tire easily these days."

The telephone jingled in his ear.

"Hallo?"

"Mrs. Sallinger?"

"Yes?"

"Raphael Alter."

"Why Dr. Alter, you just left us!"

"I'm sorry to disturb you, but I have one more quick question for your husband. Is he available?"

"Hold please, while I find out."

The receiver clattered as Frieda Sallinger put it down. Alter heard her calling shrilly, "Erich! Erich!" The cries faded away and a few moments later the psychiatrist picked up on an extension.

"Yes, Mr. Alter?"

"I apologize for bothering you, but I have a question that didn't occur to me to ask before . . . It's, uh, been so long, as you say, and one's memory sometimes—"

"You are concerned about the stroke," Sallinger interrupted irritably. "My memory is excellent."

"I'm sure. I was wondering though . . . Would you allow me to look through your treatment notes on Max? I'm especially interested in the last year or so of his life. You were among the very few people who saw him regularly then. I assure you I won't quote directly without your—"

"It's not possible."

"It would only be for background, sir. I'll clear everything with you, of course." Alter searched for a stronger negotiating point. "I won't remove them from your office, if you prefer, so there'll be no question of copies. I'll read them right there."

Sallinger was quiet; only the faint rattle of his breathing indicated he was still on the line. "Listen," he said at last, "you see, it's simply not possible. A year after Maxwell's death I burned them . . . I burned all my notes."

"You didn't," Alter said, aghast, "you couldn't. Didn't you realize . . ." *That I'd be along someday! That I'd need them!*

"I realized. Naturally. And that is exactly why . . . It seemed the most prudent course, the only sure way to protect Maxwell."

"Posterity has a right to know."

"Scavenging under the guise of posterity has never impressed me," Sallinger answered coldly. "Anyway, there are no notes, so we have nothing to discuss. Good night."

Alter clung to the arms of his chair, stunned. A phantom child? But perhaps no phantom. The reality would make all too perfect sense. Consider: the letter to Linus Wagner. 1953. *You have saved me from the worst disaster.*

An impulsive homosexual episode had crossed the biographer's mind and he had vaguely conjectured that "the money, desperately needed" might have been hush money, to keep the incident quiet. But an illegitimate child! This was a far better fit, knowing Leibert. The money might not have been hush money at all but payoff money. To send the mother and child away. Or, for an abortion? . . . an abortion that, unbeknownst to Max, never took place!

Alter calculated, feverishly. The daughter, if she had lived, would be in her thirties. The thought hit him directly, with the crushing impact of a locomotive careening without brakes down the long track of the past: Chloe. Thirty-two, thirty-five, just about. Could it be? . . . *Chloe, Leibert's daughter?* If so, who was aware of it? Was she? Before his death, was he?

Alter wandered into the bathroom. He splashed cold water on his face, dried himself on a towel, and looked into the mirror. His eyes, mirrors themselves, reflected wild bewilderment. And yet he believed that if he shifted his gaze, just barely, truths long obscured would become clear.

From Maxwell Leibert's journal, another wail of regret and self-recrimination. May 1976, less than a year before his death:

Why have I been excluded from Heavan's favor? Love has granted me so little of its joy & so much of its sadness. *Madness.* By my own hand, I've lost everything—wives and children & lovers. How I yearn for some peace. Wealth would no longer satisfy me, not even fame. I have only one certain desire: to wipe out all that has happened and begin anew. But too late too late too wretchedly late.

SIX

"I'd forgotten about all this stuff."

Ulysses Leibert had a Florsheim shoe box open on the table between himself and Alter. At his elbow sat their ritual pot of steaming tea; next to the tea a package of Fig Newtons. *Like two schoolboys doing their homework,* Alter thought. It was snowing again; flakes lit on the window and vanished.

Ulysses, rummaging in the box, removed a silver pocket watch and held it out for Alter's inspection. Alter snapped it open. The time was displayed in bold Roman numerals.

"Still works," Ulysses said. "Dad bought it before I was born and gave it to me on my fifteenth birthday. He wrapped it himself, in aluminum foil with a red bow. I made a watch fob out of paperclips to go with it, and went out and bought myself a vest, and a pipe. I tried to grow a little mustache. One day I came home from school and Dad said, 'You look like you belong to a men's club for midgets.' Well, what does he know? I asked myself. He's weird, he goes to work in his bathrobe."

Ulysses took the watch back. "We never had enough

money, and I couldn't understand why he wouldn't get real work, like everyone else's father. Those stupid teaching jobs, and writing poetry no one cared about or read . . . As a teenager I couldn't figure out what compelled him. It was like he led a secret life." Ulysses rustled in the Fig Newton package for a cookie. "I used to bring my friends home from school and there he was, in his shirttails. It wasn't easy to explain. I sometimes made him into an actor, between jobs. Once, I went to see *The Guns of Navarone* with a schoolfriend, a kid who'd never met Dad. On some crazy impulse, I leaned over to him in the dark and whispered, 'See that guy standing behind David Niven?—that's my dad.' " Ulysses poured some tea into his cup, studied its hue, frowned, and put the pot down. "Word got around that my father was in *Guns of Navarone*. Someone said, 'No, Lee's father wrote *The Guns of Navarone*.' For about a week, I was a hero.

"My mother tells the story of the time she was called in to see the school guidance counselor about my brother Ben. He was around five, and all the children had been asked to describe what their fathers did. When Ben's turn came he answered, 'He sits in his study and drinks martinis.' The guidance counselor told my mother, 'We think Ben has a problem.' And my mother says she said, 'Oh no, you've got it all wrong. Ben has no problem, Ben is fine. It's his father who has the problem. My son just has his facts slightly wrong: his father drinks straight gin. The only time Max has a martini is when he makes one for me. But Ben is just a child—a drink is a drink to him.' " Ulysses lifted the teapot. "Tea?"

Ulysses poured into Alter's chipped cup. "You know, my father was in, like, self-exile from the whole world, even from his own family. He aspired to domesticity, he really killed himself trying, but then sometimes at dinner I would see him put down his fork real slowly and look at all of us—me, my mother, Benjamin, Jonathan, Hannah—with this puzzled expression. Like an actor going up on his lines, like he wasn't sure where he was in the script, or what he was supposed to be doing. If it hadn't been so sad, so devastating to me, it would have been comical."

What were you thinking, Max? . . . "Who are these people? How did I get here? I must smuggle out a note: Being Held by Family Against Will. Send help!"

Ulysses rattled around in the shoe box. "This is from Finland. They use it to skin reindeer." He offered Alter a short knife in a carved ivory holder.

Alter unsheathed it, exposing a thick, sharp blade. "Where's the rest of your father's collection?" He cleared his throat. It was the first time he had spoken since Ulysses had launched into his monologue.

"Most of it went at auction. I have a couple more knives, Benjamin has a few, and Jonathan has one of the swords, a rapier I think, French. Hannah didn't take anything."

Alter turned the Finnish knife over in his hands.

"The one you're holding is the one that cut Tamsin."

Alter looked up. "Cut Tamsin? You never told me about anything like that."

"I never showed you the knife before. I happened to recognize it when I opened the box. The police had it for a few days and Dad sent me down to retrieve it after the investigation."

"The police were involved?"

"Well, she hurt herself pretty badly, cut herself almost to the bone, sliced up a tendon. I suppose the cops just wanted to be sure . . ." Ulysses paused, then added bitterly, "Serves her right for playing with Dad's toys."

"What really happened?"

"Tamsin was drunk, fooling around, tripped on the carpet and the blade went through her hand. She drank more than my father, if that were possible. I think that's one of the things that drew them apart—he had to be first in everything. A dumb accident, at any rate . . . You've never had any luck tracking her down, have you?"

"None, and not for lack of trying. I haven't a clue as to what became of her. Nobody seems to. She just . . . disappeared."

As Max Leibert recounted it, towards the end of their year at Bennington, his second wife had simply walked out, packing her bags and stealing off while he was teaching a class. He told colleagues he had received a call from her in Barcelona where she was lodging with the nuns of a cloistered order "to regain herself." From time to time sightings by others were reported: Tamsin on Majorca, in the village of Deyá, running a gift shop; Tamsin on the Paris Métro; Tamsin spotted eating *gelato* on the Piazza del Popolo in Rome with an unidentified Italian. But the encounters were vague and indefinite, the reports second-, third-, and fourth-hand. Alter had in his possession a letter Leibert wrote to Sam Pintchik a year after his wife had left in which the poet said he had been told "by parties who shall go nameless" that Tamsin had " 'married' a German countess, a Valkyrie, and lives with her now in a castle near the Bohemian forest. So she has quit the nunnery and asserted her true nature: dyke . . . nazi."

"I for one was glad to see her go," Ulysses said, taking the knife from Alter and dropping it into the box.

"It was a strangely abrupt departure, though."

Ulysses shrugged. "They'd been together six years and the marriage had foundered irrevocably long before she took off."

"It's the sudden nature of her leaving I find a puzzle. And the fact that she never turned up again."

The poet's son looked at Alter disparagingly. "We all know plenty of people who leave their spouses and never speak again. Even in marriages of long standing . . . Besides, Tamsin always had the gypsy in her. When she met Dad she had just returned to the States after years traipsing about abroad. Three months after the wedding she was back in Africa taking pictures and she stayed away . . . I don't know how long."

"Eight weeks, I'm fairly certain."

"Oh yes?" Ulysses responded coolly.

"I have a letter of Max's to Sam Pintchik in which he complained about her absence."

Ulysses lifted his teacup and stared into it without drinking. "You know, I sometimes resent this entire undertaking. It's not just you, and your apologetic little ways of prying. If anyone's going to anatomize Dad's life for the delectation of a voyeuristic world, I'd rather it would be you. But I find myself thinking you have too *much* of him, and I have nothing . . . And once in a while I wish we could forget the whole thing and leave him alone." His eyes locked with Alter's. "Sometimes I'm afraid of what all your diligence might turn up. I'm not sure I want to know."

Alter looked away. *I'm not sure I do either.*

.   .   .

Distant noises roused him from his work. No, *voices*. Shrill, panicky, they seemed to emanate from the lobby. Alter shuddered as he opened his front door and followed the sounds where they led.

The lobby was empty. The voices he discerned were from upstairs, the second or third floor. Alter walked with a heavy tread up the steps. The hall on the second floor was also devoid of life. He made his way to the third. He heard a scream.

A knot of tenants had gathered in the public corridor under the grim light of a round flickering fluorescent ceiling tube.

"What's wrong?" he asked Clara Eres who stood gripping the elbow of Morris Bloom. Next to Bloom, Rosalba Pompanazzi wavered on her cane. They looked spectral, disenfranchised, like the inhabitants of a welfare hotel.

"He was going down to put the garbage," Mrs. Pompanazzi said.

"Oh God." Clara Eres was crying, hiccuping, holding a hand to her head.

"*Do* something," Morris Bloom demanded of the landlord. "Help."

"Help? Who? Is it an accident? What?" Alter pushed his way through the little crowd of onlookers.

"*Madre mia,*" Mrs. Pompanazzi moaned.

Then he saw: on the floor, in a pool of his own urine, lay Simon Leipzig on his back. A small grocery bag had capsized beside him; wet coffee grounds dusted the cold tiles. Over Leipzig's inert form Angel Muñoz knelt. He had apparently torn open Leipzig's shirt. The old man's chest, exposed, had turned a sick, waxy yellow. Alter, by vocation an observer, reeled, stepped backward, half hoping to be forgotten, but Muñoz spotted him.

"Come here!" he rasped.

Trembling, Alter dropped to his knees next to his superintendent, as though commanded by a higher authority.

"His heart?"

"Mus' be. He doan breathe, I think."

"Anyone called an ambulance?"

"Miz Eres. You give him mouth-to-mouth, I'll do the
chest."

"I can't . . . I don't know how . . ." Alter, ashamed,
wished he could faint.

"We gonna lose him," the other man warned.

Shoulder to shoulder with Angel Muñoz, the landlord
felt joined to him, not in grief but in brotherhood. He
gazed at Leipzig; depleted by years of active warfare against
his own body, he seemed silently to long to be set free. "He
wants to die, Angel," Alter mumbled, "that's what he
wants."

"I doan know about that, boss. But I know God ain't
gonna forgive me, ain't gonna show me no mercy, if I let
him jus' pass away." Muñoz's dark eyes blazed.

Alter took a deep breath, bent forward, licked his lips
and placed them lightly on Leipzig's. A foul odor assaulted
him, so noisome it made him dizzy. Pinching Leipzig's
nostrils, he tipped back his tenant's coarse, unshaven chin
and forced into him a lungful of air. Leipzig's chest rose and
fell once. Surprised, oddly jubilant (there was something in
the sheer mechanics of it, in its so simply *working* that
cheered him), he took another breath and exhaled into
Leipzig again.

"One . . . two . . . t'ree . . . four." As though from an
infinite distance, he listened to Muñoz's steady count. Without speaking, they coordinated their efforts. Alter turned his
head to the side like a swimmer, inhaled, put his lips again

to Leipzig's in ludicrous approximation of a kiss and breathed out. In . . . and out . . . in . . . and out . . . in . . . and out . . . mesmerized by his task, only vaguely aware of the increasing hubbub around him.

"That's okay, we're here now."

"Move aside, ma'am."

Other voices: competent, professional, crisp.

"What've we got?"

"Elderly white male, unconscious, cyanotic."

"Anyone see what happened?"

A large orange box, like a toolbox, clattered down next to Alter. Someone opened it. He was aware of shelves, stepped shelves inside the box, filled with shining objects.

"He comes out with his trash and he just collapses," Morris Bloom reported. "Boom. Down like a tree."

"He's dead!" Clara Eres moaned, "I know it."

Someone took Leipzig's wrist. Alter kept up the breathing . . . in . . . out . . . in . . . out . . . In a vision he saw himself as a boy of seven, swimming in a lake in the Adirondacks, his father on the shore in bathing trunks, hands on hips, calling to him, letting him know he could do it . . . in . . . out . . . in . . . out.

"We have a pulse. Thready."

"He's *blue*!"

"He'll be all right, ma'am. You wanna step back a little, give us some room?"

A tap on his shoulder. "You can stop now, sir. We wanna see if he'll breathe on his own." A hand, pulling. "Mister, you can stop. We got a pulse. You did good."

"Let's get a line into him."

"We're not gonna need the paddles, Mike . . ."

"Someone wanna start an EKG?"

"Throw me the jelly."

"Go on down to the bus, Joey, get the stretcher."

A pair of hands brought Alter up; he sat on his haunches. A plastic bag of clear solution was thrust at him. "You can do me a favor and hold this. Just stand up and hold it high so it drips."

Alter, dazed, got to his feet. In the commotion, Simon Leipzig himself receded: needles had been inserted into his long, naked forearms; plastic electrodes dotted his chest; he had become less than himself, under the orchestrated ministrations of the paramedics.

"Yo, this fella needs a little more help." A pair of hands worked a stiff airway down Leipzig's throat; and another pair began rhythmically to pump on a black bag attached to the airway.

A man in a green jacket and pants sidled by Alter, pushing a collapsed stretcher. It was opened on the ground and straps like seat belts were flung aside.

"Let's see if we can get him stabilized before we move 'im."

"Mike, you wanna?—"

"I only got two hands."

"Use your teeth."

All around Leipzig a mounting pile of the litter of rescue grew: plastic wrappers, discarded syringes, rubber tubing, bits of tape. He read words: Digi-Trol, Pulmanex, Lifepak. Alter knew that right outside the city throbbed with life, oblivious to the drama taking place at his feet. He tried to distract himself from the enormity of what was happening. He searched the hall for signs of dereliction or trauma and found a gaping hole in the floor where tiles were missing, and near Martin Aswith's front door a crack, nearly a rut, in the wall . . . He smelled, could not avoid smelling, the awful, chronic stink of food. Not the smell of healthy home cooking, but the pervasive, lardy, rancid stench that haunts the lives of the poor.

"Everyone ready?"

"Watch yourself there, Phil."

"Okay . . . one, two, *three*—" The medics heaved Leipzig's limp figure onto the stretcher and brought it up to its full height. An orange blanket was placed over him. The straps were fastened. A machine to monitor the beating of his ravaged heart was situated between his legs. The stretcher rattled toward the elevator. Alter, on the leash of the solution that flowed into Leipzig's veins, was pulled along. He wondered absently when he might be cut free and then thought that perhaps he would be bound to Leipzig this way into eternity.

Alter, last into the elevator cab, pressed L. The motor groaned and slowly they sank. Over his shoulder Alter noticed that the words JESUS SAVES had been scratched into the wall of the cab, and next to them the word PUSSY, so that it read JESUS SAVES PUSSY. Self-consciously, he tried to position his head over the offending graffiti. A paramedic continued to pump on the airbag; someone reached out and adjusted the drip on the bag of solution. Alter realized he must have been holding his arm over Leipzig's body for at least half an hour; it had frozen, numb and cold, in place; he could no longer feel his fingers. The clank of the elevator as it descended made an almost soothing sound, but Leipzig's titanic bulk, his shoeless feet hanging over the end of the stretcher, pressed on Alter's heart, or his soul. Angry even in unconsciousness, Leipzig seemed to accuse: Why did you not just let me die? *Life is life's answer, Simon* . . .

When the elevator landed on the ground floor Alter exited first and held the door for the stretcher bearers.

"Where are you taking him?"

"Roosevelt." The voice that answered pronounced it *Rooz-a-velt*, and also took the bag.

They passed swiftly through the lobby. Alter lowered his arm; the numbed hand flopped like a dead fish at the end of his wrist. He looked after the team of stretcher bearers until they were out of sight.

"You got a name?" A police officer had appeared out of nowhere.

"Me? Alter. Raphael Alter."

"I meant the victim."

"Ah, the victim. Simon Leipzig."

"Can you spell that?"

"L-E-I-P-Z-I-G."

"You live with him?"

"In a manner of speaking."

"Relative?"

"Relative?" Alter blinked. "Relative to what?"

"I mean, are you a relative?"

"Oh . . . no."

"Any next of kin?"

"Nooo . . ."

"No one we can notify?"

"No."

"Too bad, when something like this happens, man's all alone, no one to take responsibility."

". . . Maybe . . . I can take responsibility."

The patrolman gaped at him and the charge was clear: Who, you? You dry little man? He ran a hand around the heavy leather belt holding the tools of his trade, redistributing its weight. Handcuffs jangled.

"Who're you?" the policeman asked.

"His landlord," Alter intoned dully, "I'm the landlord."

The radio on the cop's hip squawked some urgent indecipherable message. The thought came to Alter in the form of an imperative: the staccato emergency call was for him. . . . It was not from the police station, and it was a call that must be answered.

When he heard the ambulance siren start up he stepped back into the elevator and let the door close. Quiet now: but the quiet was tangible, something that could be listened to. Blindly, he ripped the Did Not Pass Inspection sticker from where it had been posted beside the buttons. Nothing passed inspection, nothing in his life . . . He sank to his knees on the floor of the elevator. *I do not pass inspection!* Something had moved, lurched within him, and he sought frantically to understand the hortatory summons, to determine the direction, the source from which it emanated. He searched his heart.

"Raphael? Are you okay?"

"Yes. Okay . . . just." It inspirited him a little that she seemed genuinely concerned.

"You don't sound like it."

"I . . . One of my tenants had a heart attack today. I'm still shaken up, you see a thing like that . . ." It was half the truth.

"Is he going to be all right?"

"They don't know yet. He's alive anyway." He felt like the victim of combat fatigue, hardly able to get the words out.

"Well, I was calling to say that I've made arrangements."

"Arrangements?" Today, it sounded like a funeral to him. Whose?

"For our trip to Vermont. You haven't forgotten, have you?"

"Bennington. Of course not." *Nor have I forgotten the faint whiff of incest, however unconscious, that now scents our—*

"How would next weekend be?"

"Next weekend would be fine." *Neither of them could have known . . . Neither Leibert nor Chloe—*

"Have you a car?"

"I can rent one . . . When do you want to depart?"

"Depart?" She giggled; struck, Alter thought, by the formality of the word.

But the journey they were about to embark upon did feel to him like a departure. Departure: a setting off on a new heading, a deviation or divergence from long-established routine; or, Alter recalled, in nautical terms, a ship's bearing at the start of a voyage, used as the basis for dead reckoning. Dead reckoning—it was all he had now to locate his own position in his private, rapidly shifting universe.

"How about Friday, around noon?" Chloe went on. "We'll get there in time for dinner."

"I don't drive that fast." *And I'm not sure I'll have the appetite for dinner.*

"Late supper then." She sounded slightly peeved.

"May I . . . may I ask you something, Chloe? What will we find in Bennington? Why are you so eager to make this trip?"

"I'm not 'eager,' but I've come to realize I'm morally obligated . . . Now may I ask you something?"

"Anything."

". . . Did Max love me?"

Anything but that. An occupational hazard of the biographer, the informant's demand: *What did he say about me?*

"You're uncertain?" Alter hedged.

She didn't answer directly. "I need to know, from *you*. You'd know better than anyone, you know him better than anyone." She sounded like a lost child. *His child?*

"If only that were so."

"Tell me. Please."

He swallowed hard. "There's every . . . suggestion . . . from everything I've learned . . . that he did." Well, it was no lie, and, he hoped, sufficient to satisfy her. Alter felt full of trepidation, as if skating on a frozen pond in winter, where the ice may be fatally thin. One false move, and both of them could drown. If he were to reveal inadvertently her possible biologic connection to Leibert—

"Thank you," she said in a small, abject voice. There was a pause. "Raphael . . . I'm . . . scared." He felt, rather than heard, her plaint, and he had a vision of himself as a giant filter through which her fear and anguish could pass—so much bilge, that he would strain and scour, and by some spiritual process of elutriation, return to her, purified.

"I'll see you Friday, Chloe . . . Leave everything to me."

He swiveled in his chair. Night had fallen and in the lighted room he saw his face in the window. He didn't look like the man he used to be. He couldn't find himself in that wavery, watery reflection.

"I have ceased to be Raphael Alter," he said out loud, dizzily sensing new possibility. *Or maybe I never was.*

Alter waited more than a minute before Martin Aswith answered the door. When at last he did, the landlord was shocked. Aswith looked worse than usual, as if his skin had been turned inside out. His hair stood up electrically in all directions.

"Martin," Alter said tentatively.

"Raphael."

"I—is everything okay?" Alter stealthily surveyed the man's body for signs of more self-inflicted damage—a cast on a foot, a bandage on a hand. He appeared intact.

"It's Marion. She's sick."

"What's the matter?"

"Intestinal infection. I had no idea a simple infection could get so serious."

"Where is she?" Alter asked, qualmish, but no longer immune to the confidences that were forced upon him.

"Sleeping. She's on heavy antibiotics. If there's no improvement by morning, the doctor is threatening to put her in the hospital."

Behind every door I open, another crisis. From infancy to old age, lives pocked with crisis—it's a permanent condition.

Aswith took a step backwards. "Come in."

Alter dodged. "I don't want to intrude. I just came up to give you a date for the paint job."

"Please. It's no intrusion." Martin Aswith looked at him with eyes that erupted in loneliness. "I'd be grateful for the company."

They sat across from each other in two green velvet chairs, the velvet balded away on the arms. Aswith placed a cold beer in Alter's hand; it sweated into his warm palm. The small apartment was suffused with the odors of the sickroom—the slightly sour smell of vomit, stinging camphor, and alcohol. From an adjoining apartment came the rasp of hollow coughing; from the apartment above, the muted laugh track of a television comedy; from somewhere

else, kitchen noises—the clangor of pots and pans, the pat-
ter of running water. Alter tried to blunt the discomforting
oversensitivity that—as moments before on the telephone
with Chloe—allowed him to feel, as well as hear, voices and
sounds. He fancied, as with the cop's radio, that they were
being broadcast on a special high frequency meant for him
alone. He thought that with the merest fine tuning of his
internal dials he might also see through walls, but was
unsure if this would be a blessing or a curse.

"I'm helpless," Aswith revealed, "helpless alone with her.
Before, her mother was with us. Catherine knew what to
do. There were two of us when Marion was sick."

"Hmmm?" Alter gazed into his tenant's features and saw
there batterings—purplish welts and yellow-brown con-
tusions—that he imagined were visible only to his eyes.

"I can't go to sleep. I might not hear her . . . she could
throw up, choke on it . . . die."

Alter's heart turned over and he attempted to fit himself
into the terrifying shape of that.

"No, Martin. Don't even think it. Marion's going to be
as good as new."

Aswith looked at him longingly. "You think?"

Alter hesitated. "I promise." He had no idea from where
he derived the authority to make the pledge; nevertheless it
issued naturally from his lips and he believed it absolutely.
Perhaps this new high frequency also beamed to him other
messages?

"Still, I'm nervous," Aswith confessed. "When the doctor said 'hospital,' it frightened me. Even the word."

"It would be only a precaution," Alter answered with the
same unaccustomed authority. Was he on autopilot? He
stared at his feet, half expecting them to move of their own

accord. He took a breath. ". . . I feel . . ." He trailed off miserably.

"What?" Aswith inquired with a boggy, unfocused expression.

"So *inadequate*. I want to do more. What can I do? Tell me, there must be something more I can do for you."

"No," replied Aswith, waving a hand, "you're doing it, just being here, giving me hope . . . I can't stand talking to myself anymore."

"Being here," Alter murmured. "You know, until now I have never felt any real purpose in my being . . . anywhere. In my *existing*. I could see some purpose in other people's lives. My own was all . . . a kind of dream. I was simply— there. *Here*, I mean. You know?" How effortlessly the admission slipped from him!

After quite a long silence Aswith said shyly, "I've read your books. They're very good . . . delicate and humane. You understand the secret hearts of men."

Alter regarded him with something approaching wonderment. "Really. You never said."

"You never seemed to want to hear."

Aswith's words rolled around in Alter's head. He could make out faint, clashing notes of chastisement, resentment, even hurt, in the other man's tone, like a church carillon heard from a far distance—the hymn almost, but not entirely, clear.

"You were a locked house . . . with all the windows closed and the shades drawn," Aswith continued softly. "One could knock and knock, sure that someone was inside, but whoever it was, he wouldn't come to the door." Alter wondered if Martin and Al Bruno had exchanged words about their landlord. "But tonight for some reason"—

Aswith's lips curled in the semblance of a smile—"there's a light on in an upstairs window. And I think: what's going on? What's he up to, up there?"

Alter shrugged, uncomfortable. "I'm not quite sure myself," he said with an embarrassed grin.

"Forgive me," Aswith pleaded sleepily, "I presume. I'm exhausted, and when I'm this tired my brain and my tongue ramble."

"Nothing to forgive. I'm surprised, that's all. I didn't notice—that you noticed."

"I see more in you than you think I do. Maybe more than you see in yourself."

Alter blushed and shifted in his seat. "Just to change the subject for a moment, as long as I'm here, I ought to tell you that I've scheduled the painting for January second and third . . ."

"A new year, new paint." Aswith yawned and stretched. "I feel better, simply knowing it will happen."

"I'm glad," Alter said, and it was heartfelt.

"These days I celebrate the small pleasures. A walk in the park with Marion. A week when I don't hit my head or trip over my own feet." Aswith smiled sheepishly. "Fresh paint . . . kindness." He might have been recalling a favorite dessert he had not savored in many years.

"Martin? I know . . . I *do* know how much you're suffering." Alter leaned forward, extending an open hand, as if he anticipated something to be deposited there.

"Suffering," Aswith echoed ruefully, "is not all it's cracked up to be, Raphael. I mean, I'm not sure it builds character or anything. On the other hand, in some fundamental way, we couldn't live without it." He gestured toward the rear of the apartment, to the bedroom where

Marion slept. "Love . . . provokes anxiety. Suffering. Comes with the territory." His tongue was rambling again. "The older I get, the more I believe in God. It's strange, but I *believe* in His absence, in His—unknowability—that there's no *explanation*, or none that we can understand . . ."

Aswith shook then bowed his head, and placed his beer bottle on the chair between his legs, tipped against one thigh. In a few seconds Alter heard a long, shuddering sigh. He recognized it as snoring.

It occurred to him to tiptoe from the premises while Aswith slept but something kept him rooted, a certain knowledge that he must remain, must keep a steady watch, until Martin awakened.

Minutes passed, then another presence announced itself silently. He raised his eyes. Standing a few feet from him, gaping transfixed at a figure both familiar and foreign to her, was Marion Aswith. Her cheeks were fiery red, with sleep or fever he couldn't tell which, but the child did not seem nearly as ill as her father had feared. Marion, still groggy, stumbled toward her parent.

"Marion," Alter whispered.

She turned, coy, her thumb in her mouth. He could swear she was flirting with him.

"Come over here," he whispered again, "let your daddy rest. He's very tired."

The little girl debated. Her attention wandered back and forth between the men before accepting the invitation. She padded to Alter and climbed into his lap.

He inhaled her baby sweetness mixed in with the smells of recent stomach distress, felt her pajamas damp with perspiration. He placed the back of his hand to her forehead. It was cool. Her body relaxed, not rigid or stiff with pain.

Perhaps the fever had broken; perhaps this crisis had passed. He reveled in the fragile weight in his arms, the gentle heft of her against him. He felt Marion doze.

Watching the heavy rise and fall of the child's chest, Alter mourned, as if for the last time, the monotony of his dim existence, and acknowledged that never during his lifetime had he truly asked anything of himself, not anything momentous, nothing that would have caused him to alter his course.

He suddenly saw himself as having been cast, a fisherman who had lost his boat to a sudden squall, into a roiling sea of humanity, a hellish, crazy circle of disdained lives, trapped by poverty, stunted by despair, hemmed in by ugliness. He clung to a bit of wood, all that was left of his vessel, and prayed for a sextant as the storm raged.

I have always been a reasonable man, never permitted myself to become unreasonably attached to anyone. And so I cannot explain that against my will, against all common sense (are my feelings for Chloe and my acquiescence to her wild adventure commonsensical?) these people, who surround me like an army (mustered by . . . whom?) have invaded, trespassed, conspired somehow, while I wasn't looking, to set up a blockade around my (locked) house, and keep me in their sights . . .

His eyes strayed reluctantly to the brownish stain hovering on the ceiling over Aswith's sofa. The patch appeared to have grown bigger, darker, menacing the room. *Menacing us all.* Then it came to him forcibly:

Just barely existing is no longer enough. And painting over deep internal damage is not enough either. The ceiling in Martin's living room will have to be torn into, gouged, the real trouble exposed and repaired. It will not bring back his wife, or return Marion's mother to her, nor will replacing a leaky pipe, but it must be done, and that isn't all . . .

Suddenly Alter's tenants crowded into his consciousness, jostling cantankerously for elbow room . . . Morris Bloom. Clara Eres. Rosalba Pompanazzi. Roslyn and Loretta DeAngelis. *To fix their plumbing, their kitchens, their elevator, will not save their lives, or assure them of love, and yet . . . it is what I can do. (Not Quasimodo, not the Hunchback, but the Juggler of Notre Dame, am I. The wealthy leave extravagant offerings at the statue of the Virgin. But the Juggler, having only his own gifts, stands before the mother of God—and juggles.)* Detail piled on detail. The DeAngelis sink, the Pompanazzi stove, the boiler, the furnace, the stairs, the windows, the roof. *I don't know how to accomplish it all, or where in heaven's name to find the money. But somehow, soon, I will resurrect this blighted place.*

He rested his head, heavy as a watermelon, on the back of Aswith's frayed chair. Marion stirred, then resettled herself on his shoulder.

Already long, the list grew longer the more he dwelled on it, daunting in its complexity. His eyelids drooped and he imagined he could hear out beyond the confines of the sagging edifice, into the immense city, where the woe of the millions just as loudly assaulted his ears.

I have no choice . . . Salvation does not lie in holding the middle ground, and redemption will not be found in the hiding places . . . He remembered: In times of national emergency hermits and stylites alike were commanded, *"Let them emerge from their cells and descend from their columns!"*

When Martin Aswith woke, Alter bid him and his daughter a hasty goodbye. He went to his own apartment where he brewed a pot of strong coffee and stayed up all night trying to calculate his position, his longitude and latitude, in terms of dollars and cents. At dawn, he was no closer to a solution than he had been at midnight. Yet, although spent, turning over page after page of figures that proved the prospects were bleak, he felt strangely buoyant, operating under the spell of some mysterious grace.

Alter rested his elbows on the metal bar of Simon Leipzig's bed. Clara Eres, ambushing him on his way out of the building, had insisted on accompanying him to the hospital. She stood beside him now, smelling medicinal herself, hardly distinguishable from the antiseptic, clinical odor of the intensive care unit. They contemplated Leipzig mutely.

The patient's eyes were taped shut. His chest heaved mechanically up and down; a machine next to the bed forced oxygen into his lungs. An intravenous line ran into one arm; a blood pressure cuff was loosely bound around the other. A clear plastic bag hanging from the metal bar collected bright yellow urine. The hem of the sheet covering his chest was stamped PROPERTY OF ROOSEVELT HOSPITAL. *That's what you've become*, Alter thought, *property of Roosevelt Hospital. They've got you trussed like a goose.*

"I hate these places," Clara Eres whispered.

"No one likes them," Alter whispered back.

All around them men and women lay defenseless, twisted, groaning, mewling, bleating, everything most private and most vulnerable exposed. In the bed next to Leipzig's an old woman with her eyes closed, mouth agape, was motionless save for an involuntary twitching under the rumpled bedclothes. Every few moments she cried, "Help me!" No one came. Alter noticed that on her left hand she wore a thin gold wedding band. Her legs beneath the sheets were spread akimbo in gruesome mimickry of the sexual position, as if she awaited a lover. Alter looked away. A nurse came up behind them.

"How's he doing?" Alter asked.

"A little better," the nurse replied briskly. She placed a stethoscope in her ears and began to inflate Leipzig's blood pressure cuff. "Pardon me for a sec." Alter watched as the mercury slowly dropped in the sphygmomanometer attached to the wall. The nurse peeled back the cuff, removed her earpieces. "Very nice, Mr. Leipzig. Your numbers are looking nice," she said to her unconscious patient. "But he's not out of the woods yet," she cautioned Alter.

"When will you take that tube out of his throat?" Clara Eres asked.

"When he's ready for it, we'll start to turn the respirator down little by little and hope that he can breathe without help. Probably in a day or so."

"Can he hear us?" Alter questioned.

"I don't think so." The nurse started away. "But you never know."

Tentatively, Alter reached over the safety bar and rested a hand on Leipzig's forearm. The machine pumping air sounded extraordinarily loud, nearly blotting out his voice. He found himself breathing in time to it, as if the air was being pushed in and out of his own lungs. "Mr. Leipzig . . . Simon . . . it's Raphael Alter. Your landlord . . . I don't know if you can hear me, but I just want to tell you I'm here. Right here . . ."

Truman Swanberg combed what remained of his side hairs over the top of his skull. The former professor of eschatology wore trousers hiked up to his breast. His arms, white as the belly of a carp, poked from a short-sleeved shirt and under his skin dark veins were clearly visible. In his new condition, with his new powers of apprehension, Alter thought he could see the blood coursing through them. Swanberg's grimy fingernails were seamed with ridges. He chain-smoked unfiltered Lucky Strikes.

Swanberg, well known in his field, had the doleful air of a man celebrated for his erudition only by a handful of other men as obscure and outcast as himself. There were no awards given for the subject of his lifelong scrutiny; weekend conferences were not convened for cocktails and tennis and the consideration of Last Things; Swanberg had never been invited on a radio show to discuss his notion of the Fire of Cosmic Conflagration. At seventy-nine, after more than forty years of devoted scholarship, what did he possess? A single, narrow room, tiny as a cell, on Bedford Street; a kitchen-in-a-closet with a two-burner stove and a half-refrigerator, a sink with a doll-size bowl, hundreds of books with too few shelves to house them all, a nine-inch black-and-white television set with poor reception, and a curriculum vitae as long as a burial shroud, which he had set on the table in front of Alter. The biographer felt a wave of sympathy for Swanberg, that he should have so few creature comforts in his old age, and wished there were some discreet way that he might leave a few dollars when he left.

"Ghosts! All's I get is ghosts!" Swanberg slapped the cabinet of the TV. An "I Love Lucy" episode unspooled, the sound soft, almost mute. Three Lucys and three Rickys argued about how to travel to California for Ricky's motion picture debut. Lucy couldn't make up her mind—plane, train, or automobile. Swanberg sighed, "Aw, I know how it turns out anyway," and shuffled to the refrigerator. When his back was turned Alter leaned forward and lowered the volume all the way.

"Seltzer? Pepsi? Prune juice?" Swanberg scrunched in front of the little icebox, taking inventory.

"I'm fine, thanks."

"I could make coffee," Swanberg suggested, doubtful. "Instant," he warned.

Alter thought nostalgically of Frieda Sallinger's pastries; but, like a kid in summer camp, the biographer accepted whatever was offered by his various hosts.

"Instant's okay."

"*Postum*," Swanberg said, further qualifying the offer. "I'm not allowed to have real." The old man ran water into a tarnished aluminum kettle. "Doctor says it makes me jumpy. Coffee and cigarettes and booze, that's what I lived on. He wants me to lay off the smokes too, but I can't . . . Few months ago I was really bouncin' off the walls."

Alter conjured an image of Truman Swanberg bouncing off the walls of his apartment, a Lucky clenched in his teeth, soaring, balletic, from north wall to south, looping from floor to ceiling.

"It helps, I suppose."

"What helps?"

"Not drinking coffee helps, I suppose . . . with your nerves."

"Nah." Swanberg answered sardonically. "I was born high-strung, I'll die high-strung. Damn doctors don't know what the hell they're talkin' about. Nerves's the reason I'm still *around*. Don't sit still long enough to die. Had a heart attack in 'eighty, another in 'eighty-two. Last winter I kissed g'bye two feet of gut. I wear a bag. But here I am,

walkin' and talkin'. I'm miserable, but I'm movin'." Swanberg removed the kettle from the flame; he apparently didn't
notice, or care, whether the water had boiled. He shoveled
teaspoons of Postum into two mugs and poured the water.
"You take cream in this?"

"No, thank you."

"Great, 'cause it's sour. Sugar?"

"Just the way it is."

"Good, 'cause I don't have any." Swanberg set the mugs
on the Formica table between them and sat down.

"Perhaps we could begin with a few routine questions."

"Ya sound like a cop."

*I am, sort of. The biographer as patrolman: completely familiar
with the neighborhood after years on the beat, with a nose for subtle
irregularities (an open door, a broken window, a wandering child),
friendly and dependable—but ready to use force when necessary.*

Swanberg lit a Lucky, holding the match turned inward
towards his palm. "Shoot."

"You became acquainted with Max Leibert in the last
year of his life?"

"Thereabouts. We were drinking buddies."

Alter turned a page of the curriculum vitae and studied
it. "You were teaching at City College then."

"If that's what it says, that's where I was. I get the years
mixed up." Swanberg gestured at the vita with his cigarette. "Had a girl put it together for me, coupla years back,
update it. Former student. Her field's Armageddon. Nice
kid, but morbid. She's in Rome now. I got a card once—
from the catacombs."

Swanberg's wistful tone invited a response, but Alter
forged on. "You identified Leibert's body?"

"Yeah. I didn't see him for a few days, so I went over to

his place to find out what was up. I buzzed and buzzed but there wasn't any answer. I was about to leave when a neighbor came out and told me she'd heard Max'd been hit by a car the day before. She didn't know whether he was dead or alive or where they'd taken him. I figured it must be St. Vincent's. I got there and they tell me he's dead, hadn't lasted an hour after they carried him in. So I go over to the morgue and ID 'im. Probably just as well it was me, not his family, 'cause that car pretty well took off one side of his head . . . Then I called his kid, the oldest boy . . ."

"Ulysses?"

"Right. Only reason I remember, it's such a strange name—'cept for a Greek. I found him in the phone book. Ulysses Leibert." Swanberg drew on the cigarette. "He was shook up, I think, but he wasn't surprised. Like he expected his father wouldn't die quiet, in bed y'know."

Alter nodded, concurring. "Where did you meet Maxwell?"

"Oh everywhere—uptown, downtown, across town, Chinatown, all around the town." Swanberg exploded in laughter that became trapped in phlegm and gave way to a spasm of coughs.

"What I meant was, where were you first introduced?"

"We weren't," Swanberg replied. "We introduced ourselves. What happened was we were both regulars at the White Horse and we start buying each other drinks. We get tanked and we're fast friends ever since, till he dies."

"Where did you get together mostly?"

"White Horse a lot, Chumley's, the San Remo, Julius's. If we were eatin', The Grand Ticino sometimes, for Italian. I don't believe I ever saw him in the light of day." Swanberg ground out the cigarette in a saucer and had a sip of Postum. "Actually, the first few weeks I know him I don't *know* him because we don't exchange names. Then one night we're sittin' in the Cedar Tavern I think it was, and I hear someone say 'Maxwell!' I give a good hard look and a bell goes off. I recognize him. It takes me a minute, he's so fat. Oh Lord, Max was a sight, I mean compared to what he used to be, as a young man. I'd seen pictures." Swanberg fished in the package of Luckys for another cigarette. "Sometimes we'd go to Fascination, over t'Broadway. Max enjoyed the pinball, went at it for hours—like his hands were glued to the flippers. He was skillful.

"I remember he challenged a younger fellow and won. It was somethin' to watch, one of the greatest poets of the twentieth century puttin' it over on some skinny kid at the pinball machines. Jeez, we had some laughs." Swanberg struck a wooden kitchen match on his thumbnail and held it to the cigarette. "And good talk. We talked and talked. We pissed our lives away, talking."

"What did you talk about?" the biographer asked.

"Anything, everything. State of the world, baseball, football, women, women, women, books, the end of time. That's my area, you know." Swanberg drew on the cigarette, holding Alter with his rheumy eyes. "Name me a civilization, name me a tribe, I can tell you how they believe the world's gonna end . . . There's your various types of floods and fires. Your droughts. Your famines. Plagues. Pestilence. Patterns, don'tcha know? Themes. The stories differ, but they all got their common threads. This's my life, what I gave my life to." Swanberg's tone indicated vague regret. He raised himself off his chair and went to the stove, turning on a burner under the kettle. "So I used to tell Max the stories. There was one he particularly cottoned to, about the Guarani Indians of the Matto Grosso in Brazil. The Guarani say each man has inside him two souls, one peaceful and loving and one lustful and fierce. They believed the Earth was gonna be destroyed by fire and water, and, knowing this, went out on long journeys in search of a place they called 'the Land without Sin,' like an Eden. According to the Guarani, it lay somewhere on the other side of the ocean. The expeditions began in the nineteenth century and the Indians were still at it as late as 1912." Swanberg turned off the flame and carried the kettle to the table where he poured more lukewarm water into his mug.

"Max made me go through the story a few times, like he's tryin' to memorize it—his memory was none too good then, couldn't remember from one day to the next. Then one night he tells me he's writing poems, a cycle, an epic he says, about the Guarani. He wants to trace their history and tell about their odyssey to the land without sin."

"He told you what he was writing?"

"Yep."

"There's an entry in one of his journals that mentions he was working at the time, but no actual work has ever turned up."

Truman Swanberg had a swallow of Postum. "I put together a little reading list for him, for his research, that he took to the library. I loaned him some books—never got 'em back, either." Swanberg picked at his teeth with the spent matchstick. "Listen, I'm not sayin' Max was in great shape, no one would say that. He was seeking the consolations of the bottle as hard as I ever saw. Probably put away a quart a day. But he *was* writing."

"Perhaps it was wishful thinking, barroom talk," Alter ventured.

"Shit, no!" Swanberg cried, and was seized with coughing that racked the length of his frail body and left him near tears. "I saw with my own eyes. He showed me!"

"Poems?" Alter held his breath.

"Yeah *poems*," Swanberg answered dryly. "Waltzed into Chumley's one night, all excited, could barely sit still, and showed me the first batch. Pages and pages. I don't know that he finished, but he was working away, I can tell you that. He had big plans. I 'spect he knew that this Guarani stuff'd be the last thing he'd do."

"Did you actually read the poetry?"

"I looked at it. I'm no expert, it was still pretty rough, but I was impressed. It had *teeth*, y'know what I mean?"

"You don't have any idea of what became of the poems, I suppose."

"Who knows? He coulda thrown 'em away, lost 'em, burned 'em. He wasn't always straight in the head. Would-ja excuse me? I gotta use the can. I hold it in too long I wet myself."

He disappeared into the bathroom leaving the door ajar. After a minute Alter heard a weak splashing, then the hiss of a lit cigarette hitting water, and finally a gurgling flush. Swanberg reappeared, pulling at his fly. He resumed his seat and felt around inside the cigarette package. Finding it empty he took a fresh pack from his pants pocket, tearing into it with a palsied shaking.

"Max was always saying he'd done some rotten things," Swanberg remarked, lighting up again.

"Such as?" Alter leaned forward.

"Such as 'unforgivable,' is what he said." Swanberg's eyes narrowed to slits as smoke whorled before his face. "Something was eating at him, something evil, and I deduced that's how he got the idea for the poems, the land-without-sin business." Swanberg regarded Alter hopefully. "You can put that in your book if you want, my interpretation," he said, making his small bid for immortality. "Y'think you might do that?"

"I might."

Alter turned away a little, thinking. Swanberg twisted a knob on the television, raising the volume. The three Lucys had come to a decision: Little Ricky would go on ahead to Los Angeles with his grandmother; she and Ricky and Fred and Ethel would buy a car and make the drive across country.

"Max was gonna call it 'Matto Grosso,'" Truman Swanberg said, touching Alter's forearm. "You could put that in, say I gave it to you."

From Maxwell Leibert's journal, July 1976, five months before his death:

> Haven't written here in a long time bec. embarked on real work, at last. No self-centered piece. I am not hypnotized this time with *me* as subject. Actual narrative content. Life takes on a new aspect and there's a striving in me I thought dead. I renew the struggle against an indifferent world with an Eberhard Faber Blackwing pencil ("Half the Pressure, Twice the Speed") and a yellow legal pad. These are my instruments of war. My soul is sore but I raise up one last song. God!—that I might sing like an angel & strike every note absolutely right this time!

From Leibert's journal, September 1976:

Saw her on Bleecker Street last night and she looked at me for just a moment with—I think—forgiveness. She bestows it like grace, for I have done nothing to merit it.

I saw her coming a block away and a fear gripped me that she would turn and run, or walk by w/o noticing. (I have trouble recognizing myself these days. Shaving, I look in the mirror and am shocked by the face I see: swollen, white-haired, skin the color of skim milk—but the broken vessels in my nose and cheeks give me a fraudulent ruddiness.) She slowed and stopped, though. We talked. Poorly. Halting & unhappy for both of us. What she wanted to ask, I sensed, but was too proud to do so: *Why could you not have taken care of me, as you promised? Why did you abandon me to fend for myself?* Indeed, I did, I have, orphaned her . . . Perhaps it will only be with the unfurling of time that I'll make my peace with her over the past.

I copy out for you, my lost dearest, the words of the master, Gustave, to Louise: "Oh! How I should love to write great things, to please you. How I should love to thrill you with my style. Though I do not long for fame . . . I should love to have some for you, to toss it to you like a bouquet: it would be yet another caress, a soft bed where your mind would bask in the sun of my glory. . . . when I look in the glass and think you love me, I find myself revoltingly common. . . . If only I had a voice, and could sing—oh! how I would modulate those long inhalations that must now evaporate as sighs. . . . Why weren't you the first woman I knew? Why wasn't it in your arms that I first felt the intoxication of the body and the blissful spasms that hold us in ecstasy? . . . I regret all my past: I feel I should have held it in reserve, waiting, even without knowing why: then I could have given it to you when the time came. But I never suspected anyone could love me. (Even now that seems unnatural. Love for me! How strange! . . .)"

Leibert had ended there, affixing his familiar three asterisks. He continued at dawn, in his own words, scrawling in red ballpoint pen.

5 a.m. And so, *adieu* dearheart. Beloved, dove, dear sweet life, my girl, my bride, heart's blood, apple of my fading eye, golden child, my gem, cherished muse, my tragic drama and posthumous fame! You are my other, better self, my merits, my hope, the forgiveness of my sins, my future, my child of God, dear daughter of Heaven, my guardian angel, Seraph, Truth. O how I have injured you and how I love you.

Alter closed the journal, feeling heir to some ultimate intimacy—Leibert revealing himself naked, and weeping, before him.

SEVEN

He stood near the front of a long line of weekend travelers, impatient. The line advanced a few feet, snaking around metal stanchions threaded with velvet ropes. He looked out the plate glass window of the car rental agency; on the sidewalk Chloe watched over their bags. She wore her red coat, blue jeans, white sneakers. From deep within the folds of his own overcoat he smelled lavender, or jasmine, whatever soap he had used that morning in the shower when scrubbing and scrubbing under very hot water. He had washed as though sandpapering at layers of accreted grime, until his skin smarted and glowed pink. He had dressed in clothes fresh from the cleaners, starched and sharply pressed; and even his overnight bag held brand-new underwear still in its cellophane wrap.

The line moved again and Alter moved with it, stretching his arms left and right, widely, in the fullness of the day. His course had taken him to this moment, through a seemingly endless serpentine passage where little light penetrated and the walls of the maze had nearly come down around him; and although he had no notion of where this present journey might end, he recognized he had arrived at a clearing higher and more open than any he had hitherto attained.

"Insurance?" A young Asian woman behind the counter regarded him pleasantly, her pen hovering over rental forms.

He turned to look once more through the window, to make certain she was still there. Chloe stood with her back to him, a slash of sun crowning her hair, a diadem.

"The works," he said, turning back to the counter.

He loved the country at this time of year. Nature, in her annual slumber, allowed one to see deeply into the heart of things, into copses, quarries, thickets and dells—all the places that during summer were hidden in leafy masquerade, now poignantly laid bare. He relished the blue and empty horizon melting into a pale late afternoon sky, and the stark, unmoving landscape, hard and stripped of its finery. Upon this scene, this undecorated prospect, anything might be written.

Alter took his eyes from the road to glance at her. *Is she or isn't she? His daughter? Or not?*

"Can you remember the last time you saw Max, Chloe?" Straining to sound casual.

"I . . . ran into him on Bleecker Street, in the Village, years ago. You mind if I open the window a crack?"

"Not at all. Do you recall when exactly?"

"When I ran into him? Oh, sometime before he was hit by the cab, sometime that year." He sensed her staring at him. "Why do I get the feeling you're asking me questions to which you already know all the answers."

"I don't—know all the answers. Or even if there are any." Feeling chastised, he dropped the subject. "Music?"

He slipped a tape into the player in the dashboard. The car was flooded with a crackling Fred Astaire recording.

Alter, under his breath, began to sing along. ". . . *'Won't you change partners and dance with me?'* "

The automobile hurtled on. A slanting winter sun flicked through the windshield, stuttering in and out of a canopy of barren trees.

A rutted dirt road wound through woods. Alter listened to the steel springs of the car's undercarriage squeal and groan as each tire seemed to find its own way over the frozen ground. The steering wheel skidded in his ungloved hands.

"Where are we *going?*" he demanded, aggravated as much by the drive as by the ambiguous destination.

"You'll find out when we get there."

"Oh come on." His fuse was growing shorter every moment. "Is this a game, Chloe?" he demanded.

"No game. It can spoil things to know where one is going," she reminded him. "You said so yourself."

"I did?"

"You said you work like a man with a flashlight who can see only as far as the flashlight's beam."

"That's how I *work*. It's late and cold." *And I am in the dark.*

Alter depressed the brake, easing the car through a deep pothole white with hoarfrost.

"Would you be disposed to write a book," she asked, "if you knew at the outset where and how it would end?"

"Probably not."

"Well, I have every reason to believe that if you knew where we were going now you wouldn't want to go there." Chloe gasped. "Stop!"

"Stop, go, what?"

"Stop, turn, there it is." Her blithe spirits, or the semblance of them, fell away now.

He saw nothing but black. "Where? Right or left?"

"Right."

He turned as she instructed and a moment later the tires crunched on gravel. He negotiated a long drive, and stopped when the headlamps' beams fell on the lower steps of a porch. Rising beyond it was the large, looming shadow of a house. Alter leaned over the wheel, looking closer. He knew he had seen it before.

"Oh no. This is too much."

"I don't want to stay. Forget it, nothing doing."

He heard a key chew into a lock and a bolt snap.

"Then I guess you'll be sleeping in the car." Chloe threw her weight against the door and it flew open. She tramped about in the inky dark.

"I'll find a motel," he hissed. "I'll be back in the morning." He poked his head inside but remained on the porch. "You could hang meat in here."

"It will be better as soon as I find a light and turn on the heat," she called to him through the open door.

"It won't be better. Chloe, *listen* to me!"

"I am listening. You're being childish. It's just a house."

"It's *not* 'just a house.' It's his house, *Max's* house!"

An overhead light went on. Chloe stood against the far wall of a country kitchen. The floor was taken up by a round antique pine table ringed by six ladderback chairs. The previous, or current, tenant—he couldn't tell which—had left dinner plates, forks and knives, a roasting pan, in the dishrack by the sink.

"*Was* his house, a long time ago. Not really then, even. It belongs to the college. Come in."

He stepped grudgingly into the room.

"You see a thermostat?"

"Behind you." He gestured at a place over her shoulder. "Dare I ask how you came by the key or is that also privileged information?"

"I'm an alumna," she said, adjusting the thermostat. "For a hundred and fifty dollars the college rented the house to me for the weekend. They think I'm skiing. It's all very straightforward."

"No it's not. None of this is straightforward."

"Well, *life* isn't straightforward, Raphael. It twists and turns and bites you in the ass."

"You've choreographed this whole thing, and I can't decide who's crazier—you, for doing it, or me, for letting you."

"But you *did* let me."

"Yes, I guess I did." *Her co-conspirator.*

"Look, we've come all this way."

In more respects than one.

"You have to make a decision: are you in or out?"

Alter stood frozen on the edge of a fall he wasn't sure he wished to precipitate.

"Say you're in . . . please."

He looked into her face, a luminous oval in the oblique light of an overhead lamp. Her huge, lovely eyes implored him. There was something both stubbornly vigorous and imploring in her expression that recalled to him his rabble of tenants.

Although so very different from them, she has asked me to share her destiny, just as they have done. And as they have done, she has entrusted me with her life. How to be worthy of that? How to stumble toward worthiness, even in a gross, imperfect way?

He half pivoted and slammed the door behind him. Under their feet the furnace kicked in with a great thump and a rumbling so intense that the floor trembled with it.

In a small bedroom on the second story of the house a brass standing lamp with a green shade burned dimly. An oak bureau and wall of moldy-looking books sufficed for the decor. Alter lay on the bed in his traveling clothes, feet on a pile of old flannel blankets. He imagined Leibert in the room. There was a knock.

"Yes?"

Chloe entered. She had thrown a man's plaid lumber jacket over her sweater. She carried a bottle of brandy and two glasses.

"Look what I found . . . I thought you might like some extra heat."

"I'll have a sip, thanks."

She poured an inch of brandy into a glass, handed it to him, and rested lightly on the edge of the bed. He studied the jacket; he'd seen this before too, in a photograph maybe. The image was momentarily indistinct.

". . . His?" She nodded.

"The shirt off his back," Alter said dryly. He fingered the hem of the garment. "Chloe . . . why did you give in to Max in the first place? There must have been other, younger . . . more appropriate men."

She threw him a look that said he was foolish. "Well, I

mean, *really*. If you had been me, wouldn't *you?*" She thought a long time, then smiled. "Younger, sure. But none more . . . appropriate. Besides, he jumped me."

"Jumped you?" Alter said, amused.

"Haven't you ever, Raphael? Jumped a woman?"

Who? Me?

"Taken her by surprise? Caught her off balance? *Inflicted* yourself?" She got up and patted him on the knee: a rather peremptory gesture, as he assessed it. "Some men have turned it into an art form. And believe me—it works. Sleep well."

Fat chance.

Then, as she was almost out the door, he called, "Chloe?"

"Yes?"

"Was this Max's bedroom?"

"No, it was where he wrote. He moved in a desk." She fell silent, then added—unnecessarily he thought, "I'm sleeping in . . . the other room, the one across the hall."

Through the kitchen window, Alter watched as Chloe, in the back yard, performed a bizarre ritual: muttering to herself, she paced the scrubby ground—from a tall evergreen to a fir; from the fir to the porch steps; from the porch to a small rise that ended in a deadfall, a tangled mass of timber and fallen brush that defined the boundary of the property; back to the middle of the yard; then around the side of the house where he could no longer follow her from the window. In a moment or two, she reappeared around the other side of the house and stopped, still debating with herself under her breath. Hands on her hips, she took the measure of the terrain again, then resumed her ritual pacing. Alter walked to the stove and took some fresh coffee.

As he brought the mug to his lips, he paused and studied it—old, the maroon glaze cracked, chipped at its rim. He wondered if Max Leibert had sipped from the same cup. The house had obviously lodged multiple guests; the premises showed signs of wear and tear, perpetrated by many careless occupants.

Alter walked to the kitchen table and sat down. If this cup in his hands had survived the years, it might well have touched the poet's lips. Had Leibert eaten at this very table? The biographer ran his hand over the knotty grain of the wood, noting the ring stains of countless wet glasses, cigarette burns. The previous evening, he had lain awake for hours, courting sleep in vain, gazing about the little second-floor bedroom. Leibert had written several of the poems in *On Love*, his posthumously published collection, in that room; he had also revised many of the poems in his 1966 book, *elegy*, there. The book had been reissued in a new edition a year after his death. Alter drank in the aura of the chamber, the pervasive chill that did not quite dispel the fustiness, and, recalling the words of Henry James, tried simply to revel in "the tone of things."

But the tone had taken on an off-key ring for him. He had visited and recovered the past in a way he never intended. He was more than slightly uneasy at sharing the house, this night, with Leibert's lover (daughter?). His own feelings for her perplexed and worried him. And he had no notion of what she held in store for them, what was to happen next. He mused that customarily, as he crafted a biography, he had always grasped, if tenuously, what would "happen next"—what *had* happened next. He remembered his first meeting with Chloe, when he had admitted to her that he expected surprises, even hoped for them. But the situation in which he found himself now presented a twist of stupefying magnitude. It was, he acknowledged, like fiction, the enterprise he had assiduously avoided—one never knew what would happen next, and anything could happen . . . When the hands on his wristwatch glowed two o'clock, he drifted at last into a fretful sleep.

Later that morning, as Chloe showered, Alter had stolen briefly into the other bedroom, the one that the poet and Tamsin (the poet and Chloe?) had occupied. He sprawled on the high, old-fashioned double bed and tried to conjure the emotional and erotic dramas that must have been played out on it.

Now, in the kitchen, with the coffee mug (Leibert's?) in his hand, he heard her say, "Okay."

Alter started, like a man discovered in some shameful act. He turned.

Chloe stood in the open door leading to the porch. Her face was flushed red and she smelled of the out-of-doors. "Come on. I think I'm ready."

For what?

"Dig." She held out a rusting spade.

They stood in the sweet cold air of the December morning in a weedy patch on the side of the house.

"Dig?"

"*Dig.*"

He allowed himself to receive the shovel from her, although he was not prepared to obey her command.

"I don't know what to make of it, Chloe. You bring me up here, install me in Max's house, tell me nothing, not why or wherefore, and now you're asking me to dig a goddamn hole in the ground."

She toed the dirt nervously with her sneaker. "I think this is where it was—is."

"What are you trying to tell me, for God's sake?"

"Dig . . . and you'll see for yourself." She turned from him, growing distraught, seeming to want to escape from the yard and leave him alone with his chore.

"Tell me what I'm getting into here, or I won't." He put down the shovel and swiveled her shoulders, so that she could not evade him.

She averted her eyes and, obstinate, said nothing.

"This is private property. We can't go digging up property that doesn't belong to us."

"No one's around. No one cares," she said tonelessly. "We'll put the earth back when we're done."

He scrutinized the little plot, stippled in milky morning sun. "Where are we?"

". . . The garden." He could hardly hear her.

He frowned. "Max's garden?"

"This is where it was," she said, near tears.

"Chloe, let's go back inside and talk. This is lunatic—"

He was immediately sorry he had spoken. Her eyes were damp, her expression both frightened and resolute. Looking at her, Alter knew she wasn't crazy. He had referred to the task she demanded as lunatic, not the woman, but it had come out sounding otherwise.

"I'm sorry, I didn't mean . . ."

"Then just *do* it. For me."

Alter lifted the shovel. "For you." He drove it into the ground. The winter earth broke into crusty bits under his thrust; he applied the spade several times again, putting all his weight into the effort, wanting it over with quickly. He began to perspire and the sweat cooled on him as he burrowed the scoop into dirt that grew moister and heavier the deeper he tunneled. He saw some metaphor in it: while on the surface everything appeared dead, beneath the hardened topsoil, life teemed. Roots and the tendrils of plants broke away with a subdued ripping sound. A big black beetle scurried off at his incursion.

"Chloe," he panted, "I'm too old to play pirates. There's no buried treasure here—"

"Please, Raphael, you must go on. Keep trying, a little longer." There was desperation in her voice.

He attacked the now defunct garden once more, rage piling up in him, heaving soil wildly so that she took a few steps back, out of his line of fire. Then suddenly the shovel collided with something soft, something airy, that seemed to implode against the force of the blade. Alter stumbled, buckling at his knees, throwing his hands forward to break the dive. In the ditch he had created he saw that the shovel had riven through what appeared to be a length of black plastic, filthy with mud. He turned, looking over his shoulder. Chloe's face was ashen. She stared into the hole, terrified and, it seemed to him, almost incredulous. It was as if, in the end, she hadn't quite expected him to really find anything at all.

"Is this it? . . . Chloe? . . . What *is* it?" He tasted bitterness in his mouth, the onset of nausea.

Her voice shook uncontrollably.

"Tamsin."

Alter shoved the weeping Chloe through the door and into the kitchen.

Despair wrenched him. He felt barely able to see. "What happened here? What did you *do*?"

Chloe crumpled into a chair at the table. "Please don't get it wrong," she begged, crying. "I didn't—"

"Set me straight then! There's a bag of *bones* out there!"

"He did . . ." She looked at him, her face blotched and distorted with tears. "*He* killed her. *I* . . . just dug her up."

"No." But even as he spoke, he knew it to be true.

"Yes." She sounded a note of defiance. "I dug her up."

In the dead of night, like a wolf / I bury the secret of those wild hours . . .

Alter lowered himself into a chair at the opposite end of the table. He thought to go to her, to offer solace, but was unable to stir, to move a muscle or to summon understanding. He was sealed inside a coffin—and within its black, airless confines he railed against it, scratching in a frenzy at its immovable lid to be let out, to breathe the air again.

"You're telling me . . . that Max . . . murdered Tamsin?" It was a question, and an answer, and something in his tone indicted Chloe as well.

"It wasn't murder," she sobbed from behind her fingers, holding her hands over her face, hiding from him. "I don't think so."

"What was it then?"

"An accident. A horrible, unspeakable accident. He didn't mean to hurt her. I really don't think so."

"He didn't mean to hurt her," the biographer reiterated in a dull voice. "But he killed her."

Alter shifted and looked out the window. On the gravel drive next to the rented car lay the black plastic garbage bags he had unearthed. He was sick: inside, he had found other plastic bags, layer fitted clumsily inside layer, and an entire human skeleton. The bag also contained the decayed remains of clothing tangled up in twigs and crushed leaves. Why had he exhumed it, why hadn't he left it in the ground?

"He killed her," Alter repeated in the same dead voice, "but tell me what he *meant* to do." His flat, almost matter-of-fact tone was an affront; he knew it, and didn't care. "You said, 'He didn't mean to hurt her.' What then was his intention, as you see it?"

"I don't appreciate your sarcasm," Chloe blurted. She had raised her head, taken her hands from her face, and returned his look with indignation.

"Sorry. I'm in shock. It's my shock talking."

She lowered her head again, and went on in a voice that grew higher and more febrile as she talked. "They'd been drinking, there was an awful fight. Max described it, so that much I know for sure . . . It might have been about me, he wouldn't say . . . Tamsin was aware of my existence, of course, and probably suspected." Chloe sighed. "Anyway, she came at him with one of his own knives, a bowie knife from the collection. He tried to take it away from her. They struggled, right here in this kitchen. The knife . . . some-how . . . ended up in her chest."

". . . Must have been one hell of a struggle."

"Hell." Chloe nodded. "Max saw that she was dead. He panicked. He put her body in the bag, dragged it outside, and buried her in the middle of the night." She noted that Alter looked appalled. "Haven't you ever read about people doing that?" she asked, not quite pleading Leibert's case.

The biographer almost chuckled. "Yeah, I've read about people doing that—other people. People I don't know." *Not Max, not the poet I idolized, sought to immortalize, not him.* "How did you, as you say, 'dig her up'?"

Chloe took another deep, difficult breath. "Completely by chance. Or so it seemed at first—before I thought about it. About a month after Tamsin . . . disappeared, Max decided he wanted a vegetable patch. Until then, we had only grown flowers. Well, the patch kept getting larger. Max asked for more and more vegetables: different kinds of lettuce, cucumbers, tomatoes, dill, basil, chives . . . It was a sort of mania.

"Then one afternoon I went out with my tools—it was the last crop I was going to put in, zucchini—I started to dig, to turn the earth . . . I was using the hoe, chopping, and I tore through the bag. I saw . . . her hand." She shook her head, shuddering. "The wedding band, gleaming in the dirt."

Alter felt himself shudder too, her memory—full-blown and potent—communicated to him. "Oh, God . . . Where was Max?"

"In here, in the house, writing . . . You have to understand: When I began to plant, I wasn't anywhere near . . . her—the body. But the patch just kept expanding—it was his will, his necessity. If he had let me stop sooner, I never would have found—"

Alter interrupted. "I *don't* understand. Max knew, he *knew* she was out there."

"That's true. That's why, in hindsight, I suspect he wanted me to find her, at least in some unconscious way. Or maybe he had found a way to deny the whole awful thing he'd done and believe the lie: that Tamsin had run off. The more he told about her taking off, the more he embellished his story, the more real it became to him. Also, he was drinking a lot. There may have been moments when he really didn't remember what had happened."

Alter asked the inevitable question. "No one ever went to the police?"

"Obviously not. There *was* no one, but me and him."

"*You* told no one."

"Until now."

"Until now," he echoed woodenly.

Overtaken by a hot, dry grief that swept through him like a sandstorm, howling, obscuring everything, he wanted to shake his fists and rail, *Help me! I kneel before You like a dog!*

"I should have turned Max in," she said, her voice streaked with shame. "You must despise me."

"Maybe . . . maybe you should have done." He heard the dismay, the bitterness in his voice; the anger he felt towards her had finally found a small crevice through which it could slither.

"I couldn't. He was already broken, destroyed . . . Besides, if not for me, it might never have happened. I felt— responsible."

"You don't know how much, if at all, you were implicated in their fight," he said hoarsely. *Whose fault? Where to place blame, and final accountability?*

Alter gazed about the kitchen, warm and cozy now, the pot of coffee on the stove filling the room with its aroma, and saw it as it might have been on that midnight so many years ago: Leibert, blind drunk, reeling, staggering after Tamsin, trying to grab the knife, hurling curses, screaming at her to put the weapon down (picking up another knife to hold her at bay?), knowing somehow that one of them would die. He weaves and dodges; his wife, drunk and enraged as himself, parries; finally he gets to her and seizes her wrists. They wrestle fiercely, a blade glints. He slips and pitches forward violently . . . Or . . . did he hold the knife murderously before him and rip into her flesh, burying the blade in her heart?

Accident? Murder? This much is clear: The blade that Leibert ran through Tamsin he also ran through Chloe, and now I am speared on it as well. We are, all of us, skewered together, like shish kebab.

"What will you do?" she whispered, wiping her face with the heels of her hands. "The worst of it is, I've made you an accomplice too."

"An accessory after the fact, I think," he muttered, removing a clean handkerchief from his hip pocket and pushing it at her down the table. He had no answer to her question. *Max confessed to Chloe, she confesses to me, the ripples spread . . .* He suddenly saw his life twice over: all the things around him as they usually were, as he had always known them, and then again, twilit, aghast, observed by someone else, with alien eyes.

"W-well, what are you going to do?" she stammered.

He stood shakily, reaching for his strength until his joints ached. "First thing I'm going to do is get poor old Tamsin out of the driveway . . . I've got to put her back where I found her."

"What's your pleasure?"

The bartender, a slight man—his face crosshatched with hundreds of wrinkles that seemed to explode from some central point—slapped a cocktail napkin on the bar in front of Alter.

"Bourbon. On the rocks . . . Make it a double." He wondered if it showed, if his guilty secret shrouded him in visible mist, like steam rising off pavement after a summer rain. Apparently not. The bartender gave no indication that he thought it in any way odd or sinister that a man would order a double bourbon at ten-thirty on a Saturday morning. He dropped a handful of cubes into a glass and filled it nearly to overflowing with Wild Turkey. Alter admitted to disgust at how smoothly he concealed the horror of the last hour. *Have I, like my father, become an adept at crime?* But he noticed that when he lifted the drink the bartender placed in front of him, his hand trembled a little. He had two fast drafts; the liquor made his chest hot as fire. He had never tasted anything so profoundly nourishing.

Alter had left Chloe at the former Leibert residence with a promise to return after taking some time alone to ponder his next move in the matter of Tamsin. He was not by himself in this roadhouse on the outskirts of the town. Three old men threw darts at a board; smoke from their cigarettes and pipes wound around him. He keenly regretted having given up smoking. At a table, two younger men in caps with "International Harvester" stitched across the crowns drank beer. The bartender slouched along the bar wiping at it with slow, ritual strokes.

When Alter had hoisted the dirt-caked black plastic bag containing Tamsin's remains and then returned it to the earth, what he'd said to Chloe moments before was true: he was in shock. He couldn't even explain to himself quite what compelled him to lift the body out in the first place— except to verify beyond any doubt her macabre confession.

But then, what does one do in my predicament? I am new to this unholy enterprise, the integrity of the slain. Commonly, I believe the corpses are abandoned: thrown in drainage ditches, left in marshlands, tossed into Dumpsters, cut into pieces and scattered along interstates, secreted in crawl spaces slaked with lime, dropped in vacant lots or in the woods, camouflaged under leaves and the rotting limbs of trees. Consigned to shallow graves—those ubiquitous trenches, utilitarian slashes that deface ever-widening expanses of our national scenery.

Maybe you were more right than you knew, Max: maybe serial killing has become a dominant form of self-expression of the fin de siècle. A disaffected army of men, a burgeoning new breed, crisscross the land practicing . . . the Zen of sadism: the fate of victims as aesthetically correct.

We watch it unfold every night on television and read about it in our newspapers: the age of the psychopath—criminal, corporate, political—has arrived, obliging us all to learn the sociopathic arts as a second language. How long before it comes as naturally to us as our mother tongues?

Alter raised himself off his stool, leaning over the bar.

"Have you got a phone?"

"Pay phone, by the toilet," the bartender called.

"Mrs. Sallinger?"

"Yes?"

"This is Raphael Alter."

"Ah, Mr. Alter, what a nice surprise. How are you?"

He detected genuine warmth in her greeting. Had he postponed yet another confrontation between her and her husband?

". . . Hanging in. How are you?"

"Not so bad. Erich will be off next week to Hilton Head, a five-day conference. He will deliver a paper." Her report fairly bristled with relief. "The stroke does not seem to hold him back at all."

"Remarkable," Alter said without enough enthusiasm. "Is he available? I'm calling from a pay phone, you see."

"He's right here," Frieda Sallinger replied, downcast all at once, reluctant to terminate their conversation. "Erich and I were about to sit down to a late breakfast."

"I'm sure we'll get to talk more at another time."

"Of course," she said, in the manner of one who knows an empty pledge when she hears it.

The psychiatrist's wife covered the mouthpiece to announce his name. Her muted voice made him think that she clasped the receiver to her breast. A moment later Sallinger was on the line.

"Dr. Sallinger, Raphael Alter." He lowered his voice as one of the men who had been playing darts emerged from the bathroom and took in the stranger with wary eyes. "I'll get directly to the point because there's no easy way to say this—I know why you burned your notes."

"I'm sorry, I don't understand."

"I *know*, Doctor. I know everything."

"You are rather too vague for me, Mr. Alter. What do you mean you 'know everything'?"

Alter lost his nerve briefly and took a gulp of bourbon, his second drink, which he had carried to the phone. "Tamsin Leibert, her disappearance. Am I ringing any bells?"

"She left Maxwell. Of her own volition. This has been well established."

"No, she didn't. You've known all along what became of her. Maxwell confessed to you too—and that's why you destroyed your treatment notes, to protect him."

"Frieda, close the door," Sallinger instructed coolly. "No. Close it with you on one side, Frieda, and me on the other. *You* out, *me* in." Sallinger resumed the conversation in an even undertone. "Look now, make yourself plain. You accuse me, Mr. Alter, of what?"

"It's not an accusation. I only want to confirm what I know."

"Come by the office if you like, we'll talk, after my conference, the end of next week." Sallinger sounded unperturbed by Alter's severe tone.

"It won't wait that long. I've got to talk to you now."

"Well then, perhaps tomorrow I can give you a few minutes—"

"No, it's impossible. I'm calling from out of town."

"Where?"

"Bennington."

"Oh . . . Bennington."

Alter could almost see his mask of indifference drop. "Do we understand each other now?"

There was a pregnant silence on Sallinger's end.

"Dr. Sallinger?"

"How did you find out?"

"I can't tell you that."

Sallinger exhaled, a long, sorrowing whinny. "Listen, I beg you to forget . . . It's over and done with so many years. What good can be served by opening old wounds? Who has been harmed, really?"

"Tamsin, for one," Alter said icily. "She's dead." *Chloe, for another.*

"She left nobody, I mean to say. No children, no relatives, few friends. It was an atrocious accident."

"You're sure?"

"Call it a crime of passion, if you wish. But premeditated? In cold blood? . . . no. Absolutely no." Sallinger spoke with conviction.

Shall I reduce the charge to manslaughter? Involuntary woman slaughter? Girl slaughter? Maybe we'll just plea it down to soul murder, the destruction of the other, the lingua franca of our day.

"Chloe, for another," Alter said aloud. His head was light. His heart fluttered as if he had swallowed a handful of Dexedrines.

"Who is this Chloe?"

"The name means nothing to you?"

"Nothing."

"Max's . . . daughter. I think I've found her."

"Oh for God's sake, Alter," Sallinger snorted, "there *was* no child!"

"What makes you so damned certain?"

"I have practiced for fifty years, Mr. Alter. I recognize a delusion when I see one. It is you who are deluded, sir." Sallinger enunciated slowly and precisely. "Whomever you have found, some woman you believe to be the child, you have *invented* this person—just as you chose Maxwell as your subject—to satisfy some need in your own nature."

"Some need?" Alter choked. "What need?"

"To partake of Maxwell's literary gift perhaps, to annex it as your own." Alter took a breath as the psychiatrist paused in his speculations. "But even further the need to 'bear' his child, if you will, his fictitious child. You have become Maxwell's double, Alter, his doppelgänger. You have re-made yourself in his image."

Sallinger's words reverberated through him. Silently, he assented. *My doppelgänger is—may be—more evil than I ever dreamed!*

"Ask yourself," the psychiatrist suggested, "if you do *not* hold your tongue, if you tell the entire story—what you believe to be the entire story—who will be hurt?"

". . . I've seen her corpse," Alter reported in a mono-
tone, "I . . . exhumed her—"

"You cannot be serious."

"I had to be certain . . . of the facts. Then I reburied
her." He hardly knew why he was telling Sallinger, except
that perhaps he wanted his counsel; or maybe he, too, had
to confess, to share the awful secret, as Leibert had done
with the psychiatrist, and with Chloe. The act of telling the
deed closed a circle, sealed some compact.

"Please, Alter," Sallinger gasped. "Let them both rest in
peace—"

I'm a biographer. I let no one rest in peace.

Alter said only, "I have to go now. I'm all out of . . . uh,
change."

Down the street from the bar, in his rented car, battling too
much bourbon, he turned around and, at a snail's pace,
headed back towards the house. There was only one alter-
native, the local police station—and Alter was as uncertain
as Sallinger what moral law would be served by that visit.
He knew well what would be lost: Chloe.

Out in the garden again, he leaned on his shovel to inspect
his handiwork of earlier in the day.

"How does it look?"

"Pretty good," Chloe answered mournfully. "No one
could ever tell."

"Maybe a little too good?" He hacked at the fresh smooth
grave with the edge of the spade, roughening the ground.

"Let's go inside now. I can't stand it anymore."

"You go ahead. I'll be along in a minute."

When she was gone and he heard the door shut behind her, Alter lifted his eyes. The sky had turned slate grey. For a moment he stood in silence, feeling the weight of heaven and earth on either side of him, compressing.

There, it's done, Max—my double, my strange twin. Now we are inextricably bound, one inside the other, like Edward Hyde in the person of Henry Jekyll. Or is it the other way around? Is Hyde's bloodthirsty spirit the Jekyll he carries? Alter stared at the new grave. *Well, at least where Maxwell threw her hastily, furtively, into the earth, I have tried to give her a proper burial, to make some poor amends.*

He bowed his head and began quietly. *"Yis ga dal, v'yis-kad dash, sh'meh, rabbo . . ."*

Alter paused a moment longer at the burial site, pondering their relatedness, now eternal. Like Hyde, Leibert refused to simply "pass away like the stain of breath upon a mirror," and had scrawled the final, most hideous "blasphemy," murder, across the pages of Alter/Jekyll's book. In some eerie way, as in that tale, Alter saw that he had long ago opened a psychic bank account in the name of his "twin," Leibert, and had tried to create for the poet a signature very like his own, "in many points identical," so that Leibert became Alter in reverse. But the diabolic poet, just as Hyde, refused the specious signature and signed in Alter's own hand . . . Yet, as the biographer contemplated "that ugly idol" in the mirror he held up now to his own face, he, like Jekyll, "was conscious of no repugnance, rather of a leap of welcome. It seemed natural and human. In my eyes it bore a livelier image of the spirit, it seemed more express and single, than the imperfect and divided countenance I had hitherto accustomed to call mine . . ."

He entered the bedroom, where Chloe was throwing clothes into her bag on the floor.

She looked up. "It's done?"

Alter nodded, unable to speak. All of life seemed concentrated on this moment and pierced him like a shaft. He approached, took her by the shoulders . . . and suppressed astonishment at how easily she went down, how pliant she was as she fell upon the bed . . .

Groping at first, trying to locate her mouth . . . so warm, so open to his own . . . pearly smooth inside . . . so odd . . . a human mouth . . . He turned, then she was above him and he pulled her tight. She passed her arms around his neck and kissed him all over his face and behind his ears and in the crook of his neck and in a path down his throat to where it met his chest. She undid his shirt, laved his nipples with her tongue, sucking at them, making wet little noises.

His hands moved over her body as he loosened and removed sweater, jeans, underwear, fumbling buttons and zippers and hooks, and began to recognize landmarks, familiar to him in the way of a tourist who revisits a place after a long absence. He fondled the soft mound of her breast, ran his fingertips lightly up and down her legs and into the moist heat of her groin. He grasped and kneaded and tugged and stroked her nakedness with delight that made him groan, wildly seeking to maraud, consume her, *heal* her, if that were possible. They tossed in a sort of agony, in hot, accelerating rhythm. He forgot who he was, who she was, where they were. He heard her cry, distantly.

The bed creaked in painful spasms. He smelled the odor of love, the spermy saltiness of it. An image of Leibert flashed across his brain and suddenly, almost without warning, he was gushing all his love and he arched sharply, enraptured. Then slowly, slowly, they let themselves down together, along a gentle incline of release.

He rolled over and listened to their mingled breathing as they slipped from passion. Tears cooled his cheeks, his hand locked with hers, in gratitude.

Later in the day as the sun set and her regular exhalations told him she was still asleep, he rose. The room was cold but he stood at the window, naked.

There are facts and there is truth and I see it now: in fact, she may or may not be his child; but in truth, she is—created by him out of love and madness and given me, his gift, to re-create, preserve, protect. My charge, my ward, my most beloved . . .

The deep, generous silence of the dusk enfolded him and he filled the near darkness with his prayer. *I thank You for Your blessings and for the terrible mysteries of Your joys. With what mightiness You choose to teach a man's soul Your immense lessons!*

At his back Chloe stirred and called his name. He turned, making no move to cover himself. "Raffi . . ."

"Yes."

"I thought you had gone."

He returned to the bed and pulled the blankets over them.

"What will you do?" she asked, "now that you know?" He heard the uneasiness in her tone and saw in his mind the edge of a sheet of newsprint curling as it begins to burn.

"Now that I know . . ." He smiled crookedly. "Now that I know—I don't *know*. It's not just Max, or Tamsin, or even you. It's that I myself am so . . . entangled, I wonder how to complete the book honestly. Remember my little flashlight?—it's become floodlights. I'm playing center field and I'm blinded by the glare."

"Well," she started, as if challenging him, "at last you have your ending."

"Ah, yes. But I must ask myself: is it an ending I can use? And how can it be told?" He looked away. "It may sound paradoxical, coming from a biographer, but now I feel I know too much." He turned to her again, his brow wrinkled, his face seeming older and tired.

Chloe raised herself on an elbow. And in her next words Alter sensed the impulse to draw him away from his dilemma. "There's something I want you to have when we get home." His pulse quickened. "I haven't mentioned it until now because I had to be sure of you first." She hurried on before he could reply. "A few weeks before Max died a package came in the mail—a long manuscript with a letter attached, asking me to keep it for him. I don't know why. Maybe he had a premonition that he might not live." She sighed. "Maybe he planned . . . to walk in front of that taxi. Anyway, I think it's his last work."

"Is there a title?" Alter's mouth watered in spite of himself. ("I made this choice perhaps with some unconscious reservation," wrote Dr. Jekyll of his impossible decision to renounce his alter ego, "for I neither gave up the house in Soho, nor destroyed the clothes of Edward Hyde, which still lay ready in my cabinet.") "What sort of work is it?" the biographer inquired, wishing he cared less.

She shook her head. "I haven't looked at it in years. But

I remember that some of the poems were about long journeys over water . . . It bewildered me a little."

"The poems?"

"No. I was surprised that he would leave them with *me*
instead of with someone in his family—one of his children, say."

He did. "In a way he did." Alter gathered her in his arms.
"He left them to his natural widow."

She gave him a questioning glance.

"A man may leave a wife—in the eyes of the world, his
widow—but sometimes he leaves as well another woman,
the secret woman of his truest heart. That's you, Chloe.
Max's child . . ." He caught himself. "Max's *bride*, his
natural widow."

"Ohhh . . . Well, the poems are yours now."

She shifted in his embrace and her warm breasts fell into
palms open to receive them. He reached for her other mouth
and dreamed a new dream: that his living fruit, long dor-
mant, might still spring up! He gazed at her as if from a
glorious height, faint with the altitude. A vision of a tiny,
dusty figure scuttled across the vast view, and, as he fell
upon her, he felt a tremendous surge of pity for the lonely,
frightened, dry little man, so far below.

EIGHT

"Put down: plaster, fifty pounds."

"How do you know that's enough?"

"I don't. I'm guessing."

Angel Muñoz, seated next to Alter on Alter's living room sofa, wrote on a long yellow legal pad. Alter paged through his own lists, the names of the tenants and the repairs required in every apartment. With each name he saw one of the wards of the building, and they trampled on the newly raw places in his heart.

"We'll need screwdrivers, won't we? Put down screwdrivers."

"What kind?"

"What kinds are there?"

"You got square-bar standard, spiral ratchet, Phillips head—"

"One of each, then, all different sizes. We're not sure what we're up against here."

Muñoz shrugged. "Whatever you say."

"And hammers."

"I *have* a hammer." Muñoz was trying hard to remain reasonable.

"*I* need one, Angel. And also a ball-peen hammer."

"Whatta we need a . . . ball-peen for?"

"You never know. This is virgin territory we're entering. I won't feel secure without it. And some ball cocks."

"Some *what?*"

"You know—ball cocks. They go in toilet tanks, control the supply of water."

"Oh. Them. Yeah."

"I'd say we'll want at least five, but let's get ten to be on the safe side. And caulk. It comes in tubes, doesn't it? Let's start with ten tubes."

"How d'you spell that?"

"C-A-U-L-K." Alter turned a page of his list. "I want to replace the linoleum on everyone's kitchen floor." The land-lord looked at the superintendent contemplatively. "Put down: linoleum, something cheerful."

"Cheerful? *Man* . . ." Muñoz moaned.

"You know what I mean, Angel. A nice color, nothing drab, maybe with sparkles in it," Alter said lightly. "They'll think they're walking on stars. And, oh yes, no-wax, easy care."

"Nice color," Muñoz recited, "sparkles, stars, no-wax. How much?"

"We'll have to measure all the kitchens, but make a note so we don't forget. And light bulbs. We'll need fluorescents and standards, one hundred watts—no, make it one hun-dred fifty. I want it so bright in here, they'll complain they need sunglasses to take out the trash."

"Whoa-eee." Muñoz eyed his employer with a combina-tion of concern and alarm.

"And what about mops and buckets and sponges?"

"I *got* those!"

"I want *new*. We're starting fresh. We're going to wash—

sanitize, hygienize, and purge," he fairly sang out, and was put in mind of a refining fire, everything burned to fine white ash.

"Wait a minute." Muñoz screwed up his face in suspicion. "We're *cleaning* these people's apartments too? I ain't cleaning anyone's apartment if that's what you got in mind. I'm no *maid.*"

"Okay, sure, I'll do it. Just write this down: mops, buckets, sponges. Now paint . . ."

"What about paint?"

"Mr. Law has agreed to get into Martin Aswith's place right after New Year's and I'm going to strike a deal with him to paint the other apartments too. The public areas I think we should handle ourselves."

"Christ," Muñoz muttered under his breath, "I didn't sign on to be no painter."

"Put down fifteen gallons white enamel and ten gallons green. Seafoam green. I'd like to begin with the elevator."

"Maybe get it fixed first, huh?"

"That's taken care of. I spoke to the company. We're wait-listed. It'll be a few months . . ."

"A few months?"

"Six months." Alter smiled apologetically. "My name's not Lefrak, you know. In the meantime, we'll spruce up the interior. I'm also thinking of putting in new windows. Most of them are warped. And I'm buying a new furnace. We'll get estimates next week." Even to himself he sounded a little mad with power he did not possess.

"Mind if I ask how you're planning t'pay for all this? Somethin' happen around here lately I don't know about? You win the Lotto?"

Angel had him cornered. "As to money, nothing has changed. I haven't worked out—yet—how to finance the renovations," he admitted, grinning broadly, intoxicated on some internal brew. "Banks make loans, don't they?"

"To tear the place down, maybe, not to fix up no junk heap." Muñoz rubbed his face thoughtfully. "You really think you can go through with this, don't you?"

"Yes. I'm going through with all sorts of things I never imagined, Angel."

"So what about your book? Where you gonna fin' the time to finish it?"

Alter hesitated. "I'm, well . . . I've decided, I'm not going to finish it."

Muñoz's eyes clouded with disbelief. "You been workin' a year. A whole *year*."

"Two," Alter corrected.

"No more writin'?" Muñoz asked, almost angry. "That's your job, man, it's what you *do*." Alter's abdication was as remarkable and unacceptable to the superintendent as if he himself had proposed quitting the building to spend the rest of his days beachcombing in Puerto Rico, his first home.

"I didn't say I was going to stop writing, Angel. I'm just not going to write *that book*."

"I'm sorry, man." Muñoz sounded genuinely regretful, and not a little baffled.

"Oh no, don't be. I'm not."

Alter kept from Muñoz his true feelings. He *was* sorry, more than sorry, to relinquish the biography, to give up what he had come to consider his entitlement to the poet's history. The work had been the most interesting and exciting part of his own life; indeed it had *been* his life. But in the days since his return from Vermont he had agonized over the decision and slowly grew to recognize it as the inevitable culmination of the skein of events that had raveled to this moment. The complications were overwhelming: Could he "extricate" himself from the matrix of the work? Could he redeem, or even explain, the poet now? Did he even wish to try? He would not fall into the biographer's trap described by Dr. Freud, binding himself "to lying, to concealment, to hypocrisy, to flummery and even to hiding his own lack of understanding."

(Although, as Alter debated it with himself, the thought had occurred that Maxwell Leibert would likely have been the one person most distressed by his abandonment of the book. "Tell all!" he could hear Leibert drunkenly cry, as, day after day, he wrestled with the question of proceeding. "Hold nothing back!" Then, morbidly engrossed with the labyrinthine turns of his own soul, the poet would have read it raptly, generously—albeit with a thick red pencil in hand— including the account of the death of his second wife. Nor would it have troubled Leibert an iota that the biographer had landed in the middle of the biography: the queer literary product that would have been the result would have downright amused him. Yes, Leibert would have encouraged Alter to take the experiment to its outrageous conclusion, regardless of the consequences to anyone.)

But above all, there was Chloe. She might or might not turn out to be the complete and perfect woman she presently seemed to him; he could not assay the future, nor quite assess the vulnerable, enchanting, yet somehow enigmatic girl who had torn him from his hiding place. No matter. The biography belonged to that other, previous era that she herself had brought to closure—and so closed the book. It had no place in this new incarnation.

Muñoz had leaned back on the sofa and was picking uncomfortably at his work-hardened, grimy fingernails.

"I know you a long time, right? Since your father was alive."

"More than twenty years," Alter agreed. "We practically grew up together."

"So you forgive me if I say I'm *worried*. You get a little *loco* in your old age. You're not the same man I use t'know. You've changed."

Alter thought about it. "Changed?" *Or maybe I've become . . .*

"You goin' *bananas* here. No book, no money, an' you think you gonna fix this place up like you some kinda superman." Muñoz regarded him dolefully. "You ain't no superman."

"You're right. I'll try to calm down. It's just, I feel so . . . full."

"Of what?" Angel grinned. "Shit?"

"Of the world," Alter said, suddenly shy. "I want to swallow it whole."

"Careful les' you choke," the super chided.

"Well . . . a man can't live on pabulum all his life."

Muñoz ran a hand through his hair in frustration. "I doan get it—you doan even *like* some a'these folks."

"That's not the point. Or maybe it's *precisely* the point." *The more threadbare the soul, the more attention it deserves . . .*

"What?—you think they gonna *thank* you for what you do? They believe they got it comin'—"

"No, most of them won't thank me. I don't want their thanks."

"What *do* you want?" Angel goaded him.

Then it began: with a soft, plangent boom—low and ominous—that lasted only a second or two. At first they weren't sure they had heard anything at all. But several earsplitting, heart-stopping reports followed like cannon fire or bombs. Still, it was uncertain whether the noises were coming from far off or were meant for them. They sat rigid on the sofa, poised.

All of a sudden the west wall of Alter's apartment vibrated visibly and the crack that had been there for months split like a seam. Bricks and cement roared through the gash.

"What the *hell!*" Muñoz screamed, leaping to his feet.

"Run, Angel!" Alter yelled, pushing him toward the door.

They reached the lobby and, as they did, the corridor leading back to the landlord's apartment collapsed in a clamor of mortar and beams. For an instant, Alter paused and looked—the way was completely blocked, his apartment demolished. Some force of nature certified: there was no going back.

"Come!" Angel cried.

The lobby billowed with whitish dust. Tiles, shaken loose from the walls, lay shattered in heaps on the floor. A new detonation rocked the ground like an earthquake.

Muñoz and Alter bolted through the lobby and hurled themselves out onto the street. Now they saw the source of the debacle. The building next door that had been undergoing renovation was destructing like a huge Erector toy, its roof apparently caved in. It was coming apart in massive chunks that seemed to explode as they fell. The edifice had accordioned in on itself and partly buckled Alter's building, shearing away sections of the common wall.

"Angel!" Alter seized Muñoz's arm roughly. "We have to go back."

"There's all our people in there!" the superintendent panted.

The scaffolding that surmounted the adjacent building wavered, then teetered and crashed to the sidewalk. Timber, planking, rivets and steel plates ricocheted. A board careened high in the air and fell across the street, plunging into the roof of a parked car, slicing it raggedly in two.

Alter pulled Muñoz behind him into the lobby. "Now listen, Angel: the east side is okay—it's still standing." He waved furiously in the direction of the intact portion of the building. "So we'll take the west side first!"

"We start on the secon' floor and work up!" Muñoz said.

They mounted the staircase; the entire structure, compromised by the calamity, swayed.

"We've got to move fast," Alter called over his shoulder. "God knows how much longer the rest of the place will hold!"

The east wing of the second-floor hallway was a mass of rubble. The lights had gone out and the only illumination came from the open flight of steps leading to the main floor. They picked their way over the debris.

"Miss Eres!" Alter bellowed, beating with his fist on her door. "Clara Eres! Are you in there?"

"Oh . . . dear Lord," came a barely audible reply.

"It's Raphael Alter, Clara. Open the door. Can you do that for me?—*unlock* the door."

At the far end of the corridor Muñoz tried to rouse Jeremiah Crust.

"Mr. Cruss! Cruss! *Cruss!*"

"Angel! Your passkey!" the landlord barked. "He probably can't hear you."

Alter heard the jangle of Muñoz's big key chain. Inside Clara Eres's apartment, bolts snapped. The door opened. She held her little dog, both of them blanketed in plaster dust.

"I was sitting . . . reading the afternoon paper . . . watching the TV . . . the whole wall . . . like the end of the world—"

The landlord held out his hand. She took it gratefully, clutching the poodle in her free arm.

"It's not the end of the world," Alter reassured his tenant. *Or is it?*

Like mountain goats, they began a harrowing climb over the ruins. It seemed to him interminable.

"I'm going to lose Honey. I'm dropping her!"

"Give me the dog."

When they arrived at the head of the staircase Muñoz called him back.

"Hey! Alter!"

He whipped around. Angel Muñoz was carrying Jeremiah Crust in his arms, wrapped in a chenille bedspread. The superintendent had stumbled with his charge as far as the last few feet of the corridor where a jagged slab of cement impeded his progress.

An incessant shivering against his chest reminded Alter that he still held Honey. At the top of the stairway he returned the pet to Clara. "It's just one flight. When you get downstairs go directly outside and *stay* there."

He watched as Clara Eres, terrified into compliance, started down the steps, then ran to Muñoz.

"I'm gonna hafta han' this poor guy over t'you," the super said, breathing hard. "I think he got somethin' broke." Awkwardly but gently Muñoz managed to pass Crust in his bedspread across the divide of cement.

The old man, in Alter's arms, felt lighter than air, a feather.

When he reached the stairs again, with Crust blocking his vision, he took each step deliberately, feeling the treads and risers with the soles of his feet. *You may falter, but you may not fall . . .*

On the sidewalk, Alter lay Crust down. He tore off his

tweed jacket, balled it up, and made a lumpy pillow for the man's head.

"Keep an eye on him, Clara," Alter said, aware of the woman standing over him. In the far distance, getting closer, he heard sirens. *Please God, help is on the way.*

As the landlord bounded toward the third floor, he met Muñoz and Al Bruno descending. Between them, with one arm slung over each of their shoulders, was Bruno's companion, Henry Arnold, in striped pajamas. Supported by the men, Arnold's head lolled listlessly, as if he were only semiconscious.

"A piece of ceiling fell on him." Bruno's voice quavered and his eyes shone with tears. "Henry was lying on the couch."

"Get him outside." Alter lay a hand on Bruno's shoulder. "He may be just stunned."

From somewhere indeterminate came a thin, muffled groan. "Help! Somebody! Help me!"

Alter followed the weak cry. It did not grow louder but more distinct until at last he found himself standing in front of the elevator door. Outside, a brace of sirens pulled onto the street and then fell silent.

Alter called through the door. "Is someone there?"

"Mrs. Pompanazzi! I'm stuck! No light, no air in here!"

"Hold on, Mrs. Pompanazzi, I'm going to try to open the door!"

Clawing with his fingers, he attempted to pry the heavy steel door. It gave an inch or so and then he lost his grip and it slid shut again. He heard heavy footfalls on the stairs.

"Elevator?" a voice asked.

Alter turned. Two Emergency Service Unit policemen stood behind him. He nodded and stepped aside. Using a crowbar, one of the men forced the door. The cab had stopped overhead, between floors. In the grey light, Rosalba Pompanazzi's feet and the three prongs of her aluminum cane were visible on the floor of the cab.

As Alter left them to their work and made his way upstairs, another loud boom rocked the building. He hugged the wall and waited for the rolling to subside. More sirens converged outside, their screams and whoops chorusing, comrades in disaster. The amplified blast of a fire truck cut through the din.

The building's third story was in a state of destruction even worse than the two below. Alter stopped to peer down the darkening hallway, his view obstructed by several big beams, fallen and snapped like toothpicks. Behind him, more tramping on the steps heralded the arrival of firemen wearing oxygen tanks strapped to their backs and wielding pickaxes. On their heels, two more ESU officers held German shepherd dogs, straining at their leashes. They unsnapped the leads and their animals charged down the hall, bounding nimbly over the debris in search of survivors. A handler shined a flashlight into the rubble.

"You live here?" a fireman asked Alter.

"I own the building—"

They were interrupted by the appearance of Morris Bloom, all but strolling down the shaky stairs from the fourth floor.

"Well, it finally happened, all right," Bloom sneered as he neared the landing. "Whole damn place crashing down."

"The building next door," Alter cut him off harshly. "It's caved in, an accident."

"Sure, sure. An accident. Leave it to you to pass the buck—"

"Please move along, sir," the fireman urged Bloom. He turned back to Alter. "Check upstairs yet?"

"I'm about to. Right now. There's a woman on this floor, three-B, in a wheelchair." He pointed down the hall. "Mrs. Hovanian. Can you send someone?"

Angel Muñoz appeared, breathless, on the landing. To no one in particular he reported, "Mr. Arnol' pass out."

"You're not 'about to' go anywhere," the fireman contradicted Alter, ignoring Muñoz, "you're getting out of here, sir. Pronto."

"I cannot leave," Alter said, breaking away from him. "I own this place, I told you. Angel?"

Muñoz hesitated for a moment, caught between the conflicting claims of loyalty and authority. He eyed the firemen uncertainly, then followed Alter upstairs.

"Come back!" the fireman brayed. "There's a busted gas main next door! It could blow any minute!"

Alter and Muñoz chased up the stairs two at a time.

"It's your funeral, pal!"

"It's my house!" the landlord called down.

On the floor below he heard the dogs bark. Alter hoped that they had found Mrs. Hovanian.

On the fourth-floor landing, the sound of high-pitched screaming assaulted him. On the fifth floor, Roslyn De-Angelis clutched the bannister, her face ashen with terror.

"It's my sister! My sister!"

The men trailed her to the apartment, feeling with their hands in the dark. A nail pierced the palm of Alter's hand. He lost his footing, smacking his head on the sharp edge of something.

When they entered the dwelling Alter had to take a moment to orient himself. He hardly recognized the room. A gaping hole in the living room wall was open to the twilight. All sense of geometry, of the order of things, had been lost. Not a stick of furniture remained standing.

"Loretta! *Loretta!*" Roslyn DeAngelis wailed, crawling around the fallen chrome étagère toward a large piece of concrete.

It was a section of the outer retaining wall. Alter prowled after Roslyn, cutting his other hand on a shard of glass. He glanced down: their collection of ceramic and crystal unicorns had spilled and shattered on the floor. Dropping to his knees behind her sister he saw that, from her waist down, Loretta DeAngelis had been pinned under the concrete. She was still wearing her overcoat. One of her shoes lay nearby. A plain black handbag was open beside her head. Crushed tissues, part of a roll of breath mints, and a transparent plastic change purse had spilled out.

Another cannonade shook the building. Roslyn shrieked and buried her face in her unconscious sister's shoulder. A cry—a tremendous, concerted intake of breath—went up from the crowd that apparently was gathering outside. A voice on a bullhorn issued a flurry of fierce directives, although the words were indecipherable at this distance from the street.

Muñoz drew up next to Alter.

"That might've been the gas main," Alter whispered. "There's a ton of cement on her. What're we going to do?"

Muñoz studied the situation gravely, with the eye of an engineer. "I got an idea. Be right back."

Alter took one of Loretta DeAngelis's hands in both of his and stroked it, feeling helpless, stricken.

"We need a priest." Roslyn broke into sobs.

"No. We're going to save her." It was a gigantic leap of faith. Alter gazed up through the crater in the wall, to the early evening sky. He fastened on a flight of pigeons and held them in his sight.

Suddenly he heard Roslyn singing, brokenly, through

tears. " 'Cre-a-tor of the stars of night / The people's everlasting light / Redeemer, Savior, of us all / O hear your servants when they call.' "

He looked down. Roslyn soothed her sister, fingers stroking Loretta's hair.

"Sing with me, Loretta, sing—'As once through Mary's flesh you came / To save us from our sin and shame / So now, Redeemer, by your grace / Come and heal our fallen race . . .' "

Then Muñoz returned dragging a stout, splintered beam almost as tall as himself.

"That las' one broke loose the steps," he confided under his breath. "They jus' hanging. No way down."

Alter felt the cold chill of fright, but he spoke calmly. "The firemen know we're up here."

"I'm gonna try and liff it off 'er," Muñoz went on, all business now. "When I get the stone up, you slide 'er out, unnerstand?"

"Let's try." Alter had never felt such pure love for his deputy as at this moment.

Muñoz tested around and found the place he sought at the corner of the great slab; he wedged one end of the beam underneath. Alter snuggled on his knees as close to Loretta as he could get and, from behind, his chest grazing the floor, worked his hands under her arms. His fingers dug into the warm wool of her overcoat. Again, dimly, he was aware of sirens; it sounded like hundreds of them, converging. When one wave ceased another took up the call.

"Doan look at me, boss, keep your eyes on her, and when I say 'pull,' *pull*," Muñoz directed.

So it came to him in sounds: Muñoz's straining, animal noises, laboring desperately to budge the concrete and release Loretta DeAngelis from her tomb . . . the creaking of the floor . . . scraping . . . the ominous fracture of the beam as Muñoz started to raise the slab . . . the barking of dogs on a lower floor . . . a male voice calling from inside the building, "Stay where you are! Don't move!" . . . and, from farther away, from the street, a sudden burst of applause as, he imagined, some rescue had been accomplished . . .

He riveted on Loretta's dull flesh, robbed of color, her whitened lips and shallow breathing. The fingers of her hand were extended stiffly, seeming to reach for something just beyond their grasp. He felt a sudden, urgent need to urinate, a stabbing in his bladder.

"—*Pull.*" A strangled expulsion of air. "Ahhh!—*pull!*"

With whatever reserve of energy was left to him, Alter yanked brutally, wresting Loretta from beneath the concrete. He fell backwards on his knees, her torso in his lap, just as Muñoz released the beam. Concrete slammed to the floor, cracking in two. A torrent of dust ascended.

Roslyn went down beside her sister. "Thank heaven!" She raised her eyes to the landlord and his superintendent. "Thank *you.*"

Alter stared. A tip of bone sliced through the skin of Loretta's mangled left leg; at the end of her right limb the ankle was twisted at a sickening angle.

He looked away. Muñoz rested against the overturned étagère, wiping his brow with his forearm.

The landlord sat back on his heels and gazed up again through the enormous, angry crevice. It seemed to him that a mighty hand had punched this hole in the building so that the bearer could peer into the secret inner workings of the hive. Noises that until now had not penetrated his consciousness began to intrude. He thought he heard water running in pipes, the hiss of a steam radiator, doors opening and closing, electricity humming in wires embedded deep in the walls—life still affirming itself amid the ruins.

Then, another, closer sound: a fusillade of breaking glass.

In the dark, Alter groped his way across the room and down a cramped hall to the bedroom. Framed in the shattered window, awash in flashing lights from the street, was the figure of a fireman, hovering, as though suspended in midair.

"Thank God you've come," Alter said. "I've got a woman here who's badly hurt."

"The stairs are gone," the fireman yelled, "we're taking you down in the cherry picker. How many up here?" He bobbled a little on the end of the crane.

"Four. Myself and the superintendent and two women."

"I'll lower ya two at a time."

Alter nodded, relief spreading through him.

He returned to the living room and slipped his arms under Loretta's shoulders and the backs of her knees. She mewed, unconscious, yet aware of being disturbed. Her warm breath dampened his neck.

"Angel, hold Loretta's hand. Roslyn, hold Angel's hand."

In a daisy chain, hobbled, blackish shadows, they inched toward the bedroom. When Roslyn saw the crane, she balked.

"Oh no, I can't. I can't get on that thing."

"C'mon, I go with you," Angel offered. "It's good, like Coney Island, like a ride." He regarded her features, twisted in terror, with sudden recognition. "You never been t'Coney Island, Miss DeAngelis, never been on a ride? I take you next summer."

"Stand back," the fireman called. With his axe he hacked at ragged points of glass that still adhered to the window frame.

Exerting his next to last ounce of energy, Alter delivered Loretta's flaccid form to the fireman and climbed after her into the bucket. An icy wind whipped his face and body and he looked down as they began their descent. The street was a tangle of fire trucks, patrol cars, EMU vans and ambulances, drawn up willy-nilly in front of the buildings. From behind police barricades what seemed like hundreds of people watched with anxious, upturned faces. Television news crews trained their cameras and hot lights on the crane, and flashbulbs popped, leaving staccato, intaglio impressions on the night. The whole city seemed to have ceased its regular business to bear witness.

With a slight jerk the three figures on the cherry picker were borne outward into space, then lowered ever so slowly into the teeming, kaleidoscopic, welcoming sea of light and humanity. Alter was only vaguely aware of Loretta DeAngelis being hefted from the bucket and taken away by a team of men. Later, he would have no memory of climbing down himself. Someone threw a blanket over his shoulders; someone else thrust a cup of hot coffee into his hands. A voice said, "Looks like you may need a few stitches in that." Only then did he touch his scalp and feel the ooze underneath matted hair. He looked at his hands; the palms were cut and bloody. A murmur from the assembly caused him to look up.

The crane hovered again outside the fifth-floor window. Roslyn DeAngelis, then Angel Muñoz, got aboard and the great mechanical arm swung wide over the street. For a split second, Muñoz was caught in the last high red rays of the setting sun, bathed in an unearthly incandescence. Angel had his arm around Roslyn. Alter watched as they floated overhead, then drifted magnificently to ground.

The landlord, jostled as he wandered among the throng

of emergency workers, took into himself their particular smells of breath, and sweat, and dirt. He felt a hand on his shoulder. It was Muñoz. The stroboscopic lights played on both their faces. Alter had the incongruous sense of carnival, of celebration.

"You did great, man," Muñoz said solemnly, "you really did great."

Angel bowed his head and stood silent, reverent, sensitive to the moment. And Alter, gazing about the windy street—at the random chaos, the demolished buildings, at the people huddled against the cold before the monumental altar of catastrophe—reflected on the deep courtesy that sometimes happens between human beings. It had little to do with what the other had precisely said, or even what he did, but presumed an impeccable awareness that he had spoken, acted, that he *was*.

"Raphael!" Martin Aswith rushed up, Marion in his arms. "I just got here. I saw the fire trucks, the police . . . My God." Aswith stared, dumbfounded, at the place where he had lived for so long. "What now? Jesus, what's going to become of us now?" he said, half to himself. "We've lost everything . . . all we had."

A blade turned in Alter's heart. But he perceived that this wound need not be fatal. There was loss . . . and the antidote to loss.

". . . No, Martin, we haven't. We'll rebuild . . . You have my word, we *will* rebuild."

"You're a dreamer," Aswith said indignantly. Can't you see? It's destroyed, finished. The whole place'll have to come down!"

Filth and plaster dust had run together and hardened on Alter's face. He smiled, and the mask cracked like the shell of an egg. "Yes, I see, I *do*." Suddenly he envisioned, rising from the ruins, a simple but noble edifice of light brick, a front door with polished brass fittings, and large bay windows that opened magnanimously over the sidewalk.

"How?" Aswith pressed.

"Oh," he said softly, "there are all sorts of special dispensations, construction loans . . . and, it occurs to me, lawsuits—"

*"Law*suits?"

"Look at it logically, Martin. Their building fell into *mine*. By all rights, I ought to be able to collect damages— perhaps substantial damages." Aswith looked impressed, if dubious.

"And yes," Alter continued shyly, "let us not forget dreams . . . and love . . . and courage."

"Dreams, love, courage—you got a new Trinity! This guy's the craziest nut, but I don't put nothin' past him." Muñoz threw a protective arm around his employer.

Alter breathed in deeply. The acrid stench of fire seared into pockets of his lungs that had not been filled in a long time. He accepted the pain, and followed Aswith's and Muñoz's eyes toward the building, bathed in a radiant, harlequin glow. It all seemed fantastic, real and unreal at once. He felt immense, prepared. Exalted.

BOOKS BY RAPHAEL ALTER

Forbidden Journey: The Life of Louis Oldfield

Randall Jarrell: A Life

Lives Eclipsed: Horace Wright and His Contemporaries

A NOTE ON THE TYPE

The text of this book was set in a digitized
version of Garamond No. 3, a modern rendering of the
type first cut by Claude Garamond (1510–1561). Garamond
was a pupil of Geoffroy Tory and is believed to have based his
letters on the Venetian models, although he introduced
a number of important differences. It is to him that
we owe the letter known as "old style." He gave to his letters
a certain elegance and feeling of movement that won for
their creator an immediate reputation and the
patronage of Francis I of France.

Composed by American–Stratford Graphic
Services, Inc., Brattleboro, Vermont. Printed and bound
by Fairfield Graphics, Fairfield, Pennsylvania.
Designed by Mia Vander Els